Cast o

Amanda Beagle. The no-nonsens~~e~~
and an even better manager of the ~~L...g.. ......~~ ~~.g....j, ...~~
her sister inherited from their brother Ezekiel.

Lutie Beagle. The younger sister, Lutie is a crack shot who learned how to follow clues and order vintage champagne from reading detective novels.

Martha "Marthy" Meecham. The Beagle sisters' cousin, also our narrator and Lutie's reluctant Watson. She misses the good life in East Biddicutt.

Jefferson "Jeff" Mahoney. Their brash young assistant.

Alexandro Karkoff. A jeweler, at whose penthouse the murder takes place.

Hero "Hurry" Lynn. A beautiful heiress.

Kate Kilgallon. Hero's older sister, a widow, who was cut out of their father's will.

Charles Elliot Leland. Hero's recently acquired husband.

Elinor Lynn. Hero's stepmother, she's only a little older than Hero herself.

Sabrina Brok. She's New York's Glamour Girl No. 2 (Hero was No. 1). Her nickname is Saddie—for sadistic.

Ted Greer. A famous bandleader, the current "Sultan of Swing," according to Jeff. Hero was in love with him.

Bettine Greer. Ted's new wife, young and very innocent.

Baron Delacy. He can't dance but with a thousand oil wells who cares?

Bertha Haug. Hero and Elinor's cook, she's a very unpleasant woman.

Banks. Hero and Elinor's butler. No, he didn't do it.

C.V. Lynn. Kate and Hero's father and Elinor's husband. He's dead but his presence is felt.

Inspector Moore. A gentleman copper who enjoys tea with the sisters.

McGinnis. A not-so-gentlemanly copper.

Tabby. A cat. Amanda's pet.

Rabelais. A parrot with a colorful vocabulary. Lutie's pet.

The Beagle Sisters Duet

Our First Murder (1940)
Our Second Murder (1941)

Our Second Murder

A Beagle Sisters Mystery
by
Torrey Chanslor

The Rue Morgue
Lyons / Boulder

To Roy

Our Second Murder

ISBN: 0-915230-64-X
New Material Copyright © 2004
The Rue Morgue Press

Published by
The Rue Morgue Press
P.O. Box 4119
Boulder, Colorado 80306

Printed by
Johnson Printing
Boulder, Colorado

PRINTED IN THE UNITED STATES OF AMERICA

Meet the Author
Marjorie Torrey / Torrey Chanslor

Fame is a funny, fickle thing. Marjorie Torrey, who as Torrey Chanslor created the Beagle Sisters, was one of the major illustrators of children's books in the mid-twentieth century, achieving back-to-back Caldecott Honor awards, but today she is virtually forgotten. She was born in New York in 1899 but somewhere in the late 1950s, she seems to have quietly passed from the scene.

She wrote a few children's books herself but she was primarily an artist, whose old-fashioned style was ideally suited to illustrating books for young people. She also did the covers for the two mysteries featuring the Beagle sisters, *Our First Murder* (1940) and *Our Second Murder* (1941). Although these covers were uncredited, there's absolutely no doubt whose work it is when one compares the playful, yet extremely accurate, covers of *Our First Murder* and *Our Second Murder* (reproduced for this edition in a slightly enlarged form) with the delightful illustrations in her 1946 Caldecott Honor book, *Sing Mother Goose*.

The Beagle Sisters books were her only books written for adults. They belong to that school of elaborately plotted mysteries solved by very eccentric detectives popularized in this country by S.S. Van Dine and Ellery Queen. What makes Torrey Chanslor's books stand apart from her predecessors are her delightful and unusual sleuths. The Beagle sisters are two sixtyish spinsters from a small upstate New York town who inherit a New York City private detective agency from their brother and almost immediately plunge themselves into a spectacular murder case. Elder sister Amanda Beagle (think Margaret Hamilton or Edna May Oliver) heads up the firm and runs it with an iron hand, but most of the sleuthing is done by Lutie, the younger sister (think Helen Hayes), who honed her adopted craft by reading scores of mysteries borrowed from the East Biddicutt circulating library. The action is described by their Watson and somewhat younger niece, Marthy Meecham (picture Spring Byington). Their other cohorts in crime are Jeff Mahoney, a young, lanky redhead, (think a young Van Johnson on a Jimmy Stewart frame) who does some of the legwork and all of the heavy lifting; Tabby, a cat; and Rabelais, a parrot with a colorful vocabulary (learned from his previous owner, a sailor).

The Misses Beagle weren't the first women in the genre to assume the duties of what P.D. James called "an unsuitable job for a woman." Rex Stout, the creator of Nero Wolfe, gave us Theolinda "Dol" Bonner in *The Hand in the Glove* (1937), and Patricia Wentworth's Miss Silver earned her keep as an English private detective for many years, starting with *The Case is Closed* (also 1937) among others. But the Beagle sisters were among the earliest and certainly the most eccentric women ever to walk the mean streets as private eyes. Lutie, though several decades older, is as adept as Dol in her use of and fondness for revolvers, while Amanda and Miss Silver share a stern resolve and reliance on common sense.

Contemporary critics gave the Beagle sisters a warm welcome. "Quaint but funny," is how Will Cuppy, a major critic of the day, accurately described *Our First Murder* in *Books,* while Isaac Anderson in the *New York Times* gratefully acknowledged the arrival of "two such delightful spinsters." Marian Wiggin, writing in the *Boston Transcript*, was even more enthusiastic: "The Misses Beagle (what a name for detectives!) are charming, especially Lutie, who has stepped up to the head of the list of my favorite detectives. These two women greatly enhance what would be, anyway, a very neat case of hidden identity." In spite of those reviews, the Beagle sisters returned for only one more case, *Our Second Murder*, in 1941, after which Marjorie Torrey devoted herself almost exclusively to writing and drawing for children because, as she once commented, "what happens to children is the most important thing in the world, I think."

Marjorie Torrey herself began drawing as a child in and near New York City and entered the National Academy of Design at the age of thirteen before moving on to the Art Students League. She was inspired to draw by her father who entertained young Marjorie and her brother with his own drawings, which accompanied games he invented. An injury to her back kept her out of regular school, but she spent many years at home "drawing, painting, reading, reading, reading, and writing stories." After she started at the National Academy, her father built her a small studio beside a brook on their property where she could work during summer vacations.

Her favorite memories of her art school days involved winter evenings at the Metropolitan Museum of Art when "it was even more still and magic, and with a small group of young people—not all art students—informally led by Nicholas Vachel Lindsay (the poet), we wandered where we chose, gazing raptly at sculpture, at medieval tapestries, at Egyptian mummies, discussing what we saw, trying to express what we felt." Those excursions paid off when one of her earliest art jobs called for her to draw cartoons of medieval ladies and their courtiers for tapestries. She longed "to make a cartoon of modern young people on Riverside Drive, with the Palisades in the background, but was told this would not be salable…However, I sketched New York scenes, mostly of children playing, and painted from these during the weekends."

After she finished school, she married and had a son. Soon she was getting a great deal of illustration work from various magazines, which required two extended trips to Europe. Such work was mostly for the adult market and she soon gave it up. She moved to the San Fernando Valley in California with her husband, Roy Chanslor, a novelist who was beginning to get considerable screen work. His most famous novels were *Johnny Guitar* and *The Ballad of Cat Ballou,* both made into even more famous movies. *Our Second Murder* was dedicated to Roy, who died in 1964. Marjorie earned a screen credit herself (some sources credit Roy) for the 1936 screwball comedy *The Girl on the Front Page,* starring Gloria Stuart, who was nominated for a best supporting actress Oscar for her performance in *Titanic.*

From her hilltop home overlooking the valley, Marjorie Torrey was finally free to devote herself exclusively to creating books for children. She wrote and illustrated four of her own: *Penny* (1944), *Artie and the Princess* (1945), *Three Little Chipmunks* (1947), and *The Merriweathers* (1949). But it was her work as an illustrator that brought her fame and awards. Her first Caldecott Honor book, *Sing Mother Goose,* with songs by Opal Wheeler, came in 1946. The following year she earned another Caldecott Honor medallion for illustrating *Sing in Praise: A Collection of the Best Loved Hymns,* once again selected by Wheeler. A Caldecott historian wrote of her work: "The full-color illustrations reflect the solemnity and reverence seen in Torrey's Mother Goose collection, and these interpretations communicate the essence and importance of the songs' words…Torrey's gentle black-and-white illustrations possess the softness of pencil, some the sharp lines of pen and ink, and others a combination of both."

She also illustrated *Fairing Weather* by Elspeth MacDuffle Bragdon in 1955, *Far from Marlbrough Street* by Elizabeth Philbrook in 1944, and several books by Doris Gates, including *Sarah's Idea* (1938), *Sensible Kate* (1943), and *Trouble for Jenny* (1951). She deftly illustrated reprints of several classic children's books, including *Alice in Wonderland* in 1955 and *Peter Pan* in 1957, after which she seems to have vanished without a trace. Marjorie is not mentioned in Roy's obituary in a 1964 edition of *Variety* and he appears to have remarried.

All of her books are out of print today. Even her Caldecott honor books are difficult to find, often confined to rare book rooms or the special collections section of larger libraries. Ironically, she's perhaps best known today for her two mysteries, which have been mentioned in Carolyn G. Hart's popular "Death on Demand" mystery series and are sought after by collectors specializing in the evolution of the private eye novel, especially those featuring women sleuths.

Marjorie Torrey gave us perhaps the ultimate portrayal of the spinster sleuth. Amanda and Lutie's adventures on the streets and in the nightclubs of 1940 Manhattan might seem preposterous to the jaded reader of today, who associates private eye novels with gritty urban cityscapes and even grittier characters. In their joyful innocence they offer up a picture of time when people read murder mysteries just for fun. It was a period in which America was emerging from the Great Depression and not yet embroiled in the Second World War. The country certainly needed a laugh then. Who is to say that it doesn't need another one today?

Tom & Enid Schantz
July 2002
Boulder, Colorado

CHAPTER 1

WHEN my cousin Amanda remarked, one afternoon at teatime, that Alexandro Karkoff, the jeweler, had engaged the services of the Beagle Detective Agency for the evening of April the seventeenth, I noticed that my cousin Lutie pricked up her ears.

"Oh," she said, excitement in her tone, "that's the swank party he's giving—"

She broke off, apologetically. Amanda does not approve of slang. And Lutie has been mothered, coddled and bossed by Amanda ever since the latter was a "great girl of eight, and Sister a mere baby," when their Ma died. That was a long time ago. Amanda is sixty-six now and Lutie sixty-three, but to Amanda she still seems a mere baby.

Sometimes she seems so to me, too (though I am ten years younger), perhaps because she is so tiny, her round cheeks so smoothly pink, the blue eyes below the silvery curls on her forehead so round and bright.

They were demure now as she added, "I mean, that's the Benefit for Babytown, isn't it, Sister? I've read about it in the newspapers."

"I daresay you have," said Amanda. To me she explained primly, "The occasion is the opening of Mr. Karkoff's new jewelry store. I understand that some of Mr. Karkoff's most expensive merchandise is to be displayed on the persons of several young women—not professional saleswomen, but guests. There will also be music, dancing and refreshments. The admission fee is one hundred dollars. Even so the invitations have been issued very selectively. The money is to go to the nursery called Babytown, where the young children of working mothers are taken care of."

Amanda's manner indicated a certain disapproval of this combination of business promotion and showy charity. But she added less stiffly, "However, I've heard the nursery is a very good one, and I don't suppose the mothers are bothered by the notion of such shenanigans, so long as it buys their babies good food and care. And it's certainly none of my business!"

Jeff Mahoney, our young assistant, inherited by my cousins together with the detective agency from their brother Ezekiel Beagle, was having tea with us. He chuckled as he reached for another piece of Lutie's orange layer cake.

"Did the great Karkoff hear you call his suite at the Stuyvesant-Plaza his 'new jewelry store,' Boss?" he asked my elder cousin.

Amanda merely snorted in reply to this. But her black eyes were amused, and her lean, weathered face was touched by a suspicion of a smile at her own expense as she said, "When Mr. Karkoff ordered 'half-a-dozen of our most trusted-and personable-young men,' and added, 'white ties, naturally,' I must say I was rather stumped. Even after Jefferson explained to me what was meant. Of course, Sister, you would have realized without any prompting, from your literary studies!

This was a reference to Lutie's taste for popular fiction,especially of the most lurid kind, and her perusal of the gossip and society columns in the newspapers. She smiled, though rather absentmindedly.

There was a dreamy glitter in her blue eyes as she said thoughtfully, "April the seventeenth. That leaves us only about a week to get *our* 'white ties.' "

"What?" exploded Amanda.

My little cousin's gaze rounded.

"Why, Sister, you know we have no really formal evening costumes! And certainly we must be as correctly dressed as our staff."

"We!" gasped Amanda. She drew herself up firmly. "Sister, we are sending six young men. I have called them, seen them personally and instructed them, this afternoon. And Jefferson will be with them. Their duties will be to stand guard at certain entrances and exits, to mingle with the guests and—"

"And just what do we do if Glamour Gal Number One starts out one of those exits with this million dollar choker round her alabaster windpipe?" demanded Jeff. "That's been sort of bothering me, Boss, aside from the soup-and-fish. Do we step up and tap her on the shoulder and say, 'Hi, Miss Vander Whozit, excuse me, but haven't you forgotten something?' Or do we bop her firmly but gently as she makes off with the loot?" He added, less flippantly, "D'you think six or seven of us are really going to be enough? There's to be about a dozen of these dizzy dames running around in the Karkoff pearls and diamonds and what-all, showing 'em off. That's two to one for our boys to keep an eye on. Even throwing me in for good measure it's not going to be any cinch. Suppose they slip a bauble to a boyfriend and he leaves early? I mean, if we don't intercept the pass—and just how could we in a jam like that? It's not like when wedding presents, f'rinstance, are all set out for inspection. These gew-gaws are gonna be peripatetic."

"That," said Lutie gently, "is what I was thinking about, Sister. It's not a simple task, so of course I knew you'd want to be in charge yourself."

Which is how it happened that on a lovely spring evening, ten days later, we were alighting from a luxurious limousine, hired for the evening because Lutie said it was "only suitable, and we ought to have our own car on call," and sweeping grandly across the moss-deep carpet of New York's newest and smartest hotel, to be wafted upward in a special pri-vate elevator to Mr. Karkoff's rooms.

The elevator, which the tall, gold-braided doorman called "the lift," was scented, padded with pale rose velvet like a boudoir—or rather, like a miniature powder room, as I've since learned to say. I glanced in its mir-rors and was rather set up with what I saw. I was glad that Lutie had finagled Amanda into those fittings at Mattie Fergus's, a charming-looking little place in the Fifties. Lutie said she'd heard Miss Mattie Fergus was a very good dressmaker. Of course I'd always thought Amanda was hand-some, with her smooth, clear weather-brown skin, her thin high-bridged nose and the incisive modeling of her rugged New England features. And she held her square shoulders and her thin back like a grenadier. But I'd never seen her in heavy black slipper satin, long-sleeved and high-necked with her mother's brooch of heavy gold and rubies at the throat, and stiff, wide skirts that flared and trailed behind long, narrow black satin slippers. Her thick iron-gray hair, tightly drawn into a big smooth knot, needed no adornment. She looked regal.

Lutie was even more delicious than usual, in black net with mignon-ettes tucked into the fichu about her shoulders and above the silvery curls across her forehead. And I thought I looked pretty nice myself, in black velvet, though of course I knew I really should reduce.

Jeff said, "Ugh," and ran his finger under his collar.

Lutie said, "You look very distinguished in tails, Jeffy."

He groaned, smushed down his red hair, or tried to, and yanked his white tie straight. Jeff's ties never stay straight for more than a few min-utes, anyway.

The lift softly stopped then, and we stepped out into a square foyer, richly carpeted and beautifully lighted. Liveried servants took our wraps. And we had new ones, too, for the occasion. Mine was silver fox, a short coat, and Lutie's summer ermine. Amanda had a chinchilla cape. She'd said, "I always liked chinchilla. It's so soft. It isn't so very expensive, is it, Sister?" I'd gasped, but my little cousin had given me a sharp look and said, "No, Sister!" very quickly. You see, we weren't supposed to ask Mattie Fergus about prices. Lutie had said she was a nice woman, trying to get along, and it would be kinder not to.

Well, then our host—or perhaps I should call him our client, or our employer—anyway, the Great Karkoff bustled up just then.

He bowed before Amanda. She handed him our card. It read:

THE BEAGLE DETECTIVE AGENCY
LICENSED
Private Investigating Bureau
West 44th Street
New York City
A. BEAGLE & L. BEAGLE
Assisted by
M. MEECHAM
J. MAHONEY
SUCCEEDING EZEKIEL ABIDIAH BEAGLE

Amanda said, "I am Miss Amanda Beagle."

Mr. Karkoff looked from the square of cardboard to my cousin, swiftly taking in her regal gown, her high-bridged, aristocratic countenance. For a second he seemed startled. I don't suppose Amanda looked much like a lady detective but then, what would a lady detective be supposed to look like? Anyway, Mr. Karkoff recovered his poise very quickly, and bowed again.

"Ah, yes. Yes, of course. I knew your brother, Miss Beagle. And you are very like him, if I may say so." He turned to Lutie. "And you are Miss Lutie?"

Lutie nodded graciously.

Mr. Karkoff said, "You also are like him. In fact, the resemblance—the resemblances—are extraordinary. I am most happy to meet you. Your brother often used to speak of you. So does my friend, Mr. John Bynam, for whom you so cleverly solved a most—ah, disconcerting killing." He glanced down again at the card in his hand, then up at Lutie, and his small black eyes twinkled. "I am afraid I did not realize, when I engaged your agency for such a very routine matter, that we should be honored by your distinguished presence. But I am delighted to welcome you, and I can only hope that you will forgive me if the evening does not provide any adequate scope for your talents. In other words, we are not likely to have a really first-class murder, for which I apologize!"

Lutie laughed, but Amanda didn't. Rather stiffly and in the grand manner she presented Mr. Karkoff to me, and Jeff to him. And the gentleman bowed to me no less politely than to my cousins, though less profoundly, and then to Jeff.

Then Mr. Karkoff escorted us into the next room, while Lutie murmured in my ear, "Isn't Sister marvelous? She moves like a queen. And the way she manages her train! She might be born to the purple. But wouldn't she snort at the very idea? 'Purple, my foot! What nonsense you talk, Lutie Beagle!' I can just hear her!"

She giggled and I chuckled, and further spoiled the effect of our procession by tripping over my train.

Mr. Karkoff led Amanda to an enormous chair with a high, heavy carved back, facing a long table. It was Italian Renaissance, I knew, because I loved furniture. So was the oval mirror, blurred and dark with time, on the wall above the table, and the great sconces holding big candles on either side of it, shining down on a huge book with a cover of brocade that must once have been some Venetian Doge's robe.

"My guest book," Mr. Karkoff said, asking us to sign it. When it was my turn I saw that the parchment pages were scrawled over with names I vaguely remembered reading in the current newspapers. Many were accompanied with a flippant sentiment, a clever line or two of verse, or a sketch.

From beyond the cut-velvet curtains of this reception room came the sound of music and many voices. After we had all signed our names, we were escorted across a thronged dance floor with a raised platform for the musicians at one end, into a room only slightly smaller, done in the modern manner but with real elegance, and with soft, clever lighting that was very becoming, instead of making everybody look tired to death as the lighting does in other so-called modern rooms I've been in since. In fact, it was a perfectly devised background for beautiful women, and was even enhanced by the sharp black-and-white note of the men's attire, which seemed to have become a deliberate part of the setting for the jewellike creatures scattered here and there on the deep ivory velvet divans or clustered around a long counter of what looked like frosted ice, but was, of course, some newfangled kind of glass. This stood in a wide deep niche or alcove, which could apparently be closed off by sliding panels on either side of it. Behind it were mirrors, bottles, and three attendants busily dispensing drinks. From both dance rooms, wide French windows opened onto a terrace, with the lights of the city twinkling beyond.

I was prepared for something out of the ordinary, but not for anything as extraordinary as all this. I smiled to myself, recalling Amanda's phrase, "Mr. Karkoff's jewelry store." There was certainly no sign of his fabulous wares, nor anything whatever to suggest that these luxurious rooms were in actuality showrooms, unless you counted the lovely women milling about.

Lovely women whom *we* had been engaged to watch! Or at least twelve of them, the twelve who, as the season's most spectacular debutantes or distinguished older women of fashion, had been elected by the great Karkoff to wear and display the chosen gems of his unique collection.

As he seated us and departed, after Amanda had declined the refreshment he suggested, I wondered with a pang, which ones? Which of those butterfly girls or suave women were we supposed to keep an eye on? The thought was distasteful, and its connotation seemed ridiculous. And anyway, what should we—what could we do if—? I left the disagreeable notion uncompleted but suddenly I wished I were home in our snug little apartment in back of the offices of The Beagle Detective Agency.

Jeff was probably wishing the same thing. He yanked his tie straight again, ran his finger under his collar and groaned, "Jeepers."

Then he sat up, staring, and muttered out of the corner of his mouth nearest us, "There she is! There's our Glamour Gal Number One and the million-dollar necklace!"

He jerked his head and we stared too.

Halfway across the room we saw a girl with a halo of silver-gilt hair, a softly plump and tapering face, and brilliant eyes that slanted downward at the outer corners. Even at that distance those long narrow dark-fringed eyes were a startling green. There was no other color about her except her vividly painted lips. Her frock was white, lusterless, draped tightly about a small elaborately curved body, and her skin was like camellia petals, a perfect setting for the glittering snug rope around her neck and the huge square diamond that hung just below the delicate indentation at its base.

"That," said Jeff, "is Hero Lynn." He sounded a little breathless, and I thought only a stubborn bravado made him add, "Doing her bit for Babytown."

Lutie said, "What a wench—I mean, what a very pretty girl."

Amanda said unexpectedly, "And with a very pretty fortune. Her father, it seems, left her several million dollars."

This wasn't the sort of thing that Amanda is given to remark. I turned in surprise. Her eyes were still fixed on Hero Lynn.

She continued, "Mr. Karkoff mentioned it during our telephone conversation, possibly to suggest that Miss Lynn might be eliminated from our surveillance. However—"

She didn't finish the sentence, but her eyes were still fixed on Hero Lynn as she said, "I am expecting you, Jefferson, to point out the other females displaying our client's merchandise."

"There's one!" said Jeff eagerly, and nodded toward a girl just entering the room.

You wouldn't have thought a girl with topaz eyes and burnt-gold hair and skin could wear that particular shade of citron yellow. But she could, and it was ravishing; and the circlet of pearls around her tawny throat was exactly right too.

She was looking up into the face of a large young man, her thrilled attention hanging on the words that barely moved the lips between his fluffy black beard.

She apparently had no eyes for anyone but the youth at her side. Yet somehow, as they neared the group surrounding Hero Lynn, I knew that every bit of her was aware of the girl who was its center. And that slim figure, too, was suddenly, strangely tense, or so it seemed to me.

But there was no hint of strain in her soft, throaty voice as she said, lightly, "Hello, Sabina," and reached out a lazy graceful arm and turned the large young man quickly toward her.

"You haven't said howdy to me yet, Boy Wonder," she said, and smiled. Her smile was mocking, and provocative, and oddly tender.

He said, "Howdy." But there was no answering smile in his eyes. They moved slowly, deliberately, from the girl's silver-gilt hair to her sandaled feet, and came back to rest on the great square diamond at her throat.

"An ugly gewgaw. And not becoming," he said. Then he reached for her left hand, stared at it, dropped it carelessly and turned abruptly away.

The girl in yellow said softly, "I'm afraid he prefers pearls, darling. Pearls for purity, you know."

Hero Lynn didn't seem to hear her. She was staring after the large young man making his way toward the bar. From bare smooth shoulders to forehead a deep pink flush had risen. Then it receded, she gave herself a little shake, and laughed.

"Oh, run along, Saddie. And stop putting on airs before your betters."

The other girl said, "Oh, you—" Her parted lips drew back over her white even teeth, and I saw that her hand made a clenched fist. She drew a long breath and said slowly, "You really are an unpleasant person, my sweet. And some day it's going to be just too bad—"

She turned, stumbling a little, and a moment later had joined the tall young man at the bar.

Jeff said, "Whew. Well, that's our Glamour Gal Number Two, Boss. Sabina Brok, but wearing only five hundred thousand dollars' worth of jewels. And merely pearls. The guy with her is Ted Greer, by the way. The current Sultan of Swing. Can he give! And does he get! And he's our band leader, donating his services for the evening, for Babytown." Jeff thrust his fingers through his red thatch and added, "Creepers. Both those gals are nuts about him, aren't they?"

"He is really a very impressive looking young man," murmured Lutie. "Personality, magnetism, plus a decided mind of his own, I should think. But why, I wonder," she added, "does he wear that beard? It's rather effeminate looking, don't you think?"

At this absurdity I giggled, though rather hysterically, because the encounter between the two glamour girls had oddly shocked me. It had been more than childish and petty. There had been something quite viciously spiteful about it.

That Amanda had felt this painfully also, I saw by her bleak expression.

But something else had attracted Lutie's attention. Her blue eyes were alert and bright. "Look!" she whispered.

CHAPTER 2

HERO LYNN, her eyes curiously hard and gleaming like the diamonds at her throat, was moving swiftly, purposefully, toward the girl in yellow.

Sabina Brok shrank backward against Ted Greer. But Hero didn't even glance at the girl, nor at the young man. Resting her pointed, red-tipped fingers on the broadcloth shoulders of two youths who had been leaning against the bar, she nodded a sharp command. Quickly their locked palms made a stirrup for her sandaled feet. A moment later she was on the wide frosted counter. The thick white folds of her skirt swirled, flaring from her hips like a lilycup turned upside down, and swept the long-stemmed glass in front of Greer off the bar. It struck the floor at his feet with a small tinkling crash.

He moved aside a little, took out a handkerchief, and flicked scattered drops from a coat sleeve. He didn't look up at the girl poised there above him, nor did she glance down at him. Her lips curved in a smile that didn't seem to touch her brilliant eyes. She clapped her palms sharply together.

"Ladies and gentlemen, may I have your attention, please?"

Her throaty voice, mock-solemn, interrupted the murmur of talk and laughter around the long room. Faces turned toward her, some with excited interest, others with annoyance. A dowager seated near us put up a lorgnette, stared, and muttered sharply to her companion, "A pity someone can't stop that girl from making an exhibition of herself! If her father hadn't been a fool he'd have married a woman old enough to keep her in hand, instead of—"

The companion, a plump woman in purple, obviously less interested in her friend's moralizing than in Hero Lynn, whispered raptly, "Sshh, Hetty!"

The girl on the bar bowed to left, right, center, like an actress before the footlights. Then she folded her hands demurely, and said:

"My friends and others: Being without, ah, suitable family auspices, I have a little announcement to make for myself—the announcement of my marriage, which took place yesterday, April the sixteenth, without benefit of Saint Thomas but otherwise quite firmly, to Mr. Charles Elliot Leland. Hi, bridegroom!"

Smiling across the startled faces upturned to her, she waved and beckoned. I followed her smiling glance across to a wide doorway.

A tall young man stood there, blond and conventionally handsome, beside a girl in mist gray with hair like a cap of lacquered autumn leaves. They stood close together, motionless, gazing back at the slim figure on top of the bar.

The woman in purple clutched the dowager's arm. "My dear, that's Katy with Charles! I haven't seen her for ages. Isn't she lovely!"

She was lovely, arrestingly so. And in some odd way, there was a striking resemblance between her and Hero Lynn. I say it was odd, because they differed so. The girl in the doorway had that smooth russet-red hair and a skin like peaches warm in the sun and gray eyes that turned up at the outer corners instead of down. But they, too, were long narrow eyes, dark-fringed and determined-looking. The face of each girl, wide at the cheekbones, tapered to a firm arrogant little chin. It was there, mostly, that the likeness lay.

Anyway, I wasn't surprised when Hero called, "Sorry, my dear sister! May I have my husband for a moment?" Except that there was something mocking and not at all sisterly about the tone in which it was said. And something ambiguous in the older girl's unsmiling expression as she gazed back at the girl on the bar as well as in the long, steady, questing look she turned on the man beside her.

But I mustn't give the impression that those three stood there, motionless and silent, for minutes. It was only a matter of seconds. I recall that

Jeff had barely time to murmur, "The redheaded lovely is Kate Lynn Kil-gallon, our Hero's widowed sister, with Charles Leland," before the girl in gray smiled suddenly at her companion and gave him a quick little shove toward his wife. He grinned back at her, blushing and looking rather shame-faced and very young, but happy. Then he had crossed the room and reached the girl standing there on the frosted bar and was swinging her lightly down from her perch.

A babble of exclamations and laughter broke out then from the group at the bar. I heard Hero say, "My sweets, you look too, too silly for words! Don't you know this is the consummation of a romance? Why, Charley's been my beau ever since I was an infant! Of course he couldn't tote my slippers to dancing school—I was a little too young."

Near us, the plump woman in purple whispered, excitedly, "Did you hear that, Hetty? And everyone knows it was Katy and he—"

Her dowager companion muttered, "Hmmph. I've heard that he and Elinor Lynn—"

"There's Elinor now!" interrupted the purple lady, as a tall slender girl in severe black chiffon strolled into the room. She had a beautiful pale oval face and crisp black hair swept back from a deep point on her fore-head. Emeralds gleamed in her small white ears.

Jeff murmured, "That's Elinor Lynn, boss, Hero's stepmother. And more of the Karkoff jewels."

Elinor Lynn walked toward the group at the bar, which was now gaily toasting the happy couple and the bride. After each drink they tossed their glasses to the floor.

But Greer hadn't called for another drink since Hero's skirt had swept his glass from the bar, and Sabina Brok hadn't touched the one in front of her. Then someone said, "To the bridegroom!" and she lifted it. She said, in a tone that reminded me of poisoned candied violets, "Aren't you going to drink to your husband, Hero dear?"

Elinor Lynn was passing right in front of us at that moment, and she stopped short. Perhaps she was only startled, and I merely imagined that expression of blank shock. It certainly was banished in an instant, if it had been there at all, and she was moving forward again toward the group around her stepdaughter.

As she approached them she said, "Hero never drinks except on re-ally important occasions, such as funerals." Her voice was light, smooth and gentle.

There was a split second's sharp hush. Then Hero said, "Thanks, Mama. You're always so, so right!" And then the clamor of voices and laughter broke out again.

In the midst of it Ted Greer left the bar, and presently music came to us from the farther dance room. The group from about the bar surged toward it, and soon the velvet divans were nearly empty.

But the dowager and the lady in purple had not left. And we couldn't help but hear the former say sharply, "Well! I suppose you saw Elinor's face? So there was something, just as I thought! But what did she mean about funerals? And the way she—"

The purple lady said eagerly, "My dear, don't you know? It's quite true about Hero's drinking, she doesn't. You know it's rather gone out with the younger set. Some of them do drink beer, and some of them only drink milk! Well, anyway, at her father's funeral a year and a half ago—a very quiet one, from their house on Sixty-eighth—and what a house, McKinley period, lights in grapes held up by bronze figures and walls done in red or green brocade or embossed leather, my dear! Well, as I was saying, at the end of the ceremony Hero appeared in a flame-colored frock with a glass of champagne in her hand and stood there looking down at her father in his coffin, and then she said, 'Here's to you, old boy!' and drank down the champagne. Rather shocking, wasn't it? And awfully crass of Elinor, bringing it up, no matter how much she dislikes her step-daughter."

We didn't hear any more, because Amanda rose abruptly. We followed her into the next room and found seats at a round glass table next to the wall. It was rather too near the band, but I must say I loved it. The old familiar tunes they were playing sounded gayer, yet somehow sadder, in that strange rhythm. And the dancers dipping, gliding, whirling past us. The high-coiffed heads of the women, their slim waists and flaring skirts reminiscent of bygone times, gave me a peculiar dreamlike feeling, a kind of nostalgia, not for the past, but for this present scene, this present time that would soon be gone too.

Then the music stopped, snapping me sharply out of my reverie

Jeff said rapturously, "Ain't that something? The hottest, best swing band in the country. In the world! Boy, no wonder Greer's rolling in yachts and—"

Lutie nodded. "Yes, he's tops, although I've heard he's not a bit ostentatious. It's only one yacht, and not a big one. Sshh!" she admonished herself, and added in a whisper, "He's going to make a speech or something. And he seems very earnest. Look!"

We looked. Ted Greer was advancing to the front of the musician's shallow, slightly raised platform. And when I say he advanced I don't mean he just came forward. There was something definitely formal about his measured steps, his manner. Lutie was right; he did seem very earnest.

He bowed, and the whole room was more quiet than it had been when Hero had claimed attention from her audience.

Then he turned to his left, and said quietly, "Bettine."

From behind the curtains that framed the platform a girl came to join him. Her childishly modeled face was white, with tiny gold freckles spattered across it, her pale brown hair, swept up on top of her little head, looked like a baby girl's topknot pinned up for a bath, and her eyes were dark and round. I thought they looked scared.

The bandmaster took her hand in his. He said, gravely, "I just wanted to tell you all that Bettine and I were married today. She's my darling." He leaned and kissed her bare round forehead very gently. He smiled, and swung her left hand in his.

Then he raised it. We were sitting very close by, so that we could plainly see the bands circling the fourth finger, a narrow ring of pearls and a wide pale gold one.

He said, "A poor thing, maybe, but her own. Not a million-dollar necklace, but she's wearing it for keeps."

He bowed again, said, "Thank you for your attention, everybody," put his arm around the girl's shoulders, and they left the dais.

Lutie said, "Dear me. Quite a charming little scene! Or was it? Now, I wonder—"

Amanda snorted, "These children! They have no sense of privacy. No doubt in 1950 they'll be setting up their wedding beds in hippodromes."

I gasped. Turning to stare at Amanda I saw her cheeks redden with annoyance, and perhaps with her own flight of fancy. Of course it was true. These marriage proclamations had been extremely public and not in the best of taste. But I had been feeling rather touched by the manner of the young bandmaster's announcement. It had been grave and dignified, after all, and the little bride was so plainly sweet and adoring. I'd felt as women are supposed to, and as I guess they generally do, at weddings

Then Lutie gripped my wrist. I turned to follow her bright blue gaze.

I saw Hero Leland, standing against the farther wall. Her small pointed face was awful. I thought, that's how she'll look when she's old. The eyes seemed deep-sunk, the skin tight over the cheekbones and the lips drawn down and in. She was holding onto her husband's arm, as if she really needed it for support.

He looked down at her, and I can't describe the expression on his face. Or can I? It seemed to me a desperate mixture of despair and— was it longing, or anger? I didn't know.

Then she turned to him and grinned. Her voice wasn't shrill, but it carried across the room. She said, "Copycats!" and laughed, and they left the room together, in the direction of the terrace.

A moment later the bandmaster's new little bride passed us. Her lips were faintly smiling, and yet her eyes still held that babyishly frightened look. She was alone.

Lutie rose quickly and said, "Sister, I'm going to powder my nose. Marthy, do you want to come too?"

Of course I followed her, and I soon saw that she was following the little brown-haired girl, Bettine Greer. We skirted the dance floor and reached the powder room.

Bettine was already there, seated in front of one of the silk-framed mirrors and staring in it at her small pale face, her hands pushing her light brown hair back from her forehead. Then abruptly she grabbed a lipstick out of her handbag as we came into the room, and leaning forward began carefully rouging her small full lips.

Lutie sat down in a far corner and took out a tiny puff. She touched it to her nose and chin and forehead and ran a dampened finger over her lips and eyebrows.

I saw that my nose was shiny and my cheeks flushed, and I fished out the vanity case that Lutie had given me for Christmas and dabbed my face with powder. It looked much too floury—I don't use powder often, I have a nice pinkish skin and don't need it—and I was wiping off white patches when Hero Lynn Leland came into the room. She went straight up to Bettine Greer and said, "So. *You're* the other woman. I've wondered. But I didn't know."

Bettine stood up quickly. Her large eyes grew wider, and suddenly they were not childish any more but fierce.

"I'm *his* woman," she said, very quietly. Hero stared back at her.

Then she said, "You mean, he married you. But you know why he married you, don't you?"

The other girl didn't answer.

Hero said, "He took you because I married someone else."

I coughed. Lutie and I were at the far end of the room and I wasn't sure if the girls knew we were there. Hero looked sharply across at us and then dismissed us. She turned back to the other girl.

"It's true I never expected to find you up his sleeve. Poor sap! But don't be ridic, presh. You know I always have ways of keeping what I really want."

Bettine pressed her lips together and then opened them. She stared back at Hero, with fright and fury in her eyes. Then she shut her little red mouth again, snatched up her evening bag and ran out of the room.

We left Hero delicately rouging her lips and went back to join Amanda.

The musicians were coming back again as we took our seats around the glass table. The band leader moved to his place at the front of the platform, took up his violin, tucked it under his chin, and waved his bow. At that moment a girl in dead-white draperies went past our table, her silver-gilt hair swirling like the flame-tip of a candle carried swiftly forward.

In front of the dais, directly below the band leader, Hero stopped. Her long green eyes looked up at him. There was a soft, gentle yet mocking smile on her red lips. And the green eyes were resolute, compelling. But the young man's face, looking down at her, was unresponsive.

Her smile deepened. She reached up, her hand gripping his sleeve, tugging at him. He leaned forward, though stiffly and with reluctance. Standing on tiptoe she said something, very swiftly, close to his ear.

Then she let him go, moved back a step, and said aloud, gravely, "Mr. Band Leader, will you please play for me? My song, please, *Lament for a Dead Romance*!"

Her young voice, throaty and yet clear and thrillingly sorrowful, carried across a sudden stillness in the dance room. Then someone laughed, an abrupt shrill sound broken off sharply. A girl, but who it was I couldn't see.

Ted Greer stood there, looking down at the small straight figure in front of the dais just below him. He didn't say anything, nor smile. He didn't move; the fiddle still rested against his neck. After a long moment he drew the bow across the strings. Presently his band followed—the pianist, the bass viol, the drummer, and three men with wide-mouthed horns, one with its brass tubes curling in great loops, one crescent-shaped like a shepherd's, one long and slender and straight. The notes tripped, and throbbed, and sobbed, and wailed, and laughed and sighed and whimpered and moaned.

My little cousin clutched my arm. Her eyes, wide and ecstatic, were fixed on the young leader of the orchestra.

"Man, man," she breathed, "is he sending! Man, is he in the groove! He's out of this world."

I turned to glance at her, wondering what this gibberish meant—if she'd gone crazy, or if I had. Then it came to the chorus and Ted Greer sang, softly, so that I caught only a few of the words. But it wasn't just the words that mattered. It was the tune. I'd never heard anything like it. I never want to hear it again. Yet it was banal enough in a way, a parody of callow grief. I can't tell why it seemed to hold the poignancy of a thousand childish sorrows and the knowledge that they were dying or dead. And it mocked at their death. I thought, it should be called *The Funeral March of Youth*. And fervently I wished it would stop.

Suddenly it did. Without fanfare or finale, it ended on a sudden short sharp note, like a broken laugh, from the trumpet.

Ted Greer walked to the piano and laid down his violin. The other musicians looked slightly surprised. I gathered that they had expected to go on playing some other selection. Their leader said something to them, and they settled back in their places.

Then the young man who had sounded that last hoarse laugh on his trumpet suddenly grinned, walked to the center of the platform, raised his horn, placed it to his lips and played *Taps.*

He played it through once, simply, standing like a soldier, the horn held stiffly horizontal. Then he pointed it upward, and between the familiar notes trilled the chirrup of birds, loud sounds like sighs, and bits of *La Misericordia, Sweet Alice,* and *Rockabye, Baby, in a Treetop.* He waved the horn and bent and swung his body in extravagantly mournful gestures, and ended, finally, on a last long drawn-out, wailing note.

And as the note faded into silence a clear little voice said loudly, "Corn!"

It echoed through the room.

The blond young horn player stood, his trumpet in his hand. His somewhat startled stare was riveted on our table. Lutie gazed back at him, her cheeks very pink indeed, her blue eyes slightly abashed, but unwavering.

Then he grinned, raised his hand and ringed his thumb and forefinger into an O, bowed deeply toward my small cousin, and retired from the dais.

CHAPTER 3

HOW long that strange, silly, mournful tune, and the *Taps* following it, had lasted, I don't know. When Hero went away, or which way she went, I've no idea, nor of anything else around me. Vaguely I know what happened on the platform, but that's all I was aware of, besides that mawkish, macabre, mocking music, from the moment when the band leader drew his bow across his fiddle in those first painful, pitiful strains.

Whether or not he left the dais when he laid his violin on the piano I cannot recall. The piano was close to the curtain that framed the stage, but I couldn't be sure that he left. He might have been standing there, and afterwards some people said he was, but I was watching the young man playing *Taps,* and feeling dreadful, and wishing these young people wouldn't be like that.

I suppose I was in some sort of maudlin daze. Anyway, when I first became aware of my surroundings a waiter was putting glasses before us, another was twirling a gold-necked bottle in a silver bucket.

Our glasses were filled. Then a long table (like a sort of streamlined tea-wagon) was wheeled up, and silver covers removed from smoking dishes.

Jeff peered and murmured, "Mmm. Chicken liver, lobster, sausage, pressed duck, hot dog. Mmm. I'd heard this was to be something very special. Wasn't our host, I mean Mr. Karkoff, supposed to be importing a chef from—where was it? France? Or Madagascar or Russia?"

The waiter said, "Yes, sir."

Jeff said, "Well, I always take what I don't get at home," and pointed to the grilled frankfurters, which indeed did look very delicious.

At that moment we heard a scream. It was a woman's voice and very terrifying. Amanda and Lutie were on their feet. I followed, and so did Jeff, with a look backward.

It seems rather humiliating to remember that I, too, really did cast a regretful backward eye on that wagon of viands. But it did look delectable, and it smelled so good.

And then we were across the dance floor, headed toward that frightful cry. I was hanging onto Lutie's arm and Jeff was stumbling on my velvet train.

The scream led us to the small room off the foyer—the room into which we'd been ushered by Mr. Karkoff to sign our names in his guest book.

A girl stood there facing us, her arms stretched out on either side of her clutching the draperies at the arched doorway. She was surrounded by a group of men and women. The men looked bewildered and frightened. I heard one of them say, "She won't stop yelling. She's hysterical. Somebody ought to get a doctor." A woman was saying, "Sshh, sweet, you're drunk," and another with her arms around the girl said sharply, "Quit it, you little fool! Can't you take it?"

I had just time to notice that the girl standing in the doorway screaming was the one whom the band leader had introduced as his bride, and that the girl pinioning her outflung arms was Sabina Brok, before Amanda strode up and smartly slapped Bettine's cheek.

She said sharply: "Stop yelling, child. What's the matter with you?"

Bettine's face went backward at the swift slap. She gulped, and shook her head.

Then she gasped, "She looks so—horrible." and jerked her head toward the room behind her. She shuddered, and her hands went to her trembling mouth, repressing another scream.

Amanda said, "Take care of her, Sabina," and pushed the curtains aside and went into the room. Lutie and Jeff and I followed, just as Mr. Karkoff dashed up and past us.

And we stood there, staring around us. At nothing.

I mean, there was the room of course, but apparently it was empty. Evidently the little girl who had screamed was merely hysterical, or as her friends had suggested she had imbibed too much, or—

Then I saw a face, dimly, just over the back of the tall Italian chair, as though it were peering into the room from a window in the wall beyond. But of course there was no window there. That small face, motionless, horridly dark, its eyes like emeralds circled in pearl, was staring at us from the blurry surface of the antique oval mirror hung above the table. The scarlet mouth was open, the head tilted oddly sideways and forward, and a thick lock of pale gold hair, brilliant in the light of the two big candles, fell across one cheek.

I shrank back, dragging at Lutie, but as she moved quickly forward I tottered after, clinging to her. Amanda and Karkoff were before us, gazing at something in that great Venetian throne, something still hidden from us by its tall carved back.

Then we reached them and saw it too—the burnished head twisted, the small, delicately curved body, limp as a doll stuffed with sawdust, propped like a broken puppet in the huge chair.

And then, with an added shock of horror, I realized that the long white folds of the girl's frock barely touched the floor and her sandaled feet dangled above it. She wasn't sitting in the chair, but hanging in it, hanging by the neck from a rope of diamonds caught on a carved scroll near the very top of the massive chair back. The fingers of one hand, tipped with vermilion lacquer, clutched the stem of a wine glass. The amber stain of spilled champagne spread over her white dress. The shattered bowl of the glass gleamed from the rug.

All that, and the tripod beside her holding a silver bucket of ice and a gold-necked bottle, the quill pen lying on the vellum pages of the guest book, another champagne glass beside it, the gleaming candles that made the staring eyes in the time-darkened mirror seem to move, to roll in their sockets—all was printed on my sight and on my memory for always, in a flash, in the brief instant before my cousin Amanda and Sandro Karkoff had sprung to the girl's side and were lifting her in their arms.

Karkoff muttered through clenched teeth, "Hold her—hold her up!" and his short strong hands wrenched at the diamond necklace, straining in the violent effort to tear it apart.

"Stop that! Unhook it from the chair!" said Amanda sharply.

A moment later he had unloosed that terrible shining chain, and they were carrying the girl to a couch at the side of the room.

Karkoff said hoarsely: "Get a doctor! Get Dr. Emmanuel, he's here! Quickly!"

It wasn't till then I noticed other people in the room, a huddled, silent group in the doorway, standing there staring curiously and stupidly just as I was doing. But they couldn't see the head and shoulders of the girl on the sofa, as Amanda was bending over her. Someone said, "Who is it? What happened?"

Karkoff said, "It is Miss Lynn. She is ill. Get the doctor, get him at once. And tell her sister."

A man said briskly, "I'll get Dr. Emmanuel!" and went.

Amanda straightened and turned. She was pale and her jaw was set like iron, but her voice was rigidly steady as she said, "The girl is dead."

She walked to a chair and sat down.

I thought, she ought to have smelling salts or water or something, and wondered if Lutie had the little bottle of apple brandy that her father, my Uncle Abidiah, had made by freezing cider in the keg long years ago, and which we use for medicinal purposes. When we had dashed off on our first big case she had carried it with her in her reticule. But of course that was different; that night she had reason to expect something distressing, while tonight . . .

These jumbled thoughts, if you can call them thoughts, went through my head but I didn't even move toward Amanda. I just stood looking at her foolishly, and hanging onto Lutie.

I guess my knees were weak and I was leaning on her, for she said, "Stand up, Marthy dear!" and sat me down firmly, just as there was a movement in the group near the doorway and a girl in gray came through it. She went swiftly to the figure, on the couch, pushing past Karkoff, who said something to her in an undertone and tried to hold her back. She shook off his restraining grasp, kneeled and took the hand from which the stem of the broken wineglass had fallen now. It seemed a long time that she knelt there, tightly holding those limp tapered fingers with their gaily painted tips.

Then Katherine Kilgallon put down her dead sister's hand, very carefully. She stood up.

She said, "Hero is dead, isn't she? Who killed her?"

She stood there, without any expression on her face at all, so far as I could see. No horror, nor grief. Just nothing; like a lovely, pale bronze mask tinted with color on the wide cheekbones beneath the long dark quiet eyes.

No one spoke. Then the draperies at the doorway parted suddenly, and Ted Greer came through them. He stopped short, gazing at the girl on the couch.

Katherine Kilgallon said, "You didn't do it, did you, Ted? She's dead, you know. Someone has killed her."

He turned slowly, facing her. And when he spoke it was to her only. His voice, mellow and rich and surprisingly deep for so young a man, and used, I thought, as he handled his violin, was grave.

"Do you think so, Katy? She always said she would do it herself, when she wanted to. She said that was the smart way to die."

He left the room, and Kate Kilgallon went with him, just as Charles Leland and Elinor Lynn entered it.

CHAPTER 4

CHARLES LELAND'S face was flushed and his breath short, as though he'd been running. "What's happened? Someone said Hero's ill."

He looked around, but from where he stood the body on the couch was screened from him by a knot of people. They shifted as Karkoff came forward, saying sharply, "Stand back, please! No one must go near her." And to the man in the doorway: "Mr. Leland, a very terrible thing has happened. Someone has gone for a doctor."

Leland saw that still figure then, and violently thrusting the jeweler away went toward it. He stooped, cried out, "Hero! Hero?"

Elinor Lynn was at his side. She put her hand on his arm, looking across his bent shoulder. I saw her flinch back, her thin white fingers gripping the broadcloth sleeve.

She said, "Don't! Charles, don't touch her!"

"What is it? What's happened to her? She looks dreadful." He turned, jerking his arm roughly from Elinor's grasp.

"She's horribly ill, as if—" His voice rose shrilly. "Where's the doctor? Why hasn't something been done?"

"I'm afraid nothing can be done for her," Karkoff said gently.

"Here's Dr. Emmanuel! I found him!" announced the brisk cheerful voice of the young man who had gone on that errand some minutes before.

Two men came in, an elderly gentleman with a neat Vandyke beard, erect shoulders and an authoritative manner, and the lad who had fetched him. The latter stopped in his tracks as he heard his own hearty tone fall incongruously on the strained silence. His jaw dropped ludicrously.

"Is anything serious the matter?" he stammered.

No one replied. We were all tensely waiting, watching the physician bending over the figure on the sofa.

Presently he straightened and turned.

"There is nothing I can do. The young woman was Miss Hero Lynn, was she not? She is dead."

"Dead," repeated Charles Leland in a whisper. "Dead? Why, that's crazy, she's never even been sick a day in her life. I don't believe it!" He seized the doctor's arm and shook it wildly. "Listen! You're lying, you don't know what you're talking about! Don't stand there. Do something!"

The doctor looked back at him gravely.

"There is nothing I can do, Mr. Leland. I am sorry."

Leland dropped his arm. "My God—oh, my God." His voice broke, and he swayed and stumbled to a chair, covering his face with shaking hands.

Elinor Lynn started toward him, but Dr. Emmanuel shook his head and held her back firmly.

"Let him alone! And fetch some brandy, someone," he commanded curtly, and to our host he said, "Mr. Karkoff, get this crowd out of here. And telephone the police at once. Spring—"

"Seven three one hundred," said a small demure voice. "I will attend to it at once, Dr. Emmanuel. I noted the phone in the foyer, when we came in. Also I will instruct our men to guard the doors and so forth even more particularly, since no one must go out, of course."

Lutie trotted from the room.

The doctor's startled gaze followed her, then reverted to our host.

"Who is that?" he asked sharply. But Karkoff was herding people from the room.

Amanda answered. "'That,'" she replied, "is Miss Lutie Beagle. I am her sister. We are The Beagle Detective Agency, a private investigating bureau employed for this evening by Mr. Karkoff to safeguard his interests—that is to say, his merchandise. And this is Miss Meecham, and Mr. Mahoney, our assistants."

She indicated myself and Jeff and continued, "As it happened, we reached this room practically at the same time as did Mr. Karkoff, and together with him removed Miss Lynn—I should say Mrs. Leland—from that large chair"—she pointed to it—"onto the sofa. She was then—she was not living when we found her."

Amanda's quiet statement of assorted facts seemed to be too much for Dr. Emmanuel to grasp all at once. He stared at her.

"You and your sister and this lady are detectives?" He frowned, shook his head as if trying to clear it from the vapors and said, "Hmm. And do I understand that you found the girl there? And that she was already—"

"Where is that brandy?" said Amanda, and went quickly across to Charles Leland, who was sagging in his chair. At that moment a frightened-looking waiter arrived with a glass and bottle on a trembling silver tray, and she seized the bottle, poured out the brandy and held it firmly to Leland's putty-colored lips.

He drank, choking as he swallowed, then raised his drawn face, A trickle of liquid ran down from one corner of his mouth.

"You mean you found her in that chair?" Charles Leland stared at my elder cousin with bloodshot, bewildered eyes. "I've been thinking. I thought she must have fallen, or—her face looked all bruised—"

"No, Mr. Leland, she was strangled. By the necklace. It was caught on a carved scroll on the back of the chair."

It seemed a cruel thing to tell the boy right then, though of course he would have to know sooner or later, so perhaps it was best to get the full shock over at once.

A voice said sharply, "Look! Look what she wrote."

Elinor Lynn hadn't gone with the others when Karkoff had made them leave. This was only natural since she was the dead girl's stepmother. But she'd been so quiet that I hadn't noticed she was still in the room until she spoke. Now she was standing at the table in front of the Venetian chair, staring down.

She murmured, "So she did it. I was often afraid she would."

The drapes at the doorway parted and Lutie came in. She said, "Mr. Karkoff is very busy. It appears that word of the tragedy has spread among his guests. He is trying to calm them. And Bettine, that is, Mrs. Greer, needs your services, Dr. Emmanuel. She has suffered a severe shock. Apparently she was the first person to—" She nodded toward the dead girl gravely, adding, "Mrs. Greer fainted. She is in the powder room. I was fortunate in being able to communicate with Inspector Moore personally. He is on his way here. Meanwhile he has asked us to assist you and Mr. Karkoff in taking charge. Sister and I, and our cousin, will remain right here. Jeffy dear, please stand outside there at the doorway and see that no one enters unnecessarily."

Jeff obeyed.

Dr. Emmanuel looked at Lutie, then at Amanda, and back to the delicately pink face of my younger cousin. Her silvery head, topped by the demure nosegay of mignonette, reached barely to the tiny boutonniere adorning his lapel. Her puffed sleeves above the long black lace gloves that rose to meet them were like little wings over her shoulders. In her spangled black net frock she looked like a fairy godmother, and a tiny witch, and a fine lady.

The doctor said, "You are acquainted with Inspector Moore?"

"He is an old friend of ours," answered Lutie demurely. "We worked together on our first murder, and he often drops in to tea. I hope you will honor us also, Doctor, when—"

She blushed at a realization that these amenities were not perhaps suited to the occasion.

The doctor opened the firm thin lips beneath his trim white mustache to speak, seemingly thought better of it, nodded—it was more like a bow, canceling uncertainty and acknowledging authority—and followed our assistant from the room.

As the curtains parted a girl's shrill voice said, "But I don't want to stay here! I want to go home!" Another answered, "And what'll you do there? Don't be a fooch. Let's go to the Stork." A childish treble piped, "No, the Savoy! I feel like Harlem." A man drawled, "But you ain't agoin' nowheres, my little chickadees. We're staying here. We're all under arrest. Anyway, we're not to, ahem, leave the premises. Or didn't you hear mine host? So keep your bras on, my dears."

Lutie stepped to Amanda, who was standing beside Charles Leland, crouched in his chair with his face buried in his hands. She took a small bottle of smelling salts from her jet-spangled evening purse and gave it to her sister. Then she crossed the room, and as she passed me I got up and followed her. We stood there together near Elinor Lynn and looked down at the scrawled-over pages of the big volume on the table.

Lutie said, "What is it you were afraid of, Mrs. Lynn?" Elinor Lynn's thin finger with its bright enameled nail pointed to the last entry in the guest book. It read:

Goodbye, goodbye, my funny sweet, my pet!
We loved so little, and let such silly things come between;
Your overalls and my silver spoon!
And yet, my little lovely, and yet,
Never will we forget
The sea, the stars, the moon,
Palm Beach—Weehawken—the Ferry in June—
Peanut brittle—our dance—our tune.
I guess, my presh, it all began—and ended—too soon.
And yet, my dumbbell, my sap, and yet,
Now you will never forget—

The last line was heavily underlined, and its first word had been blotted heavily, and the "Now you" written in again above it.

Lutie looked up from the vellum page to the tall pale girl who stood there staring at it, her lips set, her gray eyes brooding.

Elinor Lynn said slowly, "God! Poor infant! How could she?"

"How could she what?" said Lutie.

Elinor pressed her hands together. It sounds trite and like an exaggeration to say she wrung them, but really she did. And then she turned to Lutie, but not as if she were seeing her, and when she spoke it was in a barely audible voice, as if to herself.

"She loved Ted, of course. And yesterday she married Charles. Oh, I know she was fond of him, they'd been kids together, but she wasn't in love with him. I suppose she couldn't quite marry Ted, because of everything, or maybe he wouldn't. But anyway, when he married another girl she couldn't take it."

"Do you mean," said Lutie gently, "that you think she killed herself?"

Elinor Lynn looked at her as if she were seeing her for the first time.

She said slowly, "Did you see her tonight? Did you hear her? She was trying to be gay, hoping she could make a go of it with Charley, and then Ted Greer told everybody that he'd married Bettine. And then Hero asked him to play that song of theirs, that ought to be banned like *Gloomy Sunday*. And while he was playing it she came in here."

She looked down at the spread pages of the guest book and said violently, "Poor little thing!"

"You think she killed herself?" repeated Lutie.

Elinor Lynn said through tight lips, "She used to say she would if she wanted to! It always made me mad and disgusted. She'd often bring up the subject of death, for no reason at all that I could see, and she'd remark in that silly childish flippant way of hers, 'Well, angels, I'll never wait for the Sandman. I'll never be old or ugly or crossed up! Maybe I'll be a Ninon at ninety or maybe I'll go out like a light, whenever I like. But what a light!' Well"— Elinor touched the last line of the scribbled rhyme in the guest book—"there."

Lutie said, "That is her handwriting, Mrs. Lynn? You definitely recognize it?"

Elinor said, "What?" as if Lutie were slightly crazy. But she leaned over the page again and looked at it closely. "Of course it is!"

"Hanging is a rather painful way to commit suicide. But of course many people have chosen it. And possibly it might seem very smart to hang oneself with a million-dollar necklace. You gave your stepdaughter a very expensive and successful coming-out party last June, I understand, Mrs. Lynn."

Elinor Lynn looked my little cousin up and down, calmly.

She said, "You seem well informed, Miss Lutie Beagle. I suppose that comes within your province as a detective. Which, I must say, you do not look like. To reply to your question, I sponsored Hero's debut, but she arranged the details and paid for it, as doubtless you also know. Though why I should answer your questions, since—"

"—since they are not official," Lutie completed, and smiled up at the pale dark girl. "Of course there is no reason why you should. In any case that wouldn't be an official question. I'm sorry if it seemed impertinent. It was. Dear me, we Beagles did much better when we were anonymous. I suppose everybody will be on guard now, as if we were the Gestapo or the Gaypayoo or something. I begin to understand what the police are up against. I mean, the tendency to resent investigation seems a prevailing human trait. As a matter of fact, I quite understand it. I am sure I should feel the same way at any encroachment on my own privacy. That's really the worst bother about murders, to everyone concerned."

"So you think Hero was murdered? You don't believe she did it herself?" said Elinor Lynn quickly.

"I didn't mean to say that." Lutie clasped her little gloved hands. She looked embarrassed. "I don't really think—"

"Nonsense!" said Amanda unexpectedly and dryly. "You think quite well, at times. But at the moment, Sister, you are talking too much."

"I was only," murmured Lutie meekly, "talking against time, Sister. I mean, it would seem so much worse to just sit here without saying anything at all, while we are waiting. Wouldn't it?"

"Would it?" said Amanda. "I do not feel so."

But after a few minutes I certainly did.

Lutie had seated herself and folded her gloved fingers. Charles Leland sat there, his elbows on his knees and his head in his hands. I sat there, trying not to look toward the still form on the sofa and finally closing my eyes. Only when I did I saw a stark staring face, dark-hued and dreadful, printed against my eyelids. I opened them to follow Elinor Lynn's tall slender black-gowned figure nervously pacing back and forth across the room.

She stopped, and burst out, "My God! How long must we wait? Can't we move that screen over in front of her?"

She pointed to a tall screen in one corner of the room.

"We must not move anything until the authorities arrive," said Amanda quickly. But she went to the body of the girl on the couch and gently laid a white chiffon handkerchief over her face.

And somehow that made it all the more awful, because until then the face had been turned to one side and partly covered by silver-gold hair, and one could almost forget the girl wasn't sleeping. But now—

"I can't stand it! Talk! Say something, somebody!" cried Elinor Lynn, and turned desperately to Lutie. "Ask me questions, if you like! Anything! But don't just sit there!"

Lutie said softly, "I know you didn't like Hero very much, but you really are distressed, aren't you, Elinor?" The dark pale girl turned on her suddenly.

"No, I didn't like her! How could I? She'd never let me. Besides, she was always frightening me. I never knew what she'd do or say! I've often wished she were at the other end of the world so that I'd never have to see her again. But I didn't want her to be dead!"

Charles Leland raised his face and said hoarsely, "Stop, Elinor! Stop saying that word."

He was interrupted by the sound of quick firm footsteps outside the reception room and a crisp voice inquiring, "In here, Mr. Karkoff?"

At hearing Inspector Moore's calm authoritative tones I breathed a deep sigh of relief and relaxed in my chair. And as I recalled how I'd huddled back into it, ridiculously scared, on our first encounter, I felt a hysterical impulse to giggle.

But that time, of course, I hadn't known what to expect. Or rather, I'd expected some sort of brutally suspicious inquisitor instead of the quiet, keen and intelligent gentleman the inspector had proved to be. Besides, it had been our first case and I was very unsure of our status, particularly as we had delayed calling the authorities, and meanwhile my small cousin had been poking around, even in the room with that awful body on the bed, disturbing clues, for all I knew.

And then I gasped. For at this moment, as the curtains at the doorway parted, I caught a glimpse of Lutie swiftly stooping and plucking something from the rug at the foot of the huge carved chair in which we'd found the limp figure of the girl in white.

She straightened and moved back, clasping her silk evening bag demurely, her cheeks a deeper pink and her eyes shining in that way I knew only too well, as Inspector Moore stepped into the room.

CHAPTER 5

THE inspector had apparently arrived simultaneously with the ambulance surgeon. At any rate, the latter entered the reception room just behind him. Mr. Karkoff followed, holding aside the heavy curtains to admit two blue-coated, uniformed figures and another heavyset one buttoned tightly into a sack suit of chocolate brown. This was McGinnis, the inspector's right-hand man, as I knew from former experience, though why this burly fellow, with his uncouth manners and opinionated, commonplace mind, should have been chosen for his post I never had been able to understand.

He now stood in the doorway, his derby hat on the back of his head as usual, barely allowing three other men to squeeze past him.

His bulldog jaw belligerently out-thrust, he barked into the corridor, "Keep out, all of you!" and jerked the draperies together. Keeping his large fist on them he turned, planting himself solidly as his suspicious scowl surveyed the room before him. The three other men ranged themselves beside him, glancing with curiosity at the rich exotic appointments of the reception room, lighted only by the two huge candles, and at our assembled group. One of them grinned suddenly and delightedly at Lutie, who nodded demurely back. I recognized him then as Detective Dougherty, the stenographer; and the others as the fingerprint expert and the photographer, both of the homicide squad.

The ambulance surgeon and Inspector Moore, immaculate as always in gray worsted of faultless cut, had crossed to the slim, still figure on the couch. Gravely the inspector lifted the chiffon veiling the face and stood looking down. After a moment he moved aside with a gesture to the doctor to take his place. Their two figures hid the head and shoulders of the body from me, but the young surgeon's profile was toward me, and as he leaned forward I saw its brisk, businesslike expression change to one of horror and amazement.

"My God, it's Hero Lynn!" he muttered incredulously and straightened up abruptly.

The group in the room, which had been almost as quiet as the dead girl, stirred at her name. The men waiting near the doorway craned forward. Charles Leland groaned. Inspector Moore said sharply, "Mr. Karkoff, can we have more light?"

Karkoff moved quickly to a switch, and a bright diffused radiance from bulbs concealed behind the cornice filled the room. The young surgeon hastily set down hisbag, knelt and unfastened it. He was still staring at the dead glamour girl as his hands fumbled among his instruments and drew out a stethoscope.

I looked away and down at my own tightly clasped hands. I was holding them so to keep them from shaking. And they were cold and wanted to tremble partly because I was seeing again that dark, dreadful image in the mirror as we'd first seen it, and partly because I was frightened and, yes, angry.

For the thought of Lutie, swiftly stooping to pick up whatever it was she had spied there on the floor hadn't left me for a moment. I was telling myself, bitterly, that this death—suicide, murder, whatever it was—was none of our business. The Beagle Detective Agency had been engaged merely to guard Mr. Karkoff's merchandise. And obviously, from the glint I'd caught in her bright blue eyes, my little cousin had no intention whatever of simply minding her business.

Of course it was idiotic to expect that she would. This spectacular death had happened almost under her nose. Undoubtedly she intended not only to thrust that little nose in where it didn't belong but to follow it on secret and mysterious trails, and naturally I would be dragged along willy-nilly into dangers and difficulties and I didn't know what-all. In fact I was already being made a party to whatever she was up to, and she was up to no good, or she wouldn't be concealing whatever she had found from the authorities!

I thought, crossly, that I ought to nip her notions right in the bud! What if I said, quite casually but firmly, "What did you find on the floor just now, Lutie dear? Anything that would interest Inspector Moore?"

I glanced at the inspector, who was quietly watching the young surgeon as he pressed his instrument close to a wild young heart that would never beat again. I waited. This was no time to speak.

At last the doctor stood up. He took the rubber tubes from his ears, dropped the stethoscope into his bag and clicked it shut.

"Dead," he said, and swallowed and added automatically, "D.O.A. "

He backed away from the couch, still staring at the girl lying there. Inspector Moore drew the veil of white chiffon again over the dark face with the lock of bright hair strayed across it. Then he turned.

Now, I thought, and wet my dry lips, and looked defiantly at Lutie.

And Lutie was looking back at me. Not quite smiling, for her lips were demurely sober. But in the blue eyes under the quizzically peaked brows below the fringe of silver curls there was certainly an impish twinkle. Quite clearly she knew what was on my mind. And gently, fondly, she was laughing at me.

I felt silly. Maybe she had only stooped to retrieve the tiny scrap of lace and linen in her small gloved hand, her own handkerchief. Maybe she had found something that might be relevant to Hero's death and meant to disclose it properly in due time.

However, it didn't really matter. I couldn't tell on her any more than I could fly. And she knew it just as well as I did.

I glared back at her, and her tiny smile and nod was exactly like a little approving pat on the back. Then she turned with devoted interest to listen to the inspector, who was saying, "And now, Mr. Karkoff, what can you tell me of what happened?"

Mr. Karkoff drew a long breath. He appeared to consider. Then he said slowly and carefully, "Refreshments were being served in the ball-room and in the farther room, adjoining it. I was overseeing the arrangements, and as it happened had just stopped to suggest pressed duck to Miss Valhalla Bankitt when I heard a scream. It was a woman's scream and suggested hysteria. I laughed lightly and made some casual bon mot. I believe I said, 'Ah, youth, youth!' I did not wish to precipitate a panic, although there was something disquieting in the shriek we had heard. Then I proceeded calmly but rapidly in its direction.

"As I left the dance room and crossed the hall I saw a group of people in the foyer. In front of the doorway of this room was the young lady who had been presented this evening by our distinguished band leader, Mr. Ted Greer, as his bride. Mrs. Greer was screaming, Miss Sabina Brok was holding her arms, and as I approached, Miss Amanda Beagle slapped Mrs. Greer's face sharply.

"Miss Beagle said, 'Stop yelling, child! What's the matter with you?' And Mrs. Greer replied, 'She—she's horrible!' Miss Beagle pushed aside the curtains as I hastened across the foyer, and we entered this room together."

Mr. Karkoff drew out a white silk handkerchief and touched it to his forehead. He went on, carefully: "I think—yes, of course. Miss Beagle's sister,and her assistants followed, for they were there immediately afterwards. I mean, after I—after we—"

He swallowed.

Inspector Moore said patiently, "Yes, Mr. Karkoff?"

The jeweler straightened himself.

"Miss Hero Lynn was in the throne chair." He jerked his smooth black head toward it. "It took only a glance to see that she was hanging in it. I dashed forward and lifted her, but I think Miss Beagle was before me. Anyway, I saw at once that the girl was caught by the necklace around her neck—my diamond necklace, worth more than a million dollars, hooked on a carved scroll on the throne's back. I was wrenching at it, trying to tear it apart with my hands."

He looked down at his short strong hands, then up at Inspector Moore.

"But the necklace was very strong. Then someone—I think Miss Beagle—said, 'Unhook the thing!' I did so, and together we lifted Miss Lynn and carried her to the couch. After which I sent for Dr. Walter Emmanuel, one of my guests and a distinguished physician."

He paused, then said, "I could not believe that Miss Lynn was dead. Especially—"

He stopped short.

"Yes?" prompted the inspector. "You were saying 'especially—' "

Mr. Karkoff's eyes slid sidewise toward Elinor Lynn, who was standing stiffly against an end of the long renaissance table. She said, "Don't talk about it now, Sandro."

He said, "Yes, Mrs. Lynn. I must. I started to. It may matter."

He turned to Inspector Moore. "What I then thought of, Inspector Moore, was a previous occasion on which Miss Hero Lynn had tried to hang herself. You see, I had been present at a small party given by Miss Lynn herself, and in the course of it we found Miss Lynn suspended in an archway by a silken scarf."

Charles Leland looked up sharply. He said, "That was all nonsense. Her feet were touching the floor, she wasn't choked at all, or anything. It was just a gag, as you know very well."

"Yes," said Mr. Karkoff, "I know that quite well. It was what I thought of as I saw her hanging from my diamond necklace in my throne. And as we laid her on the couch I still thought of it. I thought she had meant to hoax us again. But I feared that this time she had gone too far. I couldn't believe that she was dead. The thought was too awful, and on this particular occasion—yet I am afraid that in my soul I knew it, even before Miss Beagle pronounced it so. The girl's face—" The jeweler shook his head, controlling a shudder.

Inspector Moore turned to Amanda. "Miss Beagle?"

Amanda said, "Myself and my sister and my cousin and Mr. Jefferson Mahoney were here tonight because we were employed by Mr. Alexandro Karkoff to see that the ladies whom he had chosen to display his wares, or any other person, did not make off with them. We had posted our agents at the various doorways and were ourselves stationed in the dance room when we heard a scream. We hastened toward it. Outside this doorway I saw a young woman, whom I had just lately heard announced as the newlywed bride of the leader of the orchestra. She was screaming. Another young woman, whose name I had gathered was Miss Sabina Brok, was holding her arms. Mrs. Greer seemed to me to be hysterical, and I slapped her face, which stopped her shrieks. I told Miss Brok to take care of her, and then I entered this room.

"Mr. Karkoff entered also and went past me. As he says, my sister and cousin and Mr. Mahoney must have been with us, but all I noticed at the time was an empty room. Then I saw the folds of a white skirt from beside that large chair." She motioned at it. "Mr. Karkoff and I went toward it, and he has quite accurately described what he saw and what he did. I need not repeat it now in detail. I will only add that I knew the girl was dead the instant I touched her."

"Stop it! Stop talking about it, for God's sake!" cried Charles Leland.

The inspector turned and looked at him.

"I am afraid that it is necessary to talk about it, Mr.—?"

The young man stared back at him, his haggard, bloodshot eyes resentful. But he straightened his shoulders and forced his voice to a quieter pitch, though it was sullen and wavered like that of a schoolboy who has been weeping.

He said, "My name's Leland. Charles Leland. Hero"—he pressed his knuckles against lips that shook as he said the name—"was my wife."

"Oh." The inspector's eyebrows registered some slight surprise. "I did not know that Miss Hero Lynn was married."

"We were married yesterday. So maybe you can see how awful—" He stopped and got a grip on himself. "Sorry. Of course I know you've got to—"

"I've got to ask questions of you as well as others, Mr. Leland, naturally. But—" The inspector glanced toward the figure on the couch, then turned to Karkoff. "Is there another room where Mr. Leland can wait?"

"My office is just across the foyer, with my private suite beyond it. Mr. Leland will have quiet and privacy there," answered the jeweler. "And, Inspector Moore, in view of the tragic termination of the evening, I would like if possible to give my guests permission to leave. I have, of course, all the names and addresses, as there were no guests present without invitations, in case you may later wish to question any of them. But under the circumstances—"

"I shall wish to see the young woman who apparently discovered Miss—Mrs. Leland's body. Mrs. Greer, I believe you said, whose screams drew you to the room here. And of course Dr. Emmanuel. Also any relatives or close friends of Mrs. Leland's. Everyone else may go, though if anybody has any relevant information to volunteer, naturally I want to hear it. Keep your entire staff also. And please find the waiter who brought that here"—the inspector indicated the silver tripod and bucket holding the bottle of champagne—"and bring him here. Just a moment, please," he added, as the jeweler, with a nod, started to leave. He turned to Elinor Lynn, who was standing, as she had been ever since the inspector had entered, beside Charles Leland's chair.

She said now, in a rather low but quite composed tone, "I am Elinor Lynn. Hero is—was my stepdaughter. When I came in here, she was—as she is now—on that couch."

"You had been sent for?"

"Not exactly. I had been—" She stopped, then continued quietly, "I was crossing one of the large rooms and met Mr. Ted Greer, with Hero's sister. She—Kate—went on past me. Mr. Greer stopped and said, 'Hero's found the smart way to die. She's in the reception room.' I came here at once."

Inspector Moore regarded her thoughtfully for several moments.

He said then, "I should like you to wait in Mr. Karkoff's rooms with Mr. Leland. Miss Beagle and the others will join you presently. Meanwhile, Mr. Karkoff, please find Mrs. Leland's sister, and Mr. and Mrs. Greer. Also Miss Brok and any other persons who were at or near the doorway of this room when you entered to find Mrs. Leland's body. I should like them also to wait in your rooms."

Elinor Lynn put her hand on Charles Leland's shoulder. He stood up, moving like a person in a daze. They went out then, with Mr. Karkoff. McGinnis, at a nod from his chief, followed, and a uniformed policeman took his place in the doorway.

CHAPTER 6

INSPECTOR MOORE crossed to the tall throne chair, as the jeweler called it, and stood looking at it for several minutes. Presently he turned to Amanda.

"Now, Miss Beagle, I'd like you to describe, in as much detail as you can recall, the exact position and appearance of the girl's body when you first saw it in this chair. Dougherty, take this down, please."

Dougherty opened his notebook and got out his pencil as Amanda stood up, and holding up her long black satin skirts carefully so that they would not touch the fragments of broken glass on the rug, walked around to face the throne.

She began, slowly and carefully.

"The girl was in the precise center of that chair, her left hand on one arm of it, her right hand, clutching the broken stem of a wine glass, hanging across the arm. At first glance she seemed to be sitting up, very straight, though in a peculiarly strained position, with her head bent forward. I was looking at her from this angle, except that I was closer than I am now, so that—"

Amanda's face was pale. She paused to steady a slight tremor in her voice. "So that I did not see her face, because it was tilted forward, and a lock of her hair fell across it. But it took only a second or two to realize that the girl could not be sitting in the chair. The body was too high in it. The next instant Mr. Karkoff and I were both lifting her, or trying to. We could not move her up and out of the chair because she was caught by something to the back of it—by the necklace she was wearing, we saw as her hair fell aside."

Amanda pressed her lips together. After a moment she went on. "Mr. Karkoff started to wrench the necklace apart. I told him to unhook it. I could now see where it was caught on a scroll on the chair back. He slipped the thing off while I held the girl's body up with my hands under her arms. Then we carried her to the couch and laid her on it. It was not until then that I saw her face."

"And yet," put in the inspector, "you knew before that. You said that she was dead."

"Her heart was not beating. I knew that while I was holding her up in the chair," Amanda said.

There was a short silence in the room. Then Inspector Moore said, "You say that the girl's hands were on the chair arms ?"

"Her left hand was. The other dangled, holding the glass stem."

"So that she should have been able to brace herself up in the chair," murmured the inspector, though not as a question. After a moment's thought he stepped to the back of the chair, and leaning forward examined closely the carved leaf with the pointed, up-curved tip like a small strong hook in the exact center of the high back and about three feet above the brocaded seat. He touched the very point of the leaf-tip.

"This is the projection on which the necklace was caught?"

Amanda said, "Yes."

He said, "There are scratches on it and the gold leaf is chipped also." He knelt down and peered at the rug. "There are flecks, apparently of gilding, here."

He stood up and said, abruptly, "Miss Beagle, did you notice anything in particular about the girl's clothing?"

Amanda said, "Merely that there was too little of it. But that is obvious. I noticed the folds of her white skirt, on either side of the chair, as soon as, or soon after, I entered the room. But, no, Inspector, I noticed nothing else in particular about her clothing."

Inspector Moore turned quickly to my younger cousin.

"And you, Miss Lutie? As I understand, you came into the room with your sister. Please tell me what you saw and did."

"I came in just behind Sister," Lutie said. "She went straight across to the throne chair, I guess. As she says, she must have immediately noticed the folds of Hero Lynn's white frock beyond the chair. I didn't, then. I was looking at the face in the mirror."

She paused, clasping her little gloved hands together. Inspector Moore waited.

Lutie went on. "It was Hero Lynn's face. Tilted down, as Sister says, and with a lock of hair across it. The face was dark, the eyes staring. It was very shocking. I hurried forward. I saw the girl's figure hanging in the chair just a moment before Sister and Mr. Karkoff lifted it."

"And the drapery of her frock? Did you happen to notice that at all, Miss Lutie?" The Inspector watched her, intently.

"Yes, I did, Inspector. The folds of her skirt were not rucked up about her figure at all. They were hanging straight, taut and smooth. The hem touched the floor."

She gazed back at the inspector gravely.

He said, "You are quite sure of that, Miss Lutie?"

She said, solemnly, "I am, Inspector."

They exchanged a look of understanding. I didn't know what it meant, which was of course very stupid. But I hadn't time to consider the point then, because the inspector had turned from Lutie to me.

I told him, as calmly as I could, though these continued recitals were making me feel almost unnerved enough to scream, what I had seen and done after Lutie and I had followed Amanda into the room. Of course I hadn't done anything of importance, as Amanda had. My report corresponded almost exactly with Lutie's, except for one detail. As it happened, I had stood farther back than Lutie, more to the left of the girl in the chair, so that her figure was in profile and I had seen, even before Lutie did, apparently, that the girl was hanging in the chair, and I even saw the narrow tight gleaming strand that held her there.

"And the girl's dress?" asked the inspector.

"Why, it was a white dress," I said, foolishly. "And, yes, I noticed that it was splashed with fresh light stains—the champagne, I suppose. And I noticed that the hem hung down to the floor but her feet didn't."

"You are quite certain about that? About the way the girl's dress hung, I mean?"

It was all very vivid. I closed my eyes. It was then even more vivid.

I said, "Yes!" vehemently. "I can see it." I opened my eyes then, as Inspector Moore said, "Thank you, Miss Meecham," and to my great relief turned away as Mr. Karkoff entered the room, accompanied by one of the waiters, a plump little man in mulberry-colored livery.

The jeweler said, "This is Jules Duval, who served the champagne." He pointed toward the bottle in its iced bucket, the silver tripod.

Inspector Moore asked, "Just when was that, Jules? Do you know, exactly? Please tell me about it."

The waiter had a round face that looked honest and bright and as if it liked to smile. But it was very sober at the moment.

He said carefully, "M'sieu, I cannot tell you the precise moment when I served the champagne to the lady here. But it was soon after we had started to serve supper. That would be sometime after half-past eleven o'clock." He looked for corroboration at Mr. Karkoff, who nodded.

"Who ordered the champagne?" asked the inspector.

"She ordered it. I mean Miss Hero Lynn. I know her well—that is to say, I have served her often. She was coming from the terrace into the large dance room, when she stopped and told me to take a bottle of champagne and two glasses to the reception room. I asked her what champagne—what vintage—she wished, and she said, 'The oldest, the finest, the best. I leave it to you, Jules!' I had just taken an order for four sazaracs and three gin-and-tonics. After I had served these I hastened to do as Miss Lynn had told me. I chose a very fine wine. The year—"

"Yes, yes, Jules, I am certain you did. Was Miss Lynn here when you brought it in?"

"No, m'sieu. Nobody was here. I brought in the wine and put it beside the throne chair and the two glasses on the table, as she had commanded. I waited then, wishing to open the wine for her. I waited several minutes. She came in alone and sat down in the big chair. She said, 'Pull the cork, my fine-feathered friend.' I did so. I asked her if I should pour the wine. She said, 'No. Scram.' I did so."

"Did anyone enter this room while you were here?"

"No, m'sieu."

"Did you pass anyone entering it as you left it?"

"No, m'sieu."

"Was anyone in the foyer?"

"No, m'sieu."

"Or approaching the foyer, from the corridor?"

The little waiter hesitated. Then he said, "No, m'sieu. Not approaching it. But as I crossed the corridor from the foyer two ladies came out of the powder room. They came toward me, talking together, as I went into the dance room. I think they came into the dance room after me, though I cannot be certain of that, m'sieu. My mind was on my further duties. It was a busy time and I had already absented myself from the floor for too long, perhaps. I was hurrying—"

The inspector interrupted. "How long was it, Jules, from the time when you received the lady's order to serve her with champagne here in the reception room to the time when you left, having served it?"

The waiter considered. "It took me, perhaps, five minutes to fetch the champagne from the service bar to this room. Then I waited for Miss Lynn perhaps seven or eight minutes, maybe ten, though I do not think quite so long. Then I opened the wine, poured it, and scra—and left, as I have already said. It is hard to be more exact."

Inspector Moore nodded. "And now, who were the ladies you noticed leaving the powder room? Do you know their names?" he asked.

"One was Miss Sabina Brok. The other—" the waiter shook his head. "I do not recognize her. But she is a very striking young lady, in pale gray, with hair coiffured close to her head. Red hair, shining like metal."

"You would know her if you saw her again?" asked the inspector.

"But yes, m'sieu." The waiter was positive. As who would not be? Merely from the brief description I knew of course that the girl he meant was Hero's sister, Kate Kilgallon. Striking red hair, gray dress. I felt my heart contract. Why, I don't know. I'd seen the girl only twice, I had no reason for any special feeling toward her, yet somehow I didn't want her to be involved.

I brought myself up short, realizing that I was being silly. After all, why shouldn't she have been coming from the powder room? Even though it must have been just a few minutes before her sister was— Again I snapped the thread of my hurrying thoughts off short.

Inspector Moore was saying, "Jules, can you describe the lady's manner, when she ordered the champagne, and also later when you served it to her? Was she upset or excited—unnaturally so, I mean?"

"Excited?" The little waiter reflected. "Yes, m'sieu, I would say she seemed excited. But these young ladies—" He shrugged deprecatingly, conveying the inference that to these young ladies as he'd observed them, excitement was a more natural state than not.

He added carefully, "Not upset, m'sieu. On the contrary. Very gay, though—how do I say it?—wound up tight. When she stopped me to order the wine her voice was high, a little thin, not low in the throat as usual."

He blushed as Inspector Moore remarked, "You seem to have been quite a close observer of the young lady's mannerisms." The tone was slightly quizzical. Jules' plump cheeks turned an even brighter red.

"Marie, pardon, m'sieu, I mean to say my wife, she reads always about these young ladies who are so often in the magazines and papers, and she always asks me what they wear, how they speak, and behave. So I notice." He spread his palms, then added, "Besides, they are noticeable."

The inspector touched his clipped gray mustache, hiding a smile. "I see. One thing more. You say the lady's voice was not pitched low when she ordered the champagne. Were there people nearby, then, who could have overheard her speak to you?"

"We were quite near a table, with several people seated at it, and others were passing. But—" He shook his head. "I do not recall any of these people in particular."

"You are quite certain of that?"

"Yes, m'sieu."

"Well, I think that's all for the present, Jules. Leave your name and address."

The inspector nodded toward Dougherty and his notebook and said, "Hello, Doctor," as the officer at the door admitted a short rotund gentleman with twinkling black eyes behind twinkling rimless pince-nez, a black mustache, a black Homburg, and a black bag. This was the medical examiner, or the M.E., as I had learned during our first case.

As the young ambulance surgeon led the M.E. toward the figure on the couch the inspector turned to us. Then he noticed that the little waiter, having given Dougherty his name and address, was hesitating in the doorway.

"Yes, Jules?"

"Pardon, m'sieu. You asked me what I can tell you about the young lady's manner. I tell you how she seemed when she ordered the wine, then later, when I served it."

"Yes? Go on."

"It is only my impression, m'sieu. But Miss Lynn was in a great hurry to be rid of me. I could not help thinking that she expected—that she had a rendezvous here with someone. Some gentleman—"

"Thank you, Jules, that's a point. I'll think it over."

The little waiter left, looking excited and important, and Inspector Moore turned back to us and told us that we were free to leave too. "If you wish. Of course I shall probably want to talk with you again." He addressed Amanda. Then his eyes slid toward Lutie as he added, "Or if you wish to wait, in Mr. Karkoff's office, perhaps, I have no objection."

Lutie said quickly, "It's awfully late, Inspector, and my cousin and I are longing to be back in our beds. May we go, Sister? Or must we stay? Surely Jeffy, wherever he is, can attend to the duty of dismissing our men, and so on."

"You will have to manage to keep your eyes open a little longer, Sister." Amanda rose firmly. "I intend to see Jefferson, and our men, before I leave."

"Then Miss Lutie and Miss Meecham can wait in Mr. Karkoff's office. Perhaps I'll see you before you go home."

I was sure the inspector and Lutie exchanged a glance as we left the room. It meant—well, it boded no good. It meant that he was counting on her, or at least hoping, from previous experience, that her keen bright eyes and her funny little sleuthing instinct, might be useful. And of course he knew, as I knew only too well, that she was dying to use it.

We followed Amanda and Mr. Karkoff across the foyer into his office, which was paneled in expensive-looking wood, with a deep-piled carpet underfoot and a curved desk across one corner. As we entered, a tall and handsome young man in impeccable evening attire, who seemed to be lurking just inside the curtained doorway, turned eagerly to my elder cousin.

"Miss Beagle, you told me not to leave here under any circumstances!" he said. "So I didn't, even when the girl screamed."

"And quite right, Mr. Walden. But I'd like you to come with me now. I must interview each of our staff. Please wait here, Sister and Martha, until I come back," said Amanda, and went out with the gentleman who, I now realized, must be one of "our half-dozen trusted and personable young men." The jeweler, begging us to make ourselves comfortable, excused himself and followed.

Now was my chance!

As soon as they'd gone I whispered, "Lutie!" and clutched her arm. Because even though the door was open into the next room and there were other people there, I meant to make her tell me! Had she picked something important up from the floor in the reception room beneath the throne chair? And what was it? And what was she going to do with it?

"Hush, Marthy. I'll show you. Wait." She put me into the chair facing the door and took one opposite me with her back to it. Over her shoulder I could glimpse the room beyond, an odd room, furnished with Louis Philippe and golden oak furniture, with a pink-shaded piano lamp and a Russian icon on the wall in the corner. Charles Leland sat staring dully before him, just below the icon. Near him Sabina Brok impatiently turned the pages of *Vogue*. Next to her was Kate Kilgallon, her hands folded and her eyes closed. Ted Greer and his wife were together on a small brocaded sofa, his arm around her. Elinor Lynn stood at a center table, glancing through a plush-covered album. McGinnis, in a golden-oak rocking chair, watched them all. To him, they were all potential killers, and his expression plainly said so. Of course, I am convinced that McGinnis thinks all suspects guilty, even after they have been proved innocent. I have never learned to like McGinnis.

Well, anyway, while I was thinking this with my usual feeling of indignation, Lutie was fishing in her spangled reticule. She drew out a handkerchief, holding it like a small cup that contained something precious.

"That's what I found, Marthy," she whispered.

I leaned forward, peering at the tiny square of linen and lace. At first it appeared that was all there was to be seen. Then I saw, at the bottom of the little cup, a minute crimson crescent. The tip of a red enameled fingernail.

"Whose?" My lips formed the word. I didn't say it aloud.

Lutie shook her head.

"Quite likely it isn't important, my dear," she murmured.

But she folded the kerchief and slipped it back in her reticule quickly as Inspector Moore, followed by Dougherty, entered the room. So quickly that he didn't notice the gesture.

In response to her eagerly inquisitive eyebrows he said, "Well, the M.E. couldn't tell us anything much that we didn't already know. The girl was strangled, obviously by the necklace. Death was very recent. The boys are taking pictures and prints now."

He spoke rather absently. Then also in an undertone, but more sharply, he asked, "Any ideas, Miss Lutie? You were there when she was found. Could the girl have committed suicide?"

"No," said Lutie, quietly. "She was murdered."

CHAPTER 7

INSPECTOR MOORE regarded my small cousin gravely.

"You seem very certain of that, Miss Lutie." She nodded. "Why?"

"Her frock. Unless someone rearranged it, which seems unlikely. Why should they? Attempts are often made to make murders appear to be suicides but I have never heard of anyone trying to make a suicide look like a murder, unless the suicide him or herself did so, out of spite. But in this case that wouldn't be possible."

"You are quite positive about the way her gown fell?"

"Entirely positive."

"Well, we'll keep that to ourselves, until or if we find the murderer. The papers may as well call it suicide for the time being."

He looked at Lutie. She nodded sedately in agreement. Then he asked quickly, "Any notions about the murderer?"

Lutie shook her head. "No, Inspector," she said regretfully.

"Hmm." He sighed and walked slowly to the door to the inner room.

All the faces in that room turned toward him, and it seemed to me a wave of dread passed over each one. "Mrs. Greer, please?"

The girl on the sofa shrank closer to her husband. His arm tightened around her shoulders for a second, then he stood her up, gently, and came forward with her.

"Chin up, Betts!" He tucked a stray lock of soft brown hair back into her topknot. To Inspector Moore he said, "She's pretty much done up. You won't keep her long?"

"I'll try not to, Mr. Greer."

The inspector closed the door behind the small figure in the pale pink dress and led her gently to a deep-cushioned chair.

Bettine Greer had shadows like violet petals under her round brown eyes, which were reddened from weeping; the long lashes stuck together in starlike points. She looked ill, and I could see that she was trembling; but she was making a valiant effort to control herself, sitting straight in her chair and looking back at Inspector Moore with a glance that didn't waver. I remembered the scene in the powder room between herself and Hero and how she'd stood up to the other girl.

"The girl has spunk," I thought. And that isn't all I thought. There had been fury, fierceness, in that childlike face. Could she have possibly—?

The inspector was saying, "I'll try not to keep you long, Mrs. Greer. I can see you are still suffering from shock. But it will help me if you are able to answer a few questions now."

She said, through lips that shook only a little, "It was awful. But I'll try."

"Please tell me about it. In your own way will be simplest."

She drew a long breath.

"There isn't much to tell. I went into that room. The reception room. At first I didn't see—I thought it was empty. I was hurrying across to the table where the guest book is. I was right up close to that big chair when I saw Hero. It startled me, because I didn't know anybody was in the room. And she was so still. Then I saw her face. It was horrible, all dark, and the eyes staring. I think I screamed. Anyway I ran right out of the room. I guess I kept right on screaming. Pretty soon there were people around, and someone was holding me. Then somebody slapped me, to stop me from screaming, I suppose. It must have been the right thing to do, because after that I sort of came to. I knew it was Sabina Brok holding me, and she started leading me away somewhere. Then I must have fainted. I can't remember anything else until I was lying on the couch in the powder room, and the doctor was there. I started to cry. I was seeing that face again."

She stopped, shuddering, then stiffened her lips and went on, "Then Ted came, and Mr. Karkoff; and they took me to a bedroom, Mr. Karkoff's, where it was quiet. Ted stayed there with me." Color tinted her round cheeks for the first time, and her chin lifted. "He sat on the bed beside me, and told me everything was all right, that he—"

The murmur of her voice trailed off.

"Yes, Mrs. Greer?" the inspector prompted her. "Your husband told you—?"

"That he loved me."

She said the words very softly. With pride and—wasn't there also a faint hint of defiance, even of that fierceness I'd seen before in her small face? I wondered.

"Mrs. Greer," Inspector Moore asked gravely, "why did you go to the reception room? Were you on any particular errand?"

Her color deepened.

"I—yes. I wanted to write in the guest book."

"You hadn't written in it earlier?"

"Yes, I had. I'd signed my name. But only part of it—Bettine Donat. I wanted to write 'Greer.' Ted didn't want me to before—" the small chin went higher—"before he'd announced our marriage. You see, we were married today. This morning. And he wanted to announce it this evening, from the musician's platform. He said though we'd had such a quiet wedding there wasn't anything secret about it, and he wanted to tell everybody. But I didn't—I mean, I was frightened—"

"Frightened, Mrs. Greer? Why? What were you frightened about?" asked the inspector gently.

"Because I always get stage fright. Always. I know it's silly, but I never could help it. Of course I wanted to tell everybody, too, only not like that. But Ted said if we told even one person there'd be a hullabaloo and fuss anyway. And of course there would, because he's so famous. So—"

"How long have you known your husband, Mrs. Greer? I hope you don't mind my asking that."

"No, of course I don't," said Bettine. "I've known him for three years. Three years and five weeks and two days." She blushed and added hastily, "I—you see, I used to sing with him. I mean, with his band. That was before he had such a famous band, of course."

"You are a professional singer, then?"

"Well, not very. I mean I wasn't for very long, and I wasn't very good. And I didn't like it. That is, I liked to sing, but I always got stage fright. And so when I had an operation on my throat and couldn't sing any more, at least not loud enough, I was glad."

She looked glad, for a moment. Then her face saddened.

"But of course I shouldn't be. Because Mama had made me study, and she'd counted on me so. And afterwards, back home in Green Center, Ohio, after I'd lost my voice—"

She didn't go on with that, but it took no stretch of imagination to guess that life back home in Ohio with Mama, after the voice was lost, hadn't been very cheerful.

After a moment she continued, "And of course I didn't see Ted all the time, as I used to. He came out often, whenever he could. But I hadn't seen him for nearly a month before last night!"

"And last night?" The inspector's tone was smooth, gentle.

She squared her shoulders. Her round brown eyes flamed proudly.

"He flew out to see me in a special plane that he'd chartered! And asked would I marry him right away! So of course I said yes. Mama wanted us to wait till June to get married in Green Center, in her wedding dress, in church or in the parlor under a bell made of white roses. But Ted said no. He had to be back in New York to play at an important affair, and besides he didn't like fuss. And neither do I!"

She set her lips. "Mama talked and talked. She even warned me that maybe he wouldn't marry me, but that was ridiculous, and it made me mad! So we flew to Elkton, Maryland, and as soon as we got there, early this morning, we were married. I sent her a telegram, and then we had breakfast, and then we flew to New York. And Ted took me to a beautiful place with tall windows facing the Plaza and the Park. It was like pictures I've seen of French palaces, big rooms with gilt mirrors and crystal chandeliers and soft gray rugs. And he bought me this dress."

She smoothed it lovingly. It was a charming dress, a film of delicate peach-blossom net over palest blue taffeta, with tiny puffed sleeves and a bunch of trailing arbutus caught on one shoulder.

She touched these.

"Ted said he liked arbutus better than orange blossoms. And I do too. Orange blossoms are too conventional."

There was the touch of defiance again. And this time I thought, why, of course! She's just a little girl, a little-town girl. Which I'd been myself, in a way, though I'd lived in a smoky city in Pennsylvania when I'd kept house for my papa, before he died and I'd gone to live with my cousins Amanda and Lutie in East Biddicutt, and then we'd come to New York. But now I recognized the unsophistication of those who live inland and under the family wing. And the rebelliousness that goes with it.

I said suddenly, astonishing myself, "Inspector Moore, can't Bettine—can't Mrs. Greer go now? She's tired—"

I don't know why I spoke up just then, really. The child didn't look especially tired. She was less wan as she stroked her pretty frock than she'd been at any time. And she looked up at me with some surprise and no particular gratitude.

But the inspector rose and said, "Yes, I think Mrs. Greer may go. After two more questions. Mrs. Greer, did you know Miss Hero Lynn—I mean, Hero Lynn Leland? Had you met her before this evening?"

The girl said quickly, "No!"

"But when you saw her in the reception room you knew who it was?"

"Yes, I did. I've seen her pictures in the newspapers." The child's voice was low. And now it was sullen, too.

"You had never met her before?"

"No. I'd seen her, this evening. Dancing. And then when she got up on the bar and said she was married. to Mr. Leland. I guess everybody saw her then—she was making a great show of it. I didn't think it was very nice."

"You never met Hero Leland at all? Never talked with her?"

"No."

"You had no unfriendly feelings toward her?"

The girl swallowed. "Of course not. How could I? I didn't know her, even—"

"Did your husband know her?"

"I don't know. I suppose he did. She was Glamour Girl Number One, wasn't she? And he is a great band leader, on the radio and in smart New York cafés, and all. I guess he must have known her. In fact I think he mentioned her to me. He said, 'I'm glad you don't wear blood on your lips and nails like—' "

She spread her fingers, the backs upward. The small nails were a pale rose-pink.

I saw Lutie leaning forward toward the girl. But Bettine folded her small hands together quickly and stood up.

"May I go now, please?"

I wondered swiftly why she'd thought her husband had referred to Hero when he'd talked of reddened lips and fingernails. And of course I knew she had met Hero. At least that once in the powder room.

But Inspector Moore said gravely, "Yes, you may go, Mrs. Greer. I'll see your husband next. Then you'll both be free to leave."

He opened the door for her and called in Ted Greer.

CHAPTER 8

THE bearded young band leader sat with his hands clasped loosely between his knees, his eyes on Inspector Moore. He looked interested.

"What can you tell me about Hero Leland's death?" asked the inspector.

Ted Greer thought, and then said, "Very little, I'm afraid. I was drinking a glass of milk in the pantry when a waiter told me that there had been an accident. He said it was in the reception room. I asked what kind of accident? The boy said he understood Miss Lynn had fainted or something. I don't like accidents, and I didn't think Miss Hero Lynn, I should say Mrs. Leland, as I believe she should be called—I heard her announce her marriage to Charley, of course—had fainted. But I went to the reception room. Hero was lying on the couch. She was dead, as you know, and as I could see. A number of people were there. I only remember her sister, who stood looking down at the body."

Ted Greer paused and smiled faintly.

"Kate, that's her sister, said, 'Somebody's killed her. You didn't do it, did you?' I said I thought Hero had done it herself." He stopped, then continued, "It wasn't nice to think; but you see, she'd tried it before. I mean as a gag, not really meaning to kill herself. And this time—"

He pushed his hand through his thick dark hair, with the first sign of nervousness or concern he'd shown.

"This time, I was afraid,she'd slipped. Or maybe she'd honestly meant to pull it off. But there wasn't anything I could do, so I left. I wanted to find my wife."

"You didn't know that your wife had found Mrs. Leland's body and that it was her screams?"

"No. I didn't hear her screaming. I must have been in the pantry then. That's behind the door at the far end of the smaller dance room in back of the bar."

"You didn't know your wife had fainted, and been taken to the powder room?"

"Of course I didn't. I left the reception room with Kate and went to the bar. I'd told Bettine I'd join her there. We were going to have a drink together to celebrate. But she wasn't there."

"Did you meet anyone on your way?"

"Yes, I met Elinor Lynn, coming in from the terrace, I think. And I told her—I think I said that Hero had found 'the smart way to die.' That's

what she used to say she'd do, you see. Then somebody told me that
Betts was in the little girls' room, that she'd found the body and fainted. I
went there. The doctor was with her, she was just coming to. And she
was terribly upset, and people were beginning to crowd around, so we
took her to Karkoff's bedroom. I went with her there. And that's all, I'm
afraid, Inspector, that's all I know."

"Is it?" said Inspector Moore, quietly. "You knew Hero Lynn very
well, didn't you?"

The young man's black eyebrows, that naturally curved up at the
outer corners, went up in the middle.

"Yes, I knew her. Who didn't, since she's been Glamour Gal Number
One? Of course I knew her."

"But merely as an acquaintance?"

"Well, we were rather more than mere acquaintances. We'd been at
lots of parties together, at the swing spots, usually with a gang. And besides that we used to go to danceterias, just the two of us sometimes, and
last summer we'd drive out to Montauk or Coney to swim, or to the Fair.
We liked those places because there weren't so many people. I mean,
people we knew. You see, I get pretty much fed up with hot spots and the
cash-and-class clan. I have to see too much of them. And Hero seemed
to like a change too."

"Were you and Miss Lynn fond of each other, Mr. Greer? Of course
you need not answer if you feel that is too intimate a question."

"Oh, no, that isn't too intimate, Inspector. Because we weren't, you
see. In the sense in which the word is generally used. I might as well get
that said, because there's been plenty of gossip which is all going to be
raked up again now, no doubt. As for being 'fond'—" The young man
smiled, with that lift of his curved eyebrows that was like a shrug. "I don't
think you'd have found that word in Hero's lexicon. For myself, the kid
was fun to be with. I liked her very much. And she must have found me
fun to be with, too, I suppose."

"Then you and Miss Lynn were not engaged to be married?"

"Good Lord, no. The notion never occurred to either of us."

"When did you first learn of Hero Lynn's marriage to Mr. Leland?"

There was an instant's hesitation before the answer. But Ted Greer's
tone was casual enough as he replied, "I learned about it yesterday. In the
afternoon. Hero told me. She asked me not to mention it because she
wanted to make her own announcement at the party tonight."

"And you didn't mention it?"

"Of course not! She'd asked me not to."

"Not even to your wife?"

"Why, no! Why should I? Bettine didn't know Hero. She wouldn't have been interested in her."

"Wouldn't she, Mr. Greer? What about this gossip that you have mentioned, concerning yourself and Miss Lynn? Might she not, quite naturally, have been interested in that?"

"Bettine was in Green Center, Ohio, inspector. New York gossip—"

"Come, Mr. Greer! New York gossip columns, and the radio, and rotogravure, reach even Green Center, Ohio. I am only trying—"

"Look here, Inspector. I know you're only trying to find out whether Hero Lynn killed herself, or if someone else did, and if so, who. And that's all right with me. I happen to think she did it herself, but naturally you can't take my word for it, and besides I could be wrong. Anyway, I'm perfectly willing to help you get at the truth. Anything I can tell you about Hero, or Hero and myself. I've already answered your questions about our relationship, though some of them have been pretty pointed. I didn't mind, because there isn't anything I've said, or could say, that people don't know, and lots of things they've probably thought they knew weren't so. But none of that has anything to do with Bettine." The incongruous black beard jutted forward. I always suspect beards of covering a lack of chin and jaw but it was evident that this one didn't.

"Not even the fact," Inspector Moore said slowly, "that, right after learning of Miss Lynn's marriage, you flew to Ohio, asked Miss Donat to marry you, married her in Elkton, Maryland, brought her back to New York, and announced your marriage, all in a rather dramatic and hurried manner, immediately after the girl whose name has been coupled conspicuously with yours had announced her own?"

Ted Greer's hands, the long strong hands of a violin player, tightened on the arms of his chair.

"Look here, Inspector Moore. Am I getting this right? Are you suggesting that, when Hero told me she'd married Charley, I hopped a plane, proposed to Bettine, married her, and announced it, all in a pretty tizzy of jealous spite? Is that what you're thinking?"

It was so exactly what I had certainly thought that I very nearly gasped. To take the bull by the horns like that—was it clever or foolish? Or had I been wrong? But no, I couldn't have been. All too vividly I could recall that scene at the bar when Ted Greer had turned from Hero, and later, his expression when he'd touched his bride's wedding ring and said, "Not a million-dollar necklace, but—" And yet, when he had put his arm around Bettine and called her his darling his tone had been tender and proud.

And now he was grinning.

"Because, if so, Inspector, you're all wet."

"Then," said Inspector Moore, "Miss Lynn's marriage had nothing to do with your own somewhat precipitate proposal and marriage, and—"

"Well, I don't know. Maybe it had. I'd wanted to marry Bettine for a long time. We'd planned it for June. Maybe Hero's getting married did—what'd you call it?—precipitate things. The alluring jingle of wedding bells, especially in the springtime—"

Inspector Moore interrupted. "You had no objection—you felt no annoyance at Miss Lynn's marriage?"

"Well, maybe I felt she might have done better for herself. I always thought Charley rather a sap. And besides—"

He broke off, frowned, and stood up.

"And now, Inspector, I'd like to take my wife home. She's had a pretty nasty jolt."

"I appreciate that. And that perhaps a not inconsiderable part of that nasty jolt, as you call it, Mr. Greer, may have been dealt your wife when she learned that you had asked her to marry you only after Hero Lynn's marriage—"

The band leader said violently, "My wife has nothing to do with Hero Lynn, or any other dumb little débutramps, alive or dead. What Betts knows—and all she cares about—is that I love her and I married her. Karkoff knows where I live, if you want to see me again. But now, unless you're arresting us, I'm taking her away from here."

His brows drawn level above his angry eyes, he faced the inspector, who answered him quietly:

"I'm not arresting you, Mr. Greer, nor your wife. And I appreciate your answering my questions as patiently as you have. Unfortunately, I have to ask them. And I want to ask two more."

Greer, who was at the door to Mr. Karkoff's sitting-room, stopped with his hand on the knob.

"Unless you're dragging Bettine into this mess again, shoot."

"When did you last see Hero Leland alive?"

"I—when I was leading my band. She came up and asked me to play a certain song."

"You played it?"

"Yes. It was after that I went to the pantry and drank a glass of milk:'

"What was the name of the song, Mr. Greer?"

"*Lament for a Dead Romance.*"

"I understand you wrote it?"

"Yes. I wrote it."

"Under what circumstances? That is, was it not a song you wrote with Hero Lynn in mind? With her and your own self in mind?"

Ted Greer smiled, reminiscently and rather sadly.

He said, slowly: "Inspector, you know those poignant autumn days with leaf-smoke and haze and nostalgia in the air, and all sorts of silly memories? It was a day like that, last fall, when Hero told me about what she called her Great Romance. She was sixteen. There was an Annapolis cadet who wanted to marry her, but she was rich and he wasn't. She grinned a little sorrowfully as she said, 'Of course I wouldn't really have married him, but I didn't know that at the time. We had such good fun together, and I was mad about the way his hair grew and he had the sweetest nose, and I wept when we parted forever.' Which made me think of a girl I'd forgotten for years. We'd spent the summer together on the beach and she was the most wonderful brown color in her yellow bathing suit. I wanted to marry her but her pappy was the Sewing Machine King or some sort of tycoon, and I was poor but proud, and just eighteen. So I thought of all the other pathetic callow kids who 'love and part forever,' and jotted down that foolish song and wrote the music that night."

"And do you know that, on the open pages of the guest book in front of Hero, when her body was found, were the words of that song, written by her hand?"

The young man's face whitened.

"No, I didn't know it. Poor kid. Damn!" His voice was low, and it shook. The knuckles of his hand, clutching the doorknob, were white too. Then he jerked the door open and went out.

CHAPTER 9

I FELT quite miserable as the young band leader closed the door between us and the sitting room. I was sure he'd lied about something. But even if he had been in love with Hero Lynn, I felt sure he loved his wife now. And she adored him. And on their wedding night when they should be so happy, they were caught up in this awful thing

While I was thinking this and wishing Amanda would come back so we could go home, Inspector Moore stepped to the door and said, "Miss Sabina Brok?"

The girl came in, tall, beautiful and sullen-looking. She had a short coat of yellow fox over her slender citron-yellow frock. She was no longer wearing the pearl necklace. She sat down, and Inspector Moore shut the door behind her.

Facing her, and leaning against the desk, he said, "Miss Brok, will you please tell me what you know about Hero Lynn Leland's death here to-night? Anything that you think might help me to find out what happened."

"How do I know anything about what happened? She probably killed herself. Or maybe"—her wide, orange-red lips curled—"the little bride was mad, and did her in. But you can't prove it by me. And I don't know why you've kept me sticking around here. I was all ready to go home when Sandro said I couldn't. I don't know how you—"

Obviously Miss Brok was going to be difficult. "Ornery," as Amanda would say.

But the inspector said, patiently, "I thought you might care to help me. I've been told that you were one of the first persons to reach Bettine Greer after she'd discovered Hero Leland's body and was screaming hysterically. Where were you when you first heard her screaming?"

"I was"—she hesitated—"at a table in the dance room. Near the entrance, from the corridor."

"There were other people with you?

"No, there weren't! I'd just sat down. Or at least, just a minute or two before."

"How long before?"

"I just told you, perhaps a minute or two. Or maybe it was three or four. I don't clock myself." She tossed her long burnt-gold bob.

"Before that, where had you been?"

"Before that? I'd been in the little girls' room. I went there with Kate Kilgallon and left there with her."

"Did Mrs. Kilgallon come back into the dance room with you?"

The girl's eyes shifted. "I don't know. Ask her."

"You say you were near the entrance. Did you see anyone enter the dance room, Miss Brok, after you did yourself?"

"No."

"Or leave it?"

"No."

"Not even Mrs. Greer?"

"No."

"But she must have passed near you."

"Must she? I wouldn't know. Anyhow, I didn't see her. All I know is I suddenly heard some god-awful yelling and ran out, and there was that little nitwit hanging onto the curtains outside the reception room, howling her head off. I grabbed her but she kept on bellowing until a dame with a face like the Rock of Gibraltar came up and smacked her. After that the little idiot came to and began to mumble about something being 'too horrible.' I'd have dropped her then, but the Rock of Gibraltar had told me to take care of her. So I tried to. I don't know why. I'd almost got her to the ladies' room when she passed out on me. And somebody picked her up—there was a crowd around by that time—and I went back. I wanted to see what the row was about. Everybody was shoving into the reception room. When I got in there and saw Hero flat on the couch, I supposed the little bride must have slapped her down. I had to hand it to her—'a better man than I am, Gunga Din.' "

The girl's beautiful tawny face was hard, but behind the topaz eyes was—horror? Or terror? There was quivering fright of some kind, and her hand shook as she stretched it toward a jade box on the desk and fumbled for a cigarette. I saw Lutie's blue intent gaze following that gesture.

Sabina said, "Of course I didn't know then that Hero was dead." She struck a match, held it to the tip of a cigarette.

"Why did you think Mrs. Greer might have felt enmity toward Mrs. Leland?" the inspector asked.

The girl laughed, a spurt of mirthless noise.

"Mrs. Greer—Mrs. Leland! You don't know how silly that sounds! And for gosh sake, Inspector, don't hand me that dumb line! As if anyone wouldn't know what 'Mrs. Greer' had against Hero Lynn."

"And what have you, Miss Brok, against them both?"

The beautiful yellow eyes narrowed and gleamed in the tiny flame arrested below them. The end of the match charred, curling, till fire licked the orange-tipped fingers holding it. The girl jerked and dashed the match to the floor. Inspector Moore set the edge of a polished shoe on it swiftly.

Sabina's lips were drawn down and in at the corners. When she spoke the words came thinly twisting between them.

"How dare you talk to me like that, you—you cop! For that's all you are, even if you were a Vandervoort-Moore! You're an unpleasant person, and if you don't stop asking me stupid questions and let me go home it—it's going to be just too bad!"

Her voice broke shrilly and rose, and she stamped her bronze-sandaled foot, a badly spoiled brat in a tantrum.

"I tell you, I don't know anything about this stinking mess! And I want to go home to my Daddy! And if you don't let me go-right now my Daddy will break you! My Daddy's Judge Bellamy Brok—"

"—who spared the rod and spoiled a very engaging little girl. I remember you when a sound spanking might have helped. Go home now, and tell your Daddy I said so. I'll see you again." With that the inspector took her arm, led her firmly to the door into the foyer, and shut it firmly after her.

Lutie murmured, "Mercy! What a temper! But of course he is a very attractive young man. Isn't he?"

Inspector Moore made no reply to this apparent non sequitur, but strode across to the sitting-room door, opened it and called, in a voice somewhat louder and certainly more vehement than usual, "Mrs. Kilgallon!"

CHAPTER 10

"THE REDHEADED LOVELY," as Jeff had called her, came in and closed the door quietly behind her. She sat down quietly too. Everything about her had an air of rather terrible quietness, it seemed to me. And her delicate skin, that had looked like rosy peaches, was sallow now.

Inspector Moore walked twice across the floor, controlling his temper, I suspected, after that last interview, before he stopped in front of Kate Kilgallon and was able to say with a fair amount of calmness, "Mrs. Kilgallon, do you know anything? Will you tell me anything and everything you know that may help me to find out how your sister met her death?"

The girl said, "Yes, I'll tell you anything. Everything, Inspector. But I don't know what will help you." She paused, then added without evident emotion, "I only know that she was killed."

"You don't believe she took her own life?"

"No. I don't."

"Why are you so certain of that?"

"Because she never would have. Never. It wouldn't be like her."

"Yet I have been told—"

She interrupted, but without any intensity. "Yes, I know. You mean you've been told about the time we found Hero with a scarf around her neck that she'd knotted over a hook in the doorway. But that was simply childish show-off stuff. She didn't mean to kill herself. Not for a moment."

"Tell me why you're so sure of that."

"I was there. It was at our—at Hero's house. During a party. And I reached her first. We'd heard a kind of groan, and then a crash. Hero was hanging in an archway in the conservatory. There was a big broken flowerpot nearby. She'd stood on it, then kicked it over. That was the crash we'd heard."

"A dangerous bit of exhibitionism, it would seem," Inspector Moore commented grimly. "What makes you believe it was merely that?"

"Because I saw Hero before I reached her. She was holding onto the hook with both hands. She only let go when she could hear someone coming. Besides, though she'd kicked over the flowerpot, there was a taboret nearby that she could have reached if we hadn't come. And the scarf wasn't tight. And she wasn't unconscious when we got to her, though she pretended to be. It was a very silly, childish stunt."

"What was the reason for it? Have you any idea?"

The girl hesitated. Then she said, "Yes, I suppose I have. She'd given the party, really, for Ted. Ted Greer. And he didn't pay any particular attention to her. She was mad at him. At least, that's what I thought."

The inspector said, "I see." And looked as if he were seeing a very great deal.

But he didn't follow the subject up. He said, abruptly: "Where were you, Mrs. Kilgallon, when you heard Mrs. Greer screaming? Or did you hear her?"

"I heard screams, yes. I was at the bar. But I didn't pay any particular attention, except to be annoyed. I don't like hysterics. And that was what these screams sounded like. But they kept up, and everybody was going toward them, so I went too. Then the screaming stopped. But in a minute someone dashed past me and said there'd been an accident, Hero was hurt, and he was going for a doctor. He said Hero was in the reception room and I went there. She was on the couch, dead. I knew it wasn't an accident—I could see she—I saw her face. And I knew she'd been killed."

"Is your certainty of that, Mrs. Kilgallon, based on any definite suspicion of a particular person?"

She shook her head slowly. "No."

"Do you know of any persons who disliked your sister violently?"

A faintly bitter smile touched her lips. "I suppose plenty of people disliked my sister heartily. But—"

"For instance?"

"Most of this season's debs, especially her rival glamour girls. And of course—"

"Yes, Mrs. Kilgallon? You promised to tell me anything that might help me."

She nodded gravely. "I know. Well, Ted might have disliked her marrying someone else. And Bettine might have disliked her, and probably did, because of Ted. And Elinor disliked her because Hero was always rude and sometimes quite hateful to her. And I disliked her, because she was vain and overbearing and often mean."

The girl raised her gray eyes from the hands knitted tightly on her knees to Inspector Moore. Her face was resolute, hard, and sad.

"It isn't nice to say those things now, or to remember them. Just the same, they are true. But I don't think Ted, or his wife, or Elinor, killed Hero. And I didn't."

"Can you think of any motives, besides personal animosity, for your sister's murder?"

Kate Kilgallon drew a sharp breath. Perhaps at the word 'murder'— or was it something else? But she shook her head. Inspector Moore was watching her keenly.

"Your father, so I have heard, disinherited you, on your marriage, in favor of your sister?"

"Yes."

"Doesn't that account for your hard feelings toward her?"

"I don't think I had hard feelings toward Hero. She made me mad, and sometimes disgusted. Maybe that sounds hard, now that she's dead. But I felt sorry for her, too. Anyway, my feelings about her had nothing to do with Father's action."

"You did not resent that?"

"Of course I did!" She drew herself straighter, and her gray eyes flamed. "I hated him for it! Not because of the money—" She bit her lips, scowling. "Oh, I know that sounds like hooey, the principle of the thing and all that guff. But it's so. I think I've always detested money. I've heard so much about it. Besides, I never was in want of it, of course, I realize that. After I walked out on Dad and married Kip, it was wonderful to feel he made just enough money, not a horrid tiresome lot of it to make us worried and ruthless and guilty about it all the time! It was wonderful to be free."

Her breast lifted, and she clasped her hands. Then after a moment dropped them listlessly in her lap.

"And after Kip's plane crashed—he was a test pilot, you know, though Dad called him a garage hand because he had worked in his father's garage—anyway, I didn't have any trouble in getting a job right away myself. So lack of money hasn't bothered me. But even if it had it wouldn't be Hurry's—Hero's—fault. I've never forgiven Dad for the way he treated Kip or the things he said about him, that he was a fortune hunter and—"

She quieted herself. "I'm sorry, Inspector. Anyway, none of that was my sister's fault. It didn't have anything to do with her."

Inspector Moore only said, "Who inherits your sister's fortune now?"

Kate Kilgallon stared at the gentleman in stone gray so intently watching her. Her eyes seemed startled. "Why, I—"

"Yes, Mrs. Kilgallon?"

"She was married, wasn't she? And to Charley." Her wide gray eyes, still fixed on the inspector, were not seeing him now. She frowned, then nodded, lost in thought. "Yes, Charley would be all right. So I suppose—I think it's supposed to go to Elinor, and me."

She stood up suddenly. Color rushed into her smooth cheeks.

"But I don't want it! I don't want Dad's money, not any part of it. And I won't take it!"

There was a moment's long silence. Then Inspector Moore's grave voice cut into it.

"Only one more question, Mrs. Kilgallon. Will you tell me where you were, what you did, and who was with you during the half-hour, say, before your sister was found in the reception room, dead?"

"Where? Oh!" Slowly the fire died in her eyes. Silky brown brows knitted above them, as she tried to concentrate on the inspector's question. She looked very tired, and also, suddenly, very young and vulnerable.

She spoke slowly, carefully. "The half-hour before Bettine Greer screamed? I'm trying to remember. They played that song, *Lament* for something. I was on the terrace then. With Sabina, and Mimi Sylvester, Hal Broderick and Tod Wallace. We'd been there for a while. Oh, I remember now that Hero came out while we were there, too! With Charley. They'd been dancing. They sat down—not with us, we were at a table. They sat over in a big wicker settee in a corner, in the shadow. Tod made some cracks about that, and shouted across to them. Hero said, 'Oh, go pitch some woo yourself.' But pretty soon she left. Charley stayed there. I think it was after that I noticed Ted was playing the *Lament.* Then someone got thirsty, we went in, and Sabina and I went to the powder room. Hal had asked me for the next dance. He said he'd be at the bar. So when Sabina and I left the powder room—I suppose we were five minutes or so—I went to join Hal. We were standing there, drinking Scotch, when the screams started. I've told you the rest."

Inspector Moore said, "Thank you, Mrs. Kilgallon. That's all. I'll want to see you again, of course."

She said, "Of course," and went out. But as she passed Lutie she stopped for a moment and looked at my little cousin with a strange intensity. Ted Greer and Bettine and Sabina Brok had all taken Lutie and me for granted and ignored us, which I'd wondered at a little, but I suppose they were all too absorbed in their own worries to bother with us. But now I wondered more at Kate Kilgallon's intense, almost excited, stare at my small companion.

Later I understood what it meant.

CHAPTER 11

INSPECTOR MOORE called Elinor Lynn into the office next.

She looked so different that I almost gasped. Less beautiful, perhaps, but prettier. She wasn't nearly as tall as I had thought her and she was much younger. I'd taken her for around thirty. She seemed much nearer twenty now. Perhaps the white fox jacket covering her severely cut, long-sleeved black frock accounted for part of the change in her appearance. It was short, jaunty, with wide upstanding shoulders and a flat, round, youthful collar. Also the sophisticated emerald earrings were gone, and the close, set design of her ultra-smart coiffure was disarranged. The black curls were loosened now and crisply soft about her small head. But the greatest change was in her expression. Some underlying tremulous excitement, whether it was fright or pity or something else, had given her a look of appeal that made her seem almost as young and, yes, naive, as little Bettine.

I was sure the inspector felt this appeal too. Anyway his tone was gentle when he asked, "Mrs. Lynn, you'll try to help me in finding out everything I can about your stepdaughter's death, won't you?"

"Of course I will. Poor Hurry."

"Then, as a matter of routine, I'll ask you first—" He asked her the question he'd put to Kate Kilgallon last.

"Where was I and who was I with? Oh, of course; I see how you must ask us all that. Let me think. The half-hour before—I suppose I was with Baron then, that is Baron Delacy. He was having a Scotch at the bar. Then we danced to that ghastly *Lament* that Hero had asked Ted to play. I'd rather dance to it than sit and listen to it."

"You heard Hero ask for that piece, then?"

"No, I didn't *hear* her. I was in the far room. But I saw her go up to the platform and speak to Ted, and right after that he played the thing. So I supposed she'd asked for it."

"I see. And after your dance?"

"Baron and I went out on the terrace for a breath of air. It was beautiful—balmy and soft, the lights in the park, the trees just beginning to bud—"

Her low voice quivered a little. "You know, C.V., my husband, has only been gone—it will be two years in May. When I see something lovely like that, I miss him quite dreadfully."

She brushed her knuckles across her eyes. "I'm sorry to be acting like such a fool. It's because of Hero, too, of course. What was I saying? Oh, yes. Then I saw Charles sitting there on the terrace. He was alone, and I wanted to talk with him. So I told Baron to run along. I had to play Mama for a minute. I hadn't seen Hero, I mean talked with her, or Charles either, since she'd announced their marriage tonight. I wanted to ask him what their plans were."

"Had you known beforehand of their plan to get married?"

"No. Oh, of course I had sort of an inkling." She smiled faintly. "Hero and I live in the same house, you know. And Charles had been there a great deal, especially lately."

"But she hadn't confided in you?"

"Of course not." Hero's stepmother bit her lip. "Hero never confided in anybody. I used to try—I mean, I wanted awfully to be friends with her. But she wouldn't let me. I suppose that would have been natural with any girl, and Hurry had always been her father's pet. And I was only nineteen when he married me, just five years older than she was herself. She always resented me. It hurt, rather, but— Sorry, I keep wandering from your questions. Anyway, the first I heard about Hero's marriage was when she told everyone here this evening."

"And when you asked Mr. Leland about their future plans, what did he tell you?"

"He said they were starting on their wedding trip immediately, the very next day. They were going to rough it, he said. He has a yacht, a little one which he keeps it at City Island, and Hero had been out on it last week for the first time and fallen in love with it. So they were going to sail, they hadn't decided where, but that was part of the fun. Of course I thought it was a crazy idea, and said so. But it was like Hero."

Elinor smiled, a rather wan smile, then she sighed and shrugged. "Charles said he had arranged to be away for three months. Then they'd spend August at his Southhampton place, and in the fall they'd buy a house or apartment in New York. He said Hero didn't want to live in the Sixty-eighth Street house—that's where we live now—and that she intended to give it to me outright. You see, my husband left it to us both as long as we both lived in it. But I wasn't sure that I'd want to live in it alone, as I told Charles. Well, anyway, that's what we talked about."

After a slight pause Inspector Moore said, "And during your conversation Mr. Leland seemed quite natural and cheerful?"

"Natural?" she repeated, seemingly a little puzzled at the question.

"I mean, there was no suggestion that he and his wife had had a quarrel or—"

She smiled. "Heavens, no! He was perfectly beaming. Why should they have quar— Oh, I see what you were thinking." Her face sobered and saddened. "Because of what Hero did, right afterwards."

Her eyes widened then, with horror, she said, "Why, even then, while we were talking about their wedding trip, she must have been—"

Elinor covered her face for a moment, as a shudder contorted it. Then she struck her fists on her chair arms. "Damn. Damn! Oh, how could she!"

Inspector Moore said gravely, "You believe she killed herself?"

She lifted angry eyes, with tears in them.

"After that other time, and the way I've heard her talk sometimes when she was mad, or miserable? And what she wrote there in the guest book? How can I think anything else? But—"

"You believe, then, that she was really miserable, that all these plans for a wedding trip and so on were not—"

"Oh, I'm sure she meant to carry out those plans while she and Charles were talking about them! And I don't think she planned to kill herself. Oh, I knew Hero so well! How she acted on impulse, often crazy wild impulses. I can feel—I can see what happened."

The inspector watched her carefully. But she wasn't looking at him. Her eyes, wide and set, stared past him as she went on, "Charles said she'd jumped up suddenly, telling him to wait, that she'd be back in a few minutes. She was always restless. Maybe it was the music that made her suddenly want to see Ted, to have him play their song again. For of course she'd been crazy about Ted. Everyone knew that, though I think she was fonder of Charley, and besides—"

The low voice stopped, then continued, "And we all knew Ted had written that song for her. It was about the things they used to do together. And then, when he played it, it was just too much for her. Poor, crazy kid."

"Mrs. Lynn," the inspector's voice cut in rather abruptly, "while you were talking with Hero's husband out on the terrace, did you hear screams?"

"Why, yes, we did! I remember I was talking, and Charles said, 'What's that?' We listened. It was some woman, way inside, apparently having hysterics. But we didn't pay much attention. I was asking Charles then what would happen about the Sixty-eighth Street house if I moved out when Hero did, or soon after. What I thought I wanted to do was to sell it, and Hero and I divide what it brought. It's such a big house, and so gloomy since C.V. died. It was different when he was there. He seemed to fill it and animate it."

Again the inspector interrupted. "Were you still with Mr. Leland on the terrace when you heard that something had happened to your stepdaughter? Or when did you hear that, and how?"

"No, I wasn't on the terrace. I'd left Charles there and gone in. And everybody was crowding toward the hall, or somewhere, and Ted Greer passed me and said Hero had killed herself this time, or something like that, and she was in the reception room. And I ran there. And just as I got to the door Charles ran up. He must have heard the commotion from out on the terrace, or somebody'd found him and told him, I don't know. Anyway—"

"How long had Mr. Leland been waiting for his wife on the terrace when you joined him? Did he say?"

"He said she had just left, a minute or two before."

"You are certain of that?"

"Why, yes! I'm certain he said so. Why?"

"Because there would seem to be a discrepancy in time, Mrs. Lynn," the inspector said. "The waiter who served Hero Leland the champagne says there was at least fifteen minutes, and probably more, between the time she ordered it and the time he opened it for her in the reception room."

"Then," she said slowly, "Charles must have been wrong. I suppose he was sitting there dreaming and— But oh, don't you see? That must mean Ted and Hero had a date for after he'd played their song. So she ordered the champagne,and then told him to play the song. And then he didn't come to the reception room, after all. Perhaps he'd never meant to. And so—"

"What makes you so certain he did not join her there?" The inspector's tone was significant.

"Why, because if he had she wouldn't have—"

Suddenly she understood the inference. She caught her breath.

"You mean, Ted did meet her there and killed her? Oh, no. No! That's utter rot. Why, I know Ted. He wouldn't, he couldn't! No one could have done it except Hurry herself. Won't you realize that? It's like her—"

"Mrs. Lynn!" the inspector interrupted rather sharply, "do you know how your stepdaughter died?"

Her face paled.

"Yes. They said she was hanging from that diamond necklace, from the back of that big chair."

"And do you believe she could have killed herself in that way? Doesn't that seem very difficult, if not almost impossible?"

"Oh, my God. You're perfectly determined to think she was murdered, aren't you? As if it weren't bad enough that she did it, but some innocent person must be suspected and blamed!"

She struck a clenched fist on her knee. Then her black eyes narrowed. And she pointed. She was pointing directly at me! She sprang to her feet.

"Look! There's a chair. It's not heavy like the one she was in but it's got a high back. I'll show you!" She came toward me. I got up very quickly. "Give me that!"

She touched the thin gold chain, carrying a locket set with a tiny pearl, that I wore around my neck. The locket contained a curl of my mother's blond hair, and I've worn it since I was small, though the chain fits rather snugly now. I didn't want to take it off. But I glanced across at Lutie, unfastened the necklace, and handed it over to Elinor Lynn.

She clasped it around her throat.

"You see? It fits me just about like the one Hero was wearing."

She was speaking only to the cool, slender gentleman in gray, who said nothing but watched closely as she seated herself in the chair I'd vacated.

"The back of this chair is about three feet high above the seat. And there's a little knob on it. That would be just about the height of that carved scroll in the other chair, wouldn't it? Look!"

She curled her feet under her and raised herself, slowly, until her neck was level with the top of the leather chair. She drew the gold chain of my necklace backward, so tightly that it sank into the creamy flesh of her throat and hooked it over the little knob on top of the chair's wooden frame. Then she slid her feet out from under her body.

For a moment it hung there. Then the chain of my old, delicate necklace snapped. The girl's body slumped into the chair.

She didn't speak for a moment or two. She put her hand to her throat. There was a long narrow red streak across it where the gold links had dug into the skin.

She swallowed. "You see? If the necklace hadn't broken—?"

But the inspector wasn't looking at the girl's face or at the mark on her neck. He was gazing at the folds of her black frock, rucked up about her knees. Then quickly he looked at Lutie. My little cousin looked back at him. And suddenly, of course, I knew what they were thinking about.

I picked up my broken necklace without even time or emotion left to be annoyed, because I, too, knew now, that Hero Lynn Leland had not killed herself.

Elinor Lynn stood up, and the folds of her gown fell around her feet. She repeated, "You see?"

"I see." He nodded. "Thank you, Mrs. Lynn. I won't keep you any longer."

She gazed at him searchingly. Her hands fell to her sides, palms outward, in a helpless gesture.

"You still don't believe me, do you? Well, I've done what I could."

She pulled the collar of the white fox jacket around the red scratch on her soft throat, turned and went out.

CHAPTER 12

HOW I wished we could go! Not only because it was late and I ached with fatigue and strain, but because I dreaded the remaining interview. I glanced at Lutie beseechingly, as Inspector Moore went toward the inner door and said, "Mr. Leland?"

But Lutie only leaned forward and patted my knee consolingly as she murmured, "Just this last one, Marthy dear. Then we'll go home."

Charles Leland sat down heavily in the chair I'd vacated for Elinor Lynn's demonstration, which I wouldn't have sat in again for love or money. Instead I was perched on a little uncomfortable bench at my cousin's side.

Inspector Moore said, "I'm sorry to have kept you waiting so long, Mr. Leland. I'll try not to keep you much longer."

"It doesn't matter," Charles Leland said dully.

"The question I must ask you first is the question I've had to ask everyone else I've talked with. Where were you, and with whom, Mr. Leland, for the half-hour or so preceding your wife's death?"

The young man, who had been sitting staring at the floor with his hands hanging between his knees, looked up. His eyes had a strange glaze over them. They appeared not to see anything of his surroundings. He repeated the inspector's question, slowly. Then he said, even more slowly, "I was on the terrace. I suppose I was on the terrace."

"Who was with you, Mr. Leland?"

"Hero was with me."

"For how long?"

There was no answer.

The inspector repeated, "For how long?"

"How long? We were talking. I don't know. She went in to powder her nose. She said to wait there for her. So of course I waited."

"How long did you wait?"

The question was repeated before Charles Leland made any reply, then he merely shook his head.

"And while you were waiting?"

"While I was waiting?" He stared dully at his interrogator. At last he said: "Oh, yes. Then Elinor was there."

"Yes, Mr. Leland? And then?"

"Then she went in too, I guess."

"And after that?"

"Why, I just sat there, waiting. And then—"

The young man sat up abruptly. His straight blond hair, that had been neat and smoothly parted when we'd first seen him, was roughened now. A thick boyish lock fell over his forehead into his eyes. He thrust it back and said wildly, "Then someone came out on the terrace and told me that she—that Hero was hurt. So I ran in and found her, there on the couch. And at first, of course, I couldn't believe it. But it's true, isn't it? Yes, it must be true, I suppose. But who did it? Who could have done it? Who wanted to hurt her, when she was so little and gay and sweet? That's what I've kept asking myself, all the time, all the time since. Who could have killed her?"

There was a silence. Inspector Moore gravely watched. Hero's young husband, who had dropped his face in his hands.

"You do not believe your wife took her own life?"

Charles Leland stiffened. He raised red-rimmed eyes, staring at the quiet man in gray.

"Hero? You mean, killed her own self? Hero? No!"

"However, I understand that she had talked of suicide and even attempted it on a former occasion."

"That stupid story!" said Charles Leland. His jaw tightened and for the first time I noticed that there were strong, characterful bones under his smooth skin. The truth is, I had thought him rather colorless, but he wasn't now.

He said violently, "I'm sick and tired of hearing that disgusting story repeated about Hero! People only told it because they liked to talk about her. And they always exaggerated, and even lied, to make a good story. But that silly little stunt? Why, she told me all about it herself. It was just some kind of a bet. She never expected anyone to take it seriously for a moment!"

Inspector Moore said thoughtfully, "That's very interesting, Mr. Leland." He stood up. "I won't keep you any longer."

I was surprised, though relieved, at the brevity of the interview. And Charles Leland seemed to be too. "But you aren't going to drop things, are you, Inspector?"

He walked, slowly to the door, then paused in the doorway and turned. His youthful jaw was out-thrust. "Because I am going to find out who killed her if it's the last thing I do in this world!"

On this pathetically young, melodramatic speech, he went out.

"A pretty tangle," muttered Inspector Moore, and sighed.

Lutie nodded demurely, and rose. She patted a yawn but her eyes were gleaming brightly.

"And we," she said, "must find Sister and toddle home to bed. Perhaps you'll drop in for tea soon, Inspector? With cheese biscuits and strawberry tarts?"

"Thank you. I probably shall," said the gentleman, bowing good night to us gravely.

CHAPTER 13

WE ATE breakfast next morning without any mention all of last night's tragedy. And a very delicious breakfast it was. Lutie had cooked it. She'd made prune whip, popovers, an omelette with frizzled bacon and stewed tomatoes that's one of her own special inventions. Lutie has the deftest hand in the world at cookery. The omelette was light as a feather, the spiced prunes rested in a nest of cream like a tiny cloud, the popovers were golden brown and after the first crisp bite they simply melted in one's mouth. Each item was a favorite of Amanda's, though of course she'd cooked the oatmeal herself, as she always does. Not that she likes oatmeal, but she and Lutie grew up on it, so breakfast wouldn't be breakfast without it, to my older cousin.

She seemed rather preoccupied, I thought, while Lutie chattered away about the lovely spring morning, and how well our window boxes were doing. We'd planted hyacinths and jonquils and tulips, and already they were getting ready to bloom. And about the pretty sprigged percale she'd bought at a remnant sale. Oh, and she'd seen a new cage for Rab that she wanted to get

"And pray why," inquired Amanda at this, "does Rabelais need a new cage?"

Lutie looked fondly at her parrot swinging in the soft breeze from the open window.

"Why, he's finally bitten almost through three wires of his old one, and I've seen Tabby eying him very interestedly, Sister. It would be so dreadful if that cat once got at Rab—"

"Stuff and nonsense!" snorted Amanda. "Sister, you seem to think Tabby's got no common sense at all. And the way you say that cat! Anyone would think he'd the soul of a murderer. And just look at him!" Her voice softened.

We looked at Amanda's pet, so incongruously named Tabby, who was sunning himself luxuriously on a small rag rug his mistress had placed for him on the fire escape. He was huge, fat-jowled, with a thick sleek coat and battle-scarred ears, but to Amanda he was the helpless, appealing stray baby cat that had followed her home one day in East Biddicutt some half-dozen years ago.

Tabby's paws were tucked under his chest. He did not return our gaze. His yellow eyes, thoughtful and unfriendly, were fixed on the parrot in the window. His stare was unwavering. The tip of his tail twitched significantly.

"He's as gentle as a kitten!" snapped Amanda.

"But," murmured Lutie, "Rab isn't."

"Demmitall, don't try any of yer blasted tricks on me!" shrilled Rabelais. Lutie had bought him from a sailor, from whom, apparently, he had acquired most of his unpolished and extremely bellicose vocabulary. "Watch out for yerself, I tell ye, or I'll give ye one in the eye, ye danged old fool!"

The bird glared balefully back at the cat, his handsome green neck feathers ruffled, the black tongue quivering angrily in his strong hooked beak. There had never been any love lost between Lutie's pet and Amanda's.

"I was only thinking," said my younger cousin gently, "that if Rab should finally work his way through those bars— However, if you aren't worried about it—"

There was small doubt in my mind as to which creature would fare worse in any encounter, tough old warrior though Tabby might be.

"Hmmph," said Amanda.

Lutie finished her coffee, and set her cup daintily back in its saucer. She rose briskly.

"Come, Marthy. Let's hurry with the dishes. I'm so anxious to get at my new afghan."

Lutie crochets beautifully and indefatigably, and yesterday she'd bought the wool for an afghan she intended as a gift to our friend, Madame LaVelle, whose theatrical "Maison," as the proprietress termed it, had been the setting of our first murder. This brought my thoughts back to the events of the night before, which to tell the truth hadn't been very far at the back of my mind, thankful as I was that we apparently were through with them.

Yet, wasn't this really very odd? And, I thought, as we carried the breakfast things into the kitchen-pantry, was it quite right?

After all, we had been right there on the spot, one might say, when a young girl had been cruelly killed. And this morning none of us had even mentioned it. Was Lutie simply going to wash her hands of the whole matter as if it were of no consequence whatever? I thought this over as I washed the cups and saucers of a rather charming old set that Lutie and I had picked up for a song at Gabay and Kaliski's, an auction place we'd found way down town during one of our exploring trips around the city.

"Steady. Steady, son!" rumbled Lutie in a deep masculine tone, as I knocked a cup handle against the edge of our tiny white sink.

Then she giggled. "Why, Marthy dear, what's the matter? You look quite cranky! You're not discontented about anything, are you?"

She hummed a little tune as she hung her tea towel neatly on its rack. We returned to the living room, which I must admit had begun to look quite cozy and homelike since we'd moved here last fall, when the sisters had inherited their brother's detective agency together with its offices in front and its apartment here in the rear of the top floor of an old, remodeled house in the West Forties. Though of course I still missed East Biddicutt.

Amanda had not repaired to the offices, as she customarily does immediately after breakfast. She was standing beside Rab's cage.

"Well, Sister," she said brusquely as we entered, "since you're so set on a new cage for your precious parrot, I see no good reason why you shouldn't have it. In fact, I shall buy it for you for your birthday."

"G'wan," said Rabelais. He shifted on his perch and cocked a cynical eye at Amanda.

"Thank you, Sister dear!" said Lutie affectionately. "That will be lovely."

She fetched her workbasket of sweet-grass, seated herself in her little rocking chair and selected a ball of brilliant green wool. Then she looked dreamily out of the window at the one straggly ailanthus tree in the backyard.

"Oh, dear. How sweet it would be to be in East Biddicutt, now that spring is here. With our garden, and real trees. Wouldn't it, Marthy?"

I glanced at our budding flower boxes and at our ailanthus tree. In spite of the cramped space and dry hard earth in which it had to live, it was unfurling new, tender, brave little leaves.

"Of course," I answered, rather crossly; and added, "But I think you're pretty unfair to our tree here. What do you mean real trees? That's the realest tree I've ever known."

"Tree of Heaven," murmured Lutie softly, almost, it seemed, rapturously. Then she bit her lip. "But just think. To be home, away from it all, back where we belong." She sighed.

"Lutie Beagle, I'm surprised at you!" snapped Amanda. "What do you mean where we belong? We belong right here. Our duties are here!"

"Yes, I know, Sister," said Lutie meekly. She drew her crochet needle from her basket, looped green wool over her finger and sighed again.

"In fact," Amanda went on, "we have an immediate urgent duty. Will you put down that doodad? Whatever kind of fal-lal it's going to be, it can wait!"

Lutie obeyed. Looking slightly surprised but completely dutiful, she waited.

"Last night," went on Amanda sternly, "a crime was committed, practically under our noses. And this morning you chatter and sing, and putter." She added, as if to give the devil his due, for Amanda is the soul of justice, "Of course I must say you did cook a nice breakfast. A very nice breakfast. But you certainly act as if what happened last night was none of our business!"

"Why, Sister," murmured Lutie. I saw the gleam in her eye, but her tone was demure. "Is it? I mean, do you really think it's our business? Of course, if you think it is—"

"Of course I think it is!" snapped Amanda. "That is"—her high cheekbones reddened—"if it's not exactly our business, at least we have a certain duty. To use our common sense, as far as we can, to find out the truth. In point of fact, " and she squared her lean shoulders, "Inspector Moore asked me last night to do so."

"Oh," murmured Lutie admiringly. "Did he really, Sister?"

"Yes, Sister, he did. And I did."

"Yes, Sister?" Lutie's head was cocked and her expression intent, like the little fox terrier in the old Victor phonograph ads, listening to His Master's Voice.

Amanda nodded firmly. "And I was able to establish certain extremely important facts."

"Yes, Sister?"

"Our men, as you know, were stationed at all the entrances to Mr. Karkoff's jewelry store, as well as at certain points of vantage inside. When I left the room where the murder was committed, I interviewed every one of our staff. Individually."

She drew her specs and a memorandum book from the large pocket of her black bombazine office dress, which she always puts on in the morning and wears until teatime. From between its pages she took a sheet of paper and unfolded it.

"This is a plan of the Karkoff rooms, terraces and so forth, furnished us last week by Mr. Karkoff, so that I could decide where to post our men. Their posts are marked with crosses, with their names beside the crosses."

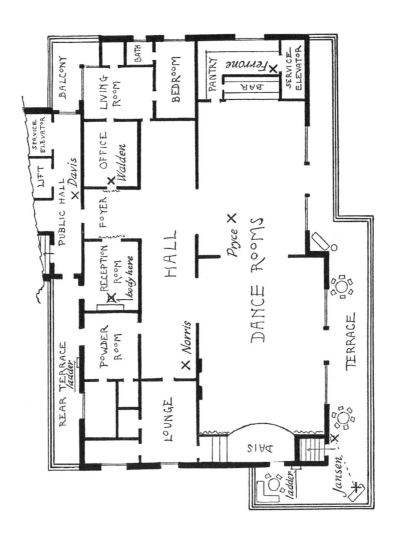

She handed us the paper. I moved my chair closer to Lutie's, and we bent our heads together over the plan.

"I verified it last night, by observation," added Amanda, "as well as interviewing our staff. Who are all, I believe, reliable men, conscientious and observant and fairly accurate."

She opened the memorandum book. "These are my notes. As you see, Davis was stationed in the public hall, near the main entrance to Mr. Karkoff's place, opening into the foyer. Besides his door, there are four others in view—to the passenger elevator, the service elevator, a stairway, and a rear terrace which is part of the Karkoff suit. Also there is a passage through to another penthouse apartment.

"Davis was instructed to take note of any persons leaving by either of Karkoff's doors, that is, before three A.M., at which time the property we were engaged to protect was all to be returned to its owner, he had informed me. Davis believed he would recognize any departing guests, as these were all prominent people. If he did not know their names he was to ask them. He assured me that he would do so tactfully, but that has no bearing on the circumstances of the death," she added.

"What has, however," she continued, "is that Davis was to note anything peculiar, in fact anything whatever about any person leaving the place, as well as the time of their departure. Naturally, I had directed all our men to be observant as to the matter of time, in connection with anything whatever they had to report. Davis did very well, I must say, in that respect. Hmm—"

She opened her notebook and read, "'At 10:53 P.M., Mr. and Mrs. Theobald Huntington and their daughter, a recent debutante, came out of the main entrance. While they waited for the elevator Mr. H. said, 'My dear, it is probably only a touch of your indigestion.' Mrs. H., who was clinging to his arm, said, 'I hope so, Theo, but I know it is my angina.' Miss H. looked sulky. She said, 'I don't see why I have to be dragged away when we've hardly got here!' Her father retorted, 'Tut, tut, Alice. Your mother is ill!'

"No one left after that until Bee Miller and Chub Olcott came out at 11:48. Miss M. said, 'What a disgusting exhibition, jumping up on the bar to announce her marriage and after that practically making a pass at Ted Greer right in front of everybody. But, of course she's got oomph, so you say! I'd like to know—' Mr. R. said hastily, 'Forget it, kid. Let's find some real hot stuff—hot, fast and dirty. Greer's too damned corny tonight. Besides, there're too many stuffed shirts. The party stinks.' "

Amanda primmed her lips. "The couple's concluding remarks are not relevant. The point is, they left. And no one else did until much later when they were given permission to do so by the police."

She drew her chair closer to ours and pointed to other X's marking the spots beside which she had written names.

"Ferrone was in the passage behind the bar, connecting the pantry with the servants' elevator which descends to the hotel kitchens. He remained there throughout the evening. Only waiters used the elevator. Jansen was on the large terrace near or watching the fire stairs opening from it. No one used that exit. Pryce sat or strolled about the two main rooms. Norris was in the large hall. They had several things to report which may or may not be of importance or interest but I'll come back to that later.

"The chief point," said Amanda, and pointed to the large X she had marked just inside the doorway of the office, "is what I learned from our man Walden. He was stationed where he had a clear view of the main door to the public hall, from the foyer,and also across it, the doorway to the reception room where the girl was found dead. The office door was open, but the curtains were drawn except for a very narrow aperture, from which Walden swears he did not stir all evening, so that, though he could not be seen by anyone in or passing through the foyer, he could plainly see anyone there."

Amanda drew a long breath. "And he tells me he saw—"

She was interrupted by a sharp excited series of raps at the door to the passage that leads through to the offices.

We all jumped, startled. Lutie turned the plan of the penthouse face down. Amanda slapped her notebook shut and thrust it into her pocket.

Then she called gruffly, "Come in!"

CHAPTER 14

THE DOOR opened. And it was only Jeff, after all. But his red hair was even more than usually on end, and his blue Irish eyes popped with excitement.

"A lovely— I mean a lady to see Miss Lutie. It's Kate Kilgallon!" he announced breathlessly.

"Oh! To see me?" Lutie sounded surprised. But I didn't think she was as surprised as she seemed. "You mean to see Sister, don't you?"

"No. She didn't ask for the Boss." He glanced apologetically at Amanda, then back to Lutie. "She asked for you."

"Well!" said Lutie. "I'm sure I cannot think why!"

Her cheeks were pink, her eyes sparkling, but her tone was demure. "Anyway, Jeffy, please ask her to come in here, will you?"

Our assistant ducked out and returned in a minute or two with Kate Kilgallon. Amanda nodded him sternly back to his post in the office. He withdrew with obvious reluctance.

Kate Kilgallon was dressed in a trim mannishly cut suit, suede gloves, pumps, pocketbook, and a wide, tilted felt hat, all of black. A tiny green-enameled watch was pinned to a lapel, her finely tucked handkerchief linen blouse was white, and her red hair, which had been coiffed into a smooth lacquered cap last night, fell to her shoulders now, shining, the ends curved under. In spite of all the black it was extraordinary what an effect of color she produced.

And so did her low, softly rich voice. She said, looking directly at Lutie, "I'd like to engage you, Miss—Miss Lutie Beagle, isn't it?"

Lutie nodded. "Please sit down, my dear." She indicated the big leather chair that had been Ezekiel's, and the girl seated herself in it.

She said, "I know John Bynam. He told me how clever you are." John Lane Bynam, as I've mentioned, was our client in our first murder case. "And besides, I' noticed you last night; so I know, myself, that you're clever. I—" the girl paused, then said steadily: "I want to find out how my sister was killed. Will you help me?"

Lutie looked at Amanda, then back at her would-be client.

"My dear, you will have to ask Sister. She is the head of our investigating bureau."

Kate Kilgallon looked at Amanda.

Amanda said, "The authorities are already trying to find out how your sister met her death, Mrs. Kilgallon." She spoke very formally.

"I know that. But I'd like you to help too."

There was a short silence. Then Amanda said, "We intend to help Inspector Moore in whatever way we can."

The girl leaned forward. "But I want you to help me. I mean—"

"Yes, my dear?" Lutie also leaned forward. Her voice was soft, but eager.

The girl turned toward her quickly. "I mean I don't trust the police. Not even that very nice, and gentlemanly, and possibly astute Inspector Moore. Didn't you notice—but of course you did!—how he kept harping on the idea of suicide? And I know Hurry never committed suicide. I know it! And besides—"

"Yes, my dear?" prompted Lutie.

"Well, besides, I don't want things to go wrong. When he finds out—and surely he will find out, there's no question about it really—that my sister didn't kill herself, then maybe the wrong person will be suspected. And I don't want that either."

Lutie didn't reply. She looked at her sister, meekly.

Amanda's face was thoughtful. It was some time before she replied. Finally she said, "We will take the case, Mrs. Kilgallon, only on one condition. You yourself will remain a suspect until we are convinced that you are not one. If the facts prove, and we come to believe, that you have any connection with your sister's death, we must proceed accordingly. In which case, naturally, you will not be obligated—"

Amanda's cheeks reddened. She does not like the idea of taking money for solving murders, but it is a part of our business, and to be businesslike is a duty also. She cleared her throat and continued doggedly, "I mean, you will pay us no fee if we are compelled to work against you. Therefore, we can only take the case tentatively. Moreover, as I told you, we were already helping Inspector Moore."

"Yes, I know. But I want you to work separately too and devote yourselves to it. It will help me so if I know you are doing that!" urged Kate Kilgallon.

"Very well, we'll try, if you are satisfied with my conditions."

"Of course I am!" The girl pulled off her wide black hat and her gloves and dropped them on the floor beside her. Her shining russet hair swung on her shoulders as she tossed her head, then leaned it on the back of the leather chair.

"Then that's settled." She sighed, closed her eyes for a moment. Then she opened them and sat upright.

"Look. I don't want you to think that this is some sort of maudlin sentimental stuff on my part. I mean, I must get the person who murdered my poor little sister if it's the last thing I do and so forth. It isn't exactly that."

She looked at us with sad and very tired eyes.

"I hate what was done to Hero. And the person who did it. But I didn't really like her very much. That's the honest truth. I have to say it. It would be false not to. Do you understand?"

There was silence for several seconds. Amanda's dark gaze was fastened on Kate's face. She said nothing. But the girl was looking back at her, and slowly the defiant gray eyes brimmed over.

"It's true that when she was a little girl she was adorable. She was an elf-thing. And you can't grow up with anyone and not feel terribly strongly about them. I suppose that's why I used to get so mad at her, too, for being a brat." She shook the tears from her eyes angrily. "Which she was, a spoiled, ruthless brat. When she started to grow up I simply couldn't get on with her. And I'm not going to be a hypocrite, now that she's dead. Only—"

She broke off, her firm chin out-thrust, though it did quiver a little.

I confess my feelings were mixed. Her unsisterly attitude seemed unnatural. Anyway its expression, under the circumstances, was shocking. The girl was too violently uncompromising and outspoken. Yet there was a passionate sincerity about her

Lutie was saying calmly, "Did your inability to get on with your sister have anything to do with your father's preference?"

"Dad's preference? How do you mean?"

"Wasn't Hero his pet? Perhaps that hurt you?"

"Oh. Oh, I see what you mean, because Dad chucked me out and left Hero his money. But don't you understand? That was because, really, he always liked me best."

She stopped short and her gray eyes grew dark and very unhappy. "I can't help it. I couldn't ever help it, but he did. Even when we were kids he used to treat me like an equal. He discussed things with me, and told me jokes, and expected me to be wonderful. But Hero—sometimes he'd pet her, sometimes he'd ignore her. But he always treated her as if she were a doll or a puppy or a kitten, as if he didn't expect her to have much sense and as if it didn't matter much whether she had or not. When I was little I didn't think much about it, except I probably liked the superior feeling it gave me. I was five years older than Hero. Maybe that's why father liked me best, I don't know. Anyway, five years give you an edge when you're a child, and you take superiority for granted. But when I grew older it often made me feel guilty, as if it were my fault, his caring most for me. Sometimes I used to pick fights with him and I always took Hero's part when he punished her, though that wasn't often. Not nearly as often as he punished me."

The girl's eyes gazed back into the past, and at the mystery of character, as she said, slowly, "I don't know if all that made Hero the way she grew up to be, or if she just was like that. When she began to grow up she was so hard. So beautiful, so recklessly gay, so crazily moody at times. And yet underneath there was that hard, ruthless, egocentric thing. I could never get close to her. No one could, I guess. Perhaps that's what attracted men to her, that peculiar aloofness, and her beauty. Apparently she only had to look at a man she wanted and she owned him."

Kate paused. "Except for Ted Greer. She really liked him, and I think they were friends. She never could boss him. Maybe that's why—"

She checked herself.

"I seem to be talking on and on, just spilling over, and not getting anywhere. I guess because I've been thinking and thinking about her, and everything, over and over, all night. But you asked me—I'm sorry, what was it?"

"Of course you feel like spilling over, and there's no reason in the world why you shouldn't," said Lutie gently. "I was only wondering, you know. I've only heard bits and rumors about your misunderstanding with your father."

Kate Kilgallon laughed, a harsh brittle little sound.

"There wasn't any misunderstanding between Dad and me! At least I always understood him very well. I don't know how much I loved Hero, but I loved him."

She looked across at Amanda, her brown silky brows lowered over smoky passionate eyes. "He was brilliant and amusing. He had such damned charm, and he loved me so much. But he wanted to own me and that"— she closed her fist slowly—"he couldn't do. When I wanted to marry Kip, I married him. And Dad couldn't take it. So he did what he did to get even. Which was all right with me, if only he hadn't said the low-down things he did say about Kip. And if it hadn't hurt Dad so himself, which made me miserable, I wouldn't have given a hoot!"

Listening to this girl, watching her resolute sensitive mouth, the wide intelligent forehead and the rebellious, passionately thoughtful eyes, I hadn't the slightest doubt that what she said was true, about herself, and about her younger sister, too. It seemed only too likely that Hero's naturally egocentric temperament had been sadly hardened by the father's attitude. Possibly, even probably, by the fortune that had been tossed to her as a kind of spite gift.

Perhaps Amanda's thoughts had followed the same line; or perhaps she felt—for the expression of intense emotion is apt to make her uncomfortable—that it was time to turn attention to the practical.

She said, abruptly, "And what was your sister's attitude toward yourself and the fortune she inherited because of your disobedience toward your father?"

"'N'yah, n'yah!'" replied Kate Kilgallon, and smiled faintly.

Then, as Amanda looked stern and unenlightened, she explained, "I mean she was contemptuous. She said I was a fool. But that it was all for the best, because she could have more fun with Dad's dough than I could."

"Did your sister inherit your father's money unconditionally?" inquired Amanda, looking flinty.

Our visitor didn't notice the disapproval, but she did look somewhat surprised at my cousin's ignorance.

"Good Lord, no! Why, it was spread all over the papers, especially the scandal sheets. Dad's will, I mean. With all sorts of would-be smart gags about the conditions. That was—"

Her full underlip shot out and the hot blood mounted under her peachy skin. "That was one of the things that made me so mad. Dad loathed that disgusting kind of publicity himself but just to take a crack at me, and Kip, and to show that he meant to boss Hero, he didn't care even if he made himself a laughingstock after he was dead!"

She stopped, as if choking on wrath, swallowed, and sat up straighter.

"I'm sorry. I'll try to hang onto myself and answer your questions decently. Father left his money, or part of it—Elinor got some, I've forgotten just how much, and an interest in the New York house, or something—to my sister Hero, on condition that, first, no scandal was connected with her before her marriage. He specified what he meant by scandal, too, in detail.

"Second, she must marry a man under forty-six years of age. That was Dad's age when he made the will. He was two years older when he died. I don't know why he put that in, unless because that still seemed young to him, and he didn't want Hero to marry an old dodo who might shuffle off too quickly or something.

"Third, she was not to marry a—" the girl's chin went up and her voice was a tight little monotone—"a garage mechanic, a lion-tamer, a shopkeeper, a clerk, a painter—either house painter or dabbler on canvas—a musician, a dancer, a writer, a chauffeur, a waiter, a maitre d'hotel, a newspaper reporter, a six-day bicycle racer, or any professional athlete, gambler, or stunt flyer."

She paused, then explained carefully, "You see, my husband was a professional aviator."

"Dear me!" murmured Lutie, and turned her face aside so that only I caught the tiny uncontrollable quiver of a smile on her primmed lips.

But Amanda's lips tightened. She was not amused. A certain paternal sternness, even at times arbitrary and carried to an extreme, seemed reasonable to her, as I well knew from my memory of my Uncle Abidiah Beagle, her father. To cut a disobedient child from one's will or one's approval might be pardonable, but to hold her up to public ridicule—no, she was not at all amused.

But she only said, woodenly, "I see."

Lutie put in gently, "And even after your husband died, your father didn't forgive you and try to make friends again?"

"Forgive me!" The girl's voice was angrily scornful. "Do you think I was the one to be forgiven after the things he'd called Kip? Not only to me, I might have forgiven that, but to Kip himself. In a letter, after we were married, he offered to buy Kip off like some gold-digging chorus girl! Oh, he wrote me, after Kip was killed, suggesting that I come back home now that I'd had my little flyer. So of course I went running home. Of course."

The gray eyes flashed. "I got me a job on a magazine as an office girl. And pretty soon I got a better job, and now I'm an assistant editor. And Dad got madder and madder, I suppose—I hope—and it served him right!"

She ground her white teeth furiously. And then suddenly she put her face down into her two hands, on her knees, and burst into a passion of tears.

CHAPTER 15

KATE KILGALLON left soon after her outburst of weeping, which was brief. When Lutie trotted in from the bathroom, where we keep our supply of apple brandy for medicinal purposes, the girl was already sitting up, mopping her drenched face angrily. She took the small glass that Lutie put into her hand, drained it in one long swallow, gulped, shivered, and said, "Thanks."

She gave a last vicious jab at her eyes, blew her nose.

"Well, that's that. I've made a fine show of myself." She glanced at her watch, reached for her hat, shook back her red mane and jammed the hat on her head, standing up.

"I'll have to run now, I'm meeting B—I've a date. When will you want to see me again? Or will you?"

She managed a crooked small smile at this, while she fished in her big square handbag. "Anyway, this is where I live." She laid a narrow white card on the table beside Zeke's chair. "I wrote the phone number on it too."

At the door she turned.

"I'll try not to make such a fool of myself again." Her slim shoulders were stiffly squared and the line of her chin was taut. But her eyes clung to Lutie childishly.

Lutie patted her arm.

"You are going to take the case, anyway, aren't you?" The girl's voice shook a little. "You promised you would."

Although she hadn't addressed Amanda it was Amanda who answered.

"Yes," said Amanda, firmly.

Lutie said softly, and I think only I caught the tiny lilt in her tone,

"We'll be seeing you, my dear." She closed the door behind our new client.

"Well, Sister," she asked eagerly, "what sort of impression did you get of Kate?"

Amanda was scanning the card the girl had left.

"Hmmph," she said, "West 11th Street. Isn't that in the neighborhood called Greenwich Village? A very unconventional place, I seem to have heard, peopled by all sorts of odd characters, bohemians and purple cows and pink elephants."

Lutie nodded. I remembered the day we'd wandered around a labyrinth of old streets, gazing at the homes of celebrities both the past and present: a saloon where once the Poet Laureate of England worked, through Tenth Street, pausing before the house where Mark Twain had lived, and, finally, under Washington Arch to the south side of the Square, where we'd stood gazing up at ancient attics, and my little cousin had told me, "That's where Albert Ryder, the great painter, lived. John Sloan lives there. That's where Rose O'Neill borned the darling Kewpies, and, once upon a time, the Father of our Country made his headquarters in a house, a little old wooden house, that stood there!"

Now she said softly: "Yes, Sister. All sorts of odd people. Artists, poets, rebels. Kate is rather a rebel, isn't she? And quite unfilial, of course."

"I daresay! However, under the circumstances her attitude may be understandable, if not excusable!" snapped Amanda.

"I do hope so, Sister," murmured Lutie meekly. She changed the subject. "When she came in, you were telling us what our man Walden had seen?"

She picked up the plan of Karkoff's place, which she had turned face down on the desk before our visitor was shown in, and pointed. "Walden was posted there, you said, behind those curtains. And he saw?"

Amanda turned her attention back to the matter at hand.

She said, "He saw a waiter taking a tripod, a bucket containing a bottle, and two goblets into the reception room. It was then thirty-five minutes past eleven o'clock. At a quarter to twelve Hero entered the room. The waiter left immediately after that. A minute or two later a young man and woman, corresponding to Davis's description of Miss Miller and Mr. Olcott, passed through the foyer and left by the main door. Soon after that—unfortunately Walden cannot be any more accurate than 'a few minutes later'—a young woman entered the foyer. Walden did not know her name but described her as a slight little girl in a pale pink dress, with light brown curls done up on top of her head. He says she was hurrying as she went toward the room. He saw her part the curtains and peer through, then dart in. Immediately afterward he was startled by a scream. The girl ran out, still screaming, and soon a small crowd collected."

"Which means that between the time the waiter left, and Bettine went into the room where Hero was found dead, no one else—" began Lutie.

"No one else entered it by that entrance. However—"

"Oh!" cried Lutie, who had been scrutinizing Amanda's sketch. "Of course! The window! And the ladders!"

I snatched the plan toward me. It was true. A window was shown opening from the rear terrace into the reception room. And as I now recalled perfectly clearly, there had been a window, heavily curtained, on that particular side of the wall. And apparently there were fire-ladders.

"Which means," I exclaimed excitedly, "that anyone might have climbed over the roof from the front terrace and onto the back one and through the window, and left the same way, and wouldn't have been seen by Walden at all!"

Lutie patted my back, approvingly, though a trifle absently.

"Exactly," said Amanda. "Which means that we must find out, if possible, who had the opportunity to do so."

"Well,'" said Lutie thoughtfully, "it seems to me almost everybody, everybody connected with the case so far, I mean—the people questioned last night—might have had the opportunity. At least a number of them were on the terrace, or—"

She looked up at Amanda then and added, "You see, Sister, Inspector Moore let Marthy and me stay in the room, Mr. Karkoff's office, while he was asking questions."

"So I gathered," said Amanda dryly, and opened her notebook.

"Well," said Lutie, and proceeded with a very complete account of the several interviews, also a description of the scene between Hero and Bettine we had overheard in the powder room. Now and then I was able to supply a small detail that she had seemingly forgotten—I have got a pretty good memory—and when I recalled the name of the man with whom Elinor said she had danced and then gone out onto the terrace, Baron Delacy, Lutie exclaimed, "Marthy dear, you're simply wonderful! I've been racking my brains and I simply couldn't recall it, and we're going to have to check everything. You're going to be most useful! Well. Except for Bettine, of course, that leaves only Ted Greer inside all the time, doesn't it? And suppose he stepped out of this window, right from the platform, and up this ladder, and—"

"Why," I said, explosively, "do we have to consider just those people, the ones we've mentioned? Why shouldn't the murderer have been somebody who wasn't connected with Hero at all? Someone who heard her order the champagne taken to the reception room and hoped she might be there alone and went up over the roof and down, and looked into that window and saw her there, and thought it was a perfect chance to steal that million dollar necklace? And tried to rip it from her neck, reaching through the scrollwork of the throne chair, but didn't quite make it because he heard someone, Bettine, of course, coming into the room? And strangled Hero, either accidentally or because she'd seen him! And ran out, darting behind the window curtains just before Bettine came in, and escaped over the roof again!"

"Martha," said Lutie solemnly, "that's perfectly marvelous. And for some reason it never occurred to me!"

"Nor to me," said Amanda. "Hmmph. Certainly we must question Jansen, our man who was stationed on the terrace, very carefully. I'll telephone him to come here immediately. Also Ferrone. He was stationed in the pantry, where you tell me Mr. Greer says he was drinking milk while his wife was finding the body and screaming. Ferrone made no mention of Mr. Greer in his report. However, his report merely consisted of the statement that no one but the waiters used the service elevator to the hotel kitchen below. I will question him again, more particularly. Meanwhile," she rose, "there's no sense in speculating further. I'll file this."

She picked up Kate Kilgallon's card, took off the apron she wears over her bombazine dress during breakfast and the morning's household tasks and left for the office.

As soon as the door had closed behind her I turned to my younger cousin. I had remembered something, and emboldened by the recent respect I had evoked I said firmly, "Lutie, whose fingernail did you find on the floor last night, there beside the body? Do you know?"

She took so long to answer that I feared she wasn't going to. But finally she did.

"It was Elinor Lynn's fingernail," she said quietly.

"Elinor's? But—but—" I stammered, "how can you be so sure? I thought perhaps it was Bettine's, after all, we know she was there. Or even that it might have been Hero's."

Lutie shook her head. "I looked very carefully at Hero's hands. Her nails were very long, a lighter red, and none of them was broken. Nor were any of Bettine's, which were pink, anyway, and she doesn't paint the tips. Neither does Sabina, though hers are dark red and all of them were long, very pointed, and undamaged. Kate's are not very long, she wears no color on them, and they were whole. You see, I took particular notice of their hands, all of them, last night. Only Elinor Lynn's nails were enameled right out to the tips, a dark crimson, and oval. And besides, one of them, the middle finger on her right hand, was snapped off, right down to the quick."

"But—but —" I faltered.

"Listen, Marthy dear," said Lutie. "This broken fingernail cannot possibly prove anything at all. Elinor was undoubtedly in the reception room before Hero met her death there. She might have broken her nail then."

"Why, of course!" I said, relieved, and a bit annoyed because I hadn't thought of that simple fact, somehow. And also—

"Then why," I snapped, "were you so darned mysterious about it? All that to-do."

Lutie nodded calmly. "May be much ado about nothing. Certainly it isn't evidence, so you see," she glanced at me demurely, "I'm not suppressing anything. Just the same," her eyes grew dreamy, "it may be a lead."

"Pish tosh!" I interrupted rudely. I didn't intend to budge from my own pet theory of the would-be diamond thief as the murderer. "We know, now, that the person who killed Hero must have come over the roof somehow. Which eliminates Elinor, in fact all the girls! Certainly you don't believe that any of them could have climbed ladders and crawled through windows in those filmy trailing frocks they were wearing last night! You can't think for a moment—"

Lutie came out of her dreamy abstraction.

"I can't think for this moment, my dear Watson, with you so vehemently excited!" She twinkled at me.

Then she rose briskly. "Let's not try to think any more till we have more to go on. So come, we'll do the marketing; and after that, a walk up the Avenue in this lovely spring sunshine, and a little visit to Mr. Karkoff's penthouse is indicated!"

A few minutes later, having changed into street clothes and informed Amanda that we were off on our usual morning errands, we were out on the brilliant busy streets. After stopping at the grocer's, the butcher's and our nice vegetable man, we were trotting east across town to Fifth Avenue. At least, Lutie trotted and I plowed along at her shoulder, for somehow, no matter how fast I manage to go, my little cousin always seems to be two little leaps ahead of me. She has a habit of walking quickly even though she makes frequent stops to window-shop, or to admire some quaint or impressive building or vista, or to point out to me an odd, or amusing, or smart-looking passerby.

Today we even made a detour, strolling past the hyacinth beds at Rockefeller City to lean on the railing with other loiterers gazing down at the roller-skating in the wide sunken square below. It was a charming sight: bright parasols shading tables in front of the English Grill and the French Cafe, massed borders of white bloom, the fountain with its poised bronze figure and the splashing fall of water gleaming in the April sunshine, and the figures of the skaters, in gay springlike apparel on this lovely day, dipping, swirling, gliding smoothly as though blown along before the balmy breeze.

Lutie and I had on our new spring rigs, too. I wore a soft gray coat, beautifully cut, over a gray silk dress with white dots that were actually tiny stars and a rakishly tilted hat with a frivolous, flattering veil. Lutie's little black jacket was very jaunty, with a nipped-in waist and perky sleeves. A single white rose perched atop of the tiny black straw bonnet tied under her chin with a wide taffeta bow. She looked adorable. I felt that we both looked smart, and I was conscious of that delightful, festive sense of well-being that comes of pretty new clothes on a fine spring day.

Absorbed in these pleasant feelings and the charming scene, I hardly noticed that Lutie was squeezing my arm for attention, until she pinched it.

"Look!" she whispered, nodding down toward the skaters. "Look who's there, Marthy!"

I followed her gesture. A girl and a boy had just come out onto the wide concrete floor below us. The girl's slender back was toward us, but there was something familiar about those erect square shoulders and the copper locks sweeping them

"Why, it's Kate Kilgallon, isn't it?" I exclaimed.

The girl pulled off her wide hat, tossed it on a bench, and shaking back her red hair turned to her companion. She was indeed the girl who had been with us, weeping, only a very short time ago. But she was not weeping now. She was laughing, and as the young man who was with her caught her hand and they glided off together, her flushed, peach-bloomy skin seemed not only to reflect the sunlight but to shine with a light of its own.

"Yes, it's Kate," said Lutie. "But who is the boy? Though he does look familiar."

I drew my gaze from the radiant face with the blazing hair streaming behind it.

"Oh. Why, it's the trumpeter! You know, the one who played *Taps* last night. Don't you remember?"

"Of course, so it is!" said Lutie. "Well, well. Now, I wonder—"

The happy-faced girl and the tall smiling boy with his thick blond hair roughed up by the wind made a very pretty picture. But—

"Lutie," I said, "don't you think that's frightfully callous? After all,

Hero was her sister. Yet now, right after the terrible thing that happened, she goes skating. I should think she'd be ashamed."

"Should you, Marthy dear?" murmured Lutie mildly. "Well, I never could see any sense in deliberate glooming. But other people have different notions, I know."

"It's not that," I insisted. "It's simply I don't see how she can feel like that."

"Don't you, Marthy?" said Lutie. Her blue eyes dwelled on the pair who, their hands linked, their faces lifted to the spring breeze, pirouetted and swooped and floated below us.

"She's in love," said Lutie.

She spoke softly. But to infer that there was anything sentimental about her tone would be quite misleading. She was stating an observed fact, thoughtfully. And she continued to think while we both watched the happy young h pair, and I, made of softer stuff than my little cousin, began to feel my heart melt toward the lovers

"Well! We'd better be going about our business, my dear!" said Lutie briskly at last, and tapped my shoulder. But just then the young trumpeter glanced up and straight at us both.

He said something, and Kate looked up and saw us too. She waved, they swerved, swept in our direction and brought up short just below us.

"Hello," called Kate, and grinned. "Miss Lutie, Miss Marthy, this is Bill Cameron!"

"Hi!" said the boy and grinned too. Then he looked at my cousin, drew his wide mouth down and scowled. "So! I'm corny, am I?"

Lutie blushed. But it was only a moment before she regained her usual demure poise. Gravely, but with a smile tucking in the corners of her mouth, she nodded. "Corny. But not icky!" she called. "Goombye!" And she took my arm, and trotted off.

"Lutie," I asked as we reached the Avenue again, "what in the world does that gibberish mean?"

"Oh, it's just a bit of swing slang, Marthy! One really can't help picking it up nowadays."

We proceeded up the Avenue.

CHAPTER 16

WE crossed the Grand Army Plaza, passing the tall warrior on his gold horse facing with noble indifference the coquettish nymph on the fountain opposite him. As I looked up at the chiseled features, stern and weary even in victory, with busy chirping city sparrows at the foot of his statue and budding trees beyond it, I thought it was a pity that anyone should have to be intent on war, or murder, instead of loveliness, on such a sweet, gay day.

I was sorry to leave the sunshine outside as we stepped within the wide doors, into the cool forenoon quietness of the Stuyvesant-Plaza. And I hated being shut into the small, plush-padded cage of the elevator that shot us so swiftly upward through dead, faintly perfumed air to the scene of last night's horror.

Lutie, however, seemed to have no such qualms. And Mr. Karkoff, who hurried toward us as we entered the foyer, seemed delighted to greet us, though he looked somewhat haggard, as if he'd had little sleep and that not restful since we had last seen him.

Which was the case, as he told us at some length.

"Such a terrible, terrible thing. So unprecedented," he explained in his neat precise English, but with a slight outward turning of palms that was distinctly foreign. "My beautiful, beautiful party ruined, all my guests so upset. Why should it have happened here? Why should it have happened at all? That pretty, and popular, and rich young girl! Why should she take her life? Why should anyone take it?" He shook his head disconsolately. "It is incomprehensible. I cannot comprehend it."

Lutie agreed that it was very puzzling indeed.

"However," she said, "we have certain ideas. They may lead to nothing, or they may lead to the truth, which I'm sure you are anxious to learn, also. So I hope, I'm certain, of course, that you'll help us. May we look around your penthouse a bit? It is just the arrangement of the rooms we wish to see and the terraces. We won't disturb anything, of course. We just want to wander around. If you are busy."

"Not at all. Not at all, in the least," Mr. Karkoff assured us. "Any way in which I can be of assistance will gratify me. Where shall I show you first?"

Lutie considered. "Well, I think we'll begin at the scene of the crime, the reception room."

We were still standing in the foyer, and she nodded toward the curtained doorway on our right. "I understand, of course, the police finished there last night; so it is all right to go in there now, if you have no objection?"

"Oh, no. No, indeed. I have no objection. None at all," said Mr. Karkoff, stepping to the doorway and drawing the curtains to one side for us to enter.

How I dreaded going into that room! Involuntarily my eyes went first to the oval mirror on the opposite wall, from which last night those staring eyes, that darkly mottled face, had looked out at us. And then to the tall carved chair. And the couch near the window where the white, still figure of the dead girl had lain.

But Lutie apparently had no thought of any of those horrors.

She walked straight to the tall French window. The cut-velvet curtains were not drawn across it now as they had been last night, and sunlight slanted into the little room, making it glow like a jewel, gleaming dully on the gilded sconces, the soft rich colors of the carpet, the crimson and blue and golden threads of the brocade covering the closed guest book lying on the table. But Lutie wasn't thinking of beauty either.

She stepped through the open steel-casement window onto a balcony outside and peered upward. I couldn't help following, and so did Mr. Karkoff. We all stared upward, following her gaze. There was nothing to see except, some four or five feet above the top of the window, the roof of the penthouse, with the clear April sky above it.

"What holds your interest, Miss Lutie?" asked the jeweler.

Lutie didn't reply. She had just spied an iron ladder against the facade of the penthouse, between two windows beyond the one we were in front of.

"I think," she said, "I would like to go up there, Mr. Karkoff."

She trotted to the foot of the ladder, hung her reticule over her wrist, grasped her long full skirts with her left hand (no matter what the fashion or time of day, Lutie wears the long skirts she did as a young girl in the Nineties) and with her right hand she took a firm hold of the side of the ladder. She put a foot on the lowest rung.

"Lutie!" I cried. "Don't! Don't go up! Stop it! You'll fall! Come down!"

Lutie slid her hand upward on the iron upright and gained another rung.

Mr. Karkoff said breathlessly, "But, my dear lady, that's dangerous! And—and why?"

He stared. We both stared as Lutie went up another rung, another, and another. She was nearing the top. But how would she manage that last difficult step over onto the roof? We both ran forward with outstretched arms.

Then she paused, and I thought perhaps she only meant to look over the housetop, which was bad enough, goodness knew. Suppose her foot slipped, or she turned suddenly dizzy way up there? I was afraid to breathe, to move.

But Lutie wasn't. With her black silk skirts and her starched embroidered white petticoat gathered snugly about her, she slid her hand forward over the curved side of the ladder, gave herself a sharp little pull, and was over the top.

My arms dropped, limply. Mr. Karkoff let his breath out in a long "Pouff."

Lutie's voice floated down to us brightly. "Meet me on the front terrace, Marthy dear!" she called cheerfully.

Mr. Karkoff and I looked at each other.

"A most extraordinary lady," he said at last. "Very, very unusual. But why?"

I made no reply. I was stepping back through the window into the reception room and hurrying across it with no thought now for the horrors of the night before. I hastened through the foyer and the wide hallway and the long room, sunny and silent and swept now, which had been filled with soft lights and music and laughter and dancing and the clinking of glasses last night. A wide French window was open onto the terrace. I dashed out of it, Mr. Karkoff at my heels.

Bright awnings, tables and chairs and shrubs dotted the terrace, but Lutie wasn't there. Nor did I see a stairway or ladder. I blinked up toward the sky and called, "Lutie! Where are you?"

"Here, my dear," called a voice to my left. I ran in its direction, around the corner of the penthouse.

Lutie was on the lowest rung of the ladder against its wall. With a little jump she landed beside me. She dusted off her gloved hands and smiled at me happily.

"So, you see, my dear Watson? If I could do it—"

"But, my dear lady," gasped Mr. Karkoff. "Why?" Then he said suddenly, "Ah. Ah, I see. You believe that someone went over the roof, and entered the reception room, and—"

"I only wanted to find out how difficult it would be to do that," replied Lutie. She brushed a fleck of dust from her skirt. "And of course it wasn't difficult at all. Now, let's see. Where does this window lead to?" She pointed to one right beside the ladder from which she had just descended, and without waiting for a reply peered through it.

"Oh, of course. That's the one onto the musician's platform. Do you see, Marthy?"

I looked and saw, nearby, a grand piano, the semicircular edge of the dais, curtains on either side of it, and the long room beyond.

But Lutie's alert glance was already thoughtfully scanning the tables and chairs on the terrace just outside the window.

"I wonder who was sitting here, and for how long?" she mused. "Well, we'll try to find out." She trotted around the corner of the penthouse and pointed to a heavy metal door in the white-painted brick wall. "That's the door to the fire stairs, and Jansen probably sat there," she gestured to a chair beside it, "most of the evening."

She walked slowly along the terrace, past two more tables with chairs grouped about them, to a jog in the wall. A settee with a high curved back stood in the jog. Beyond it the terrace narrowed. Lutie walked along it and I followed while she looked through the long windows opening from it. To our left we could see the wide archway leading into the main dance room of the night before with the dais at the end, but in this nearer room something was missing

"Why, where is the bar?" I exclaimed.

"It is closed now. It is behind those doors." Mr. Karkoff indicated the wide white panels at the end of the room and smiled. "But if you would care to have a little drink, some sherry, perhaps, or—"

"No, thank you, Mr. Karkoff; we really must be on our way. What a wonderful view!" Lutie paused for a last glance at the Plaza, almost straight down and far below us, and out across the Park, over the tops of the menagerie buildings, the long line of the Mall, and the pond, flecked with infinitesimal white dots and bordered with what, from this height, looked like clusters of nosegays, the bright frocks of the children sailing their toy boats.

Then we went back into the penthouse where, I now had time to observe, the two large rooms had been rearranged since the night before. Most of the tables with their surrounding chairs had been taken away and replaced by deep chairs with lower tables and soft-shaded lamps beside them. Thick rose-colored carpets covered the floors, a small fire glowed in the wide fireplace, and bowls of red roses were everywhere.

Lutie's alert gaze traveled about with interest and admiration.

"What a transformation, and how charming!" she murmured. "And so original."

"Is it not?" agreed Mr. Karkoff, rubbing his hands together delightedly. "My jewels, of course, are always shown singly, each exquisite creation, or set, quite by itself. Sometimes on mannikins. I employ three beautiful young women, of varying ages and with costumes for differing occasions, to suit my gems. They make a most tempting picture, I assure you. The lights on my little stage are most carefully arranged, as you see."

He switched the lights on the dais, illuminating it in an artful manner. One could imagine how softly yet brilliantly pretty faces, white arms and shoulders, gleaming gems would be thrown into relief.

"And now, perhaps, you would like to see where I keep my darlings?"

For one absurd moment I believed Mr. Karkoff was referring to his "three beautiful young women of varying ages," but was enlightened when we were shown into a room at the end of the large hall and the jeweler, sliding back several wall panels, disclosed a number of large steel safes.

"How ingenious!" exclaimed Lutie. "But didn't this room do duty as the men's lounge last night? Mightn't that have been a bit risky?"

"Risky? Oh, no. For one thing only I, I myself alone, know the combinations of my safes. Moreover, this whole room," he waved his hand around at the wall panels, the doors and the window, "is fully equipped with the very latest in burglar alarms. These can be adjusted individually to ring at the slightest touch. Last night only those connected with the panels and the safes were set, but that was all that was necessary. Would you care to see one or two of my special treasures?"

"Oh, no. No. That is, I would love to see them, but I mustn't, I really mustn't! I have always wanted a diamond necklace," added Lutie wistfully. "Oh, nothing spectacular, of course, like the one Hero was str— I mean, a few small gems set in some pretty and original design, with a platinum chain, perhaps."

"I have, I believe, the perfect creation!" said the jeweler. "If you will rest yourself in the salon, it will be a great pleasure to show it to you."

"No, oh, no!" Lutie backed hastily out of the room. "Get thee behind me, Mr. Sandro Satan!" She smiled. "Though perhaps some other time. If, say, we should be successful with this case, maybe Sister would let me have just a very teeny weeny diamond necklace as a souvenir."

Reluctantly the jeweler slid the panels across his treasures and followed us out into the hall.

As we went toward the foyer to make our departure, I hoped, Lutie suddenly spied a door at the far end of the hall.

"And that door, where does it lead? I don't believe I noticed it last night," she said.

"Oh, that door!" Mr. Karkoff shrugged. "Why, that is the door to the sitting room of my private apartment. Last night it was kept locked, simply to preserve for my little sanctum sanctorum a measure of privacy."

His tone was casual, rather elaborately casual, or so I thought. But his small black eyes slid sidewise as he took a few steps toward the door that placed him, whether intentionally or not, between it and ourselves.

Lutie glanced at him sharply.

"But it isn't locked now, is it, Mr. Karkoff?" she inquired brightly. "You know, I caught a glimpse into your sitting room last night, just a glimpse, and it was fascinating! So quaint and individual. I would love to have a real peek! May we?"

She trotted toward the door and put her hand on the knob.

I was shocked. To invade the gentleman's private apartment, not only uninvited but quite clearly for some reason against his wish, seemed a most unwarranted impertinence. Yet it was obviously his oddly dismayed manner that had provoked my little cousin's determination to intrude.

"You don't mind?" she said sweetly, as she turned the handle of the door and opened it. Then she said pleasantly, "Oh. Good morning!"

Mr. Karkoff, looking uncomfortable, and I, feeling so, followed her into the sunny, rather cluttered room, where a girl's figure, silhouetted against the light of a window, was rising from a chair.

It was Elinor Lynn, in a dark tweed suit, her crisp gleaming black hair in brushed-up curls around her small head, her oval cheeks tinged with color. "Good morning," she said, and smiled, and added, "So you, too, are doing a little investigating, I gather?"

"That," replied Lutie primly, "is our business."

"Oh. Is it?" The girl blushed then. "I didn't mean that the way it sounds. I know who you are, of course, and Sandro told me he'd engaged your agency last night to guard his treasures. But he didn't say he'd employed your services to—"

"Find out how your stepdaughter met her death?" supplied Lutie. "No, my dear, he didn't."

"But somebody has?" said Elinor quickly.

"Yes, and no," replied Lutie, carefully.

The girl said, "Who?"

"That," answered Lutie, "I'm afraid I can't say. If you wish you may ask my sister, Miss Amanda Beagle. She is the head of our bureau."

"Oh, well, it doesn't matter," said Elinor. She reached for a cigarette and lighted it. I caught myself trying to get a glimpse of the middle finger of her right hand. But I couldn't. Somehow the long fingers holding the cigarette curled in toward the palm, though seemingly in a quite natural manner.

Lutie was watching the girl too. But she was watching her face. She didn't say anything, and after a moment Elinor went on, "You see, I don't think there's anything more to find out. I almost wish there were. I couldn't sleep all night, thinking there might have been something I could have done to prevent her killing herself. And I couldn't help coming up here this morning, to see if I got any other ideas. Almost hoping I might."

"And did you?"

The girl shook her head.

"I see," said Lutie. "But tell me, my dear, why did you hide?"

."Hide?" The girl's voice sounded a little shrill. "What do you mean?

Why should you think I was hiding?"

Lutie merely raised her silvery eyebrows a fraction.

Elinor pressed out her cigarette in a china tray shaped like a cupped hand. "For that matter," she said more calmly, "I didn't care to see anybody. Can you imagine how ghastly it's going to be to see people after what happened? The commiserations and consolations, and all the thinly disguised inquisitiveness? Ugh!"

She shivered and picked up a small black hat from the center table. "I feel as if I didn't ever want to see anybody again."

"Come, that is a very wrong and unnecessary way to feel," said Lutie quietly. She seated herself in the golden-oak rocking chair. "It always seems very futile to me to brood. I'm sure you should meet your friends and acquaintances without expecting them to be unpleasant. I think that just as soon as possible you should go on with your usual life, trying not to—"

"Do you know," broke in Elinor Lynn, rather wildly, "what my usual life has been like for the last year and a half since C.V. died? Living in that big lonesome house with Hero, when she was there, and mostly she wasn't, treating me like a—like a stepmother? I tell you, it's been deadly! Why, do you know that the party last night was the first one I've gone to since—"

Her lips went down at the corners and quivered childishly.

"And I'm young. I was just beginning to feel young again. And now this."

Her hands dropped to her sides. Then she shrugged, raised them and put on her hat, pulling the small net veil down over her eyes.

"I'd like," she said, picking up her gloves and staring down at them, "to wear something besides black, and feel something besides black, for a change." She drew on the gloves and looked up at us, half piteously, half defiantly. "That's a very selfish way to feel, isn't it?"

"But quite natural," replied Lutie gently.

"Goodbye," said the girl. At the door she turned. "I daresay I'll see you again, since you seem to be working on this case. I'll find my way out, Sandro."

We heard her footsteps going along the hallway. A moment later a door closed.

Lutie said, thoughtfully, "You have known Mrs. Lynn for some time, haven't you, Mr. Karkoff?"

The man seemed a little surprised. "Why, yes. Yes. In a business way, and also socially, in a sense, I have known her for some four, five years. Since her marriage to her husband she has been a customer of mine, as he was also. And I have met them both at certain gatherings."

"Has Mrs. Lynn been an exceptionally profitable customer?"

"Profitable?" Karkoff's eyebrows shot upward.

"I mean, was she extravagantly fond of expensive jewelry?"

The jeweler shook his head.

"No. No," he said definitely and somewhat regretfully. "I would say she was unusually indifferent to fine jewels as compared to most young women, or any women, in my experience. Her husband, Mr. Caleb Vanderbrough Lynn, purchased a number of very beautiful pieces from me as gifts to his wife, as well as her engagement and her wedding rings. No doubt she appreciated them, as gifts, and she always complimented me very charmingly concerning them. But her expressions of appreciation lacked excitement, if you understand me."

"I think I do," replied Lutie thoughtfully.

"As for her own purchases," went on the jeweler, now on his own ground and carried away by his subject, "they were very modest. Gifts for friends, birthdays, Christmases, and so forth, not meager, you know, and always in good taste. But—"

Lutie nodded. "Was Mrs. Lynn wealthy before her marriage?" she asked.

Mr. Karkoff's eyebrows went up again. His palms turned outward.

"She was a DeBrussy," he said, as if that answered Lutie's question in full.

"But, Mr. Karkoff, I am not a New Yorker, you see," said Lutie meekly.

"Oh," said Mr. Karkoff, as if he saw. "Well, the DeBrussys are a very fine old family. Elinor DeBrussy, Mrs. Lynn, is their only child. They managed to put her through the correct schools and to bring her out. It was a very simple debut. But they have no money. No money at all."

"I see," said Lutie. Then she asked, "Mr. Karkoff, I suppose you saw Mr. and Mrs. Lynn together at times?"

The jeweler nodded.

"Well, would you say she was in love with her husband? Do you think they were happy together? Do you believe she married him for his money?"

Mr. Karkoff, who had perched himself on a Victorian sofa, sat up very straight.

"Yes, no, and no!" he replied decisively. And then proceeded to explain.

"I think, but definitely, that Mrs. Lynn was in love with her husband. Possibly she was dazzled by him. He was a very handsome man and a brilliant one, and though he was older than she, he was comparatively young, only forty-six when they married.

"Were they happy together? That is another question. I think not. I do not think Mr. Lynn cared for anyone except himself and his older daughter. He was always courteous and indulgently pleasant, to his wife, but I believe she felt a lack of warmth.

"As for Elinor DeBrussy's interest in money—in spite of her family's poverty I do not believe money could tempt her. I do not think she is a cold-blooded young woman!"

"Ah," murmured Lutie. She looked back, very intently, at Sandro Karkoff's small, intelligent black eyes. "You are very convincing, Mr. Karkoff."

"I saw them together," he replied simply.

Lutie said, "Thank you. You have been very indulgent. Very helpful. I hope we haven't taken up too much of your time."

She rose, and Mr. Karkoff rose, and said his time was at our service. That he too wished to get at the root of last night's tragic occurrence.

He escorted us to the padded cell, I mean the elevator, and as we descended he waved his short, square, delicately pointed hand in adieu. His swarthy face looked at us through the bars, then disappeared from our sight as the cage descended.

CHAPTER 17

WE reached home just before dinner, which we have at noon. During the meal Lutie was unwontedly silent. I, too, was busy trying to sort out my impressions of the morning, especially the somewhat varied and puzzling impressions made on me by the two young women, the sister and the stepmother of the dead girl.

Amanda, on the contrary, was rather talkative, for her, describing, not without a spice of dry humor, her handling during the morning of the ladies and gentlemen of the press who had clamored for interviews and with whom she had been courteous but firmly noncommittal. She seemed particularly satisfied as she related the attempts of "one brash young whippersnapper" who was determined to take her picture, and how she had given him his comeuppance.

Lutie listened smiling, with little nods and clucks of approval and amusement, but contributed no reminiscences of her own.

Finally Amanda, finishing her blackberry pudding and folding her napkin, remarked with a shrewd glance at her small sister, "I don't suppose it took you three hours to do the marketing. What were you up to, Lutie Beagle?

"We were up to a roof," replied Lutie. She gave a brief account of our visit to the scene of last night's tragedy but made no mention of her discovery of Elinor Lynn in the jeweler's sanctum sanctorum, nor of our encounter with the blond horn player and our new client, who had so shocked me by weeping passionately and roller skating rapturously within the same hour. Concluding with her own trip over the penthouse roof, up one ladder and down another, she said simply, "So you see how easy it would have been for anyone—"

I expected a sharp comment from Amanda on such precarious shenanigans, but instead she said thoughtfully, "Hmmph. Quite sensible, Sister. We shall have to question Jansen, our man who was stationed on the terrace, very carefully. I expect him here at one-thirty." She rose. "Come, we must hurry with the dishes."

We did so, and were seated in the inner office, Amanda enthroned in the swivel chair behind the big desk that had been Zeke's, when at exactly half-past one Jansen arrived.

He was a solid, intelligent-looking young man and reflected carefully after Amanda had explained that we wished to know anything he could tell us, in detail, concerning any guests at the party last night who had come out on the terrace while he was stationed there.

He answered that quite a number of people had come out at one time or another. He was afraid that he could not identify them all by name nor describe them in detail. Lots of couples had wandered out briefly between dances, strolled along the terrace or leaned on the parapet, then returned to the dance rooms. None of these remained for more than a few minutes at a time, until a group of five young people came out and sat down at a table quite near him.

Of these he recognized Miss Sabina Brok, who had been pointed out to him as the wearer of a pearl necklace, one of the pieces it was his job to keep an eye on. For this reason he had kept a watchful eye also on her companions: Kate Kilgallon (he had seen pictures of her in what he termed the smut sheets in connection with the stew about her father's will, and he heard the others call her Kate); a girl in a red dress, called Mimi; Harold Broderick, the polo player; and a baldish fellow they called Todquite, a card, that one. He and this Mimi did most of the talking. She was all excited about Hero Lynn's marrying Charles Leland and kept asking her sister for the lowdown. Mrs. Kilgallon said she didn't know any more about it than they did, and Tod started to sing *At the Bar, at the Bar,* with references to Hero's wedding announcement that he seemed to think howlingly funny. The Brok girl told him to shut up, that he wasn't funny at all, and anyway the whole subject was a crashing bore.

"Then Hero Lynn herself, I mean Mrs. Leland, came out, with her husband. They—"

"Just a second, Mr. Jansen," Lutie interrupted. "I've just been wondering. I understand that your particular duty was to guard the only direct exit from the terrace, the door to the fire stairs. So of course we're assuming that you kept that in sight all evening."

"Except for about five minutes once, when Pryce glanced out and I asked him to take my place," interpolated Jansen conscientiously. "But that was much later in the evening. While I was there no one touched that door. I'll swear to that."

Lutie reached for the plan of the penthouse that lay on the desk in front of Amanda.

"Is there a possibility that anyone could have gone up this ladder, "she said, pointing to the one on the front terrace, "while you were there?"

He examined the plan and said, after a moment, "Well, I certainly don't think so. A good part of the time I was here." He put his finger on a porch seat in an angle of the parapet, from which both the fire door and the ladder to the roof were in plain view. "But there was quite a stiff breeze blowing over from the East River, so some of the time I sat here." He indicated a chair against the wall, between the fire door and a group of chairs around a table. "No one went round the corner and didn't come back, I'll swear to that. But of course it's possible that someone could have sneaked out that window you've shown there, leading from the musician's platform. They'd have been taking a chance, and I think I'd have heard them, but—"

"Did anyone sit here at any time?" Amanda tapped a pencil on the group of chairs and table beside the ladder.

"No," answered Jansen, positively. "As I said, the wind was rather chilly around that corner."

"Thank you," said Lutie. "And now, to go back to what you were saying when I interrupted. Mr. and Mrs. Leland came out—?"

"Yes. They went over and sat down here." He showed a settee placed in a slight jog of the wall where the terrace narrowed. "This Tod fellow called out some wisecracks to Mrs. Leland, and she talked back. Then, some five minutes after, maybe less, she went back into the dance rooms. Right after that the other party left, the Brok girl, and the other four with her. I was pretty chilly. I'd taken myself over to the porch seat in the corner when they'd sat down at that table near me. I didn't want to seem to be listening in, so I went back to my chair against the house wall by the fire door."

"And Mr. Leland?"

"He was still sitting there where his wife had left him, smoking a cigarette. In fact he smoked several cigarettes. I noticed him lighting them, as if he felt nervous. Anyway, I thought to myself that I wouldn't like to be left cooling my heels like that by the girl I'd just got married to, while she—"

"How long did he sit there, cooling his heels?" interrupted Amanda.

The young man reflected. "Well, I'd say it was ten minutes, maybe more. I don't think it was less. There was some sort of hot dirge being played, I remember that, but I didn't look at my watch."

"Your instructions were to do so," said Amanda sternly. "However, continue."

"Then Mrs. Elinor Lynn came out. She was the one who was wearing the emerald earrings. I'd had her pointed out to me, too. There was a fellow with her, I didn't know him, medium height, medium coloring. They stood for a minute looking at the park, then she spotted Leland and said something to this fellow with her and he went on back in. She went over and sat down with Leland. They talked for a while, then she left. Pretty soon afterward someone came out and spoke to Leland and he jumped up and ran inside."

"I don't suppose you happened to overhear any of Mrs. Lynn's conversation with Mr. Leland?" suggested Lutie.

Jansen shook his head. "No. But I heard them laughing a couple of times. That was just before I heard a woman screaming somewhere."

"Ah, you could hear the screams from the terrace?" asked Lutie quickly.

"Yes. I got up and looked into the dance rooms. Some people seemed to be going toward the noise, others just acted as if there wasn't anything very exciting about some gal yelling at a party, like it was all in the night's play. I thought those screams sounded pretty bad, myself. But I was supposed to stay where I was, and I did."

"Very properly," said Amanda, and Lutie nodded, but absently.

"And Mrs. Lynn and Mr. Leland? Did they seem curious about the disturbance?" she asked.

"Well, I didn't notice exactly. But they didn't jump up or look in the window or anything, and afterwards they went on talking. Soon after that, though, she went in. He sat there till this fellow came out and spoke to him, as I said."

Which seemed to be about all the pertinent facts Mr. Jansen had to tell us. Lutie assured him prettily that he'd been very helpful indeed, and Amanda brought the interview to an end. Jeff went to the door with him, then came back excitedly, running his fingers through his wiry carrot-top.

"Jeez, Boss, we're really on this case, aren't we? I was hoping but I wasn't sure. Where do we go from here?"

"I have told you, Jefferson, not to use the expression 'jeez,' " said Amanda sternly. She rose. "I am going to buy a birdcage."

After she'd left, with her new black straw pancake clamped firmly on her head, Lutie and I, back in the apartment, looked at each other.

"Well, mercy me!" exclaimed Lutie. She added thoughtfully, "And that's not all she's up to, either! Marthy, do you know what? She's being the Mysterious Sleuth! Now, I wonder—"

So did I, but an idea of my own had occurred to me that I'd been holding onto for some time. Why it hadn't occurred to me, or to my little cousin, long before, I couldn't imagine.

Now I voiced it solemnly. "Lutie. Fingerprints. And probably you destroyed them!"

She'd taken up her crocheting, and now she looked up at me over a small green wool square that was rapidly growing larger.

"Oh. You mean on the ladder?"

So it had occurred to her. I couldn't help feeling crestfallen. I said, rather crossly, "Well, if you thought of that, why did you go right ahead and smudge them, as you must have done?"

She said, "Marthy dear, I've learned that dear Inspector Moore isn't at all a fool. He'd never have missed those ladders last night, with one almost alongside that reception room window. And I'm sure he has pretty little pictures of any fingerprints that were on them."

I took this in. So we hadn't made a special discovery.

"Well, then, why did you have to go climbing around all over the place like a monkey? Why?"

"Because one never knows what one may find out by looking for oneself. That window entrance to the room where Hero was strangled is quite obvious, and the way over the roof— But who took it? Or did anybody? That's another matter. From Mr. Jansen's report—"

She didn't finish that. She put her crocheting down in her lap. Her eyes grew dreamy.

"And as for the fingerprints on the ladder, I know that Inspector Moore would look for them there right away, but would other people know that? For instance, would Elinor Lynn?"

I jerked upright.

"Elinor? Lutie, you don't mean you think Elinor—?"

Lutie picked up her needle and wool.

"Marthy dear, I've only begun to get my thinks in order, and anyway perhaps they'll have to be all unraveled again. Like this." She pulled a thread of yarn, and in a moment or two the green wool square was demolished. "I missed a stitch, you see, somewhere at the start, and the whole thing was skew-gee. So— "

She looped the yarn over her fingers and began the square over, rocking gently and twinkling up at me.

So that was that. There was no use asking her any further questions now, I knew. So I got out my darning and retired into my own thoughts.

These, now that Lutie had dropped her enigmatic little innuendo, reverted and revolved around Hero's young stepmother.

My impressions of Elinor Lynn varied. Thinking back now I was surprised to find how nebulous the picture was. No, that doesn't express it; there were several pictures, each sharp and clear in itself; the trouble was they differed so.

First, there was a beautiful woman of the world, poised, calm, in severely draped, smart black. Then, I remembered that smooth oval face suddenly contorted, for one fleeting moment anguished, despairing. Soon after that the face was quiet, even gentle again, but the voice, though cool and light, had a thin brittle tone as it remarked, "Hero only drinks on important occasions, such as funerals." Afterward, in the room where her stepdaughter lay dead, she seemed simply a quiet, gentlewomanly person, shocked if perhaps not grief-stricken and keeping herself under admirable control.

And then, when I'd next seen her, when she was called into Karkoff's office to be questioned, there had been that extraordinary effect of tremulous childlikeness, as if a burden of years had been swept away, or— But I could analyze it no further than that.

And this morning there was still the impression of youthfulness, tempered by—fear, was it? And some sort of hard young determination. Moreover, I was quite sure now that she had been hiding, not merely shrinking from seeing anybody, as she had claimed. She had not wanted to be found there.

Why?

What did all those questions of Lutie's to Karkoff mean? Did she believe that the girl had married for money and now wanted more? The fortune that perhaps she would inherit by her stepdaughter's death? Or would she?

I was still going over and over these painful queries in a more and more muddled frame of mind when Amanda returned. She took off her hat and coat, hung them in the wardrobe, and sat down stiffly in her own special straight-backed chair. Lutie looked at her demurely but said nothing.

Amanda's lips were firmly set. I wondered if she, too, were going to keep her own counsel or tell us what her real errand had been. And, I thought crankily, they can keep their precious secrets, both of them. I suddenly felt pretty tired of floundering around in the dark.

Amanda said, "I ordered your birdcage, Sister. After which I called on Mr. Edward Williamson Holmes, the Lynn family attorney. I obtained his address this morning, also a letter of introduction to the gentleman, delivered by messenger from Kate Kilgallon. It seemed pertinent to this case to ascertain all the provisions of the will of the late C.V. Lynn."

"Oh," said Lutie interestedly, putting away her crocheting. "And what does it say, Sister?"

"It is a peculiar document, showing a brilliant mind, which, if not legally unbalanced by egotism and wrath, was certainly—" Amanda closed her lips sternly. "However. In the first place, the older daughter, Katherine, was disinherited for disobedience and—I need not enumerate her supposed offenses nor the terms in which they were described. In the second place, the widow, Elinor Lynn, inherited five hundred thousand dollars and a joint interest in two houses, one in New York and one in Southhampton, these to be shared with the younger daughter, Hero, so long as both remain in residence and the widow unmarried. Third, the bulk of the estate, totaling some nineteen million dollars, was left in a trust fund to Hero, with an annual income of twenty-five thousand dollars to be paid to her until her marriage, unless— But I won't repeat the conditions imposed on the girl in relation to her conduct while unmarried and the man she must or must not marry. Kate informed us about them, correctly, this morning."

Amanda paused, looking grim, then continued, "On the younger daughter's proper marriage, the income from the entire fund was to be at her disposal. And—"

"Excuse me, Sister dear!" cut in Lutie. "But were there any restrictions on her possible second marriage?"

"No. In point of fact—"

It was my turn to interrupt, for suddenly I had been struck by what seemed to me a ray of light.

"Then, I suppose, she inherited the whole trust fund outright? Which means that her husband, Charles Leland—"

Amanda said tartly, "Well, you suppose quite wrong. It was because there's no sense in supposing that I took the trouble to learn the facts from Mr. Holmes. The father's will left Hero no power over anything except the income from the trust fund, and specified definitely that on her death the estate was to be divided, not in the form of a fund, but unconditionally, between his widow and his older daughter, Katherine."

"Well, for mercy's sake," exclaimed Lutie. She sat back in her little chair and began to rock. Her silvery eyebrows were knitted into a tiny pucker.

Presently she nodded. "Well, of course, Kate told us that though she was very vague about it. And I had no idea the sum involved was so large. Nor that the widow's portion, unless her stepdaughter died before she did, was so small."

I too had been mulling over what Amanda had told us. And what especially surprised me—

"So Kate's father did relent, in a sense!" I burst out. "He must have had qualms, I suppose."

"Whatever was in the man's mind seems to me too ridiculously painful to try and ferret out," snapped Amanda. "What he did, however, was to scratch up a fine little garden plot, manured with the injustice of spiteful anger. And planted with the seeds of dissatisfaction, discomfort and discord. Small wonder if it grows a crop of guile and greed and is watered with blood!"

"Why, Sister!" Lutie's rocking chair stood utterly still as she gazed on her sister in amazed but unqualified admiration. "How marvelously poetical! And how true."

Amanda flushed and snapped, "Poetical, fiddlesticks!" She cleared her throat. "The point is, we now have more motives for murder in this case than we can shake a stick at!"

She rose abruptly.

"And we may as well go over what we do know in some sort of common-sense fashion, for what it may be worth."

So saying she led the way through the hallway into the inner office. Lutie and I followed. We exchanged astonished glances, and Lutie tucked her arm into mine.

"Why, Marthy," she murmured, "Sister's caught the real spirit. She really has!"

CHAPTER 18

AMANDA didn't overhear this delighted whisper. Already seated at the big desk, she opened a drawer, took out two sheets of foolscap, and adjusting her steel-rimmed specs, glanced over the blue-ruled pages, which were covered with her small, legible, angular handwriting. She inserted a note here and there, then taking a fresh sheet she wrote rapidly for several minutes.Finally she passed the pages across the desk. Lutie picked them up eagerly.

"Why, Sister!" she exclaimed, her eyes sparkling, "this is extraordinary. Absolutely in the best tradition!"

Amanda received this, as she does all praise, gruffly.

"Hmmph," she snorted. "I don't know what tradition you're talking about, Sister. Let's get down to brass tacks. I expect you'll have some of your own to offer. First, however," she said, tapping the top sheet of foolscap, "let's consider our timetable."

I leaned over Lutie's shoulder and read:

NOTES ON THE DEATH OF HERO LYNN LELAND, APRIL 17, 1940

Hero was last seen alive, by myself, when she requested the baud leader, Ted Greer, to play a certain selection. Time, 11:43.

I looked up quickly and said, "Amanda, how do you know? Do you really know that it was exactly eleven forty-three when the girl—?"

"Of course I do," replied Amanda tardy, "or I should not have set it down. I looked at my watch, fortunately, as it turns out. As it happens I had just overheard a woman nearby ask the time. Automatically I glanced to see—"

As Amanda is very time-conscious and frequently glances automatically or purposefully at the neat gold watch she always wears pinned to her bodice, I made no further comment and resumed reading:

I did not personally notice when Hero left or where she went after the music started. After it stopped and as refreshments were being served, screams were heard. We went at once in their direction. A girl (Bettine Greer) was screaming in front of a doorway. Another girl (Sabina Brok) was with her (as well as several other persons). We entered the room before which they stood (Mr. Karkoff, hastening up, entered with us) and discovered Hero, dead. We detached her from the chair in which she was hanging, strangled, and carried her to a couch. I then looked at my watch. The time was 11:53. The death, therefore, took place in the ten minutes between 11:43 and 11:53.

Lutie breathed softly: "Sister dear, that's perfectly wonderful! It narrows things down so definitely."

Amanda frowned. "It is not quite precise. I omitted to discount the interval between our first hearing the screams and the time when I looked at my watch. I will call that roughly a minute. As Hero must have been strangled before Bettine screamed, even if only an instant before, that leaves"—she reached for her schedule and corrected it—"nine minutes. Have either of you any relevant details to add?"

She handed us back her notes.

Lutie murmured, "There's the waiter's statement about when Hero ordered the champagne and when he served it to her in the reception room. Do you remember, Sister? Would that be of importance?"

"Of course I remember!" snapped Amanda. "Now that you've re-minded me. And it certainly may be important, Sister," she added more graciously. She took the schedule and inserted:

Jules Duval, the waiter, states that Hero L.L. ordered a bottle of champagne and two glasses served to her in the reception room; that "about five minutes later" he took it there. He then waited until she came in, "maybe seven or eight minutes, perhaps ten." He then opened the wine and departed.

"Hmm. Which accords very well with our man Walden, who reported that a waiter went into the reception room with champagne at eleven-thirty-five, and that Hero L.L. entered the room at eleven-forty-five."

Amanda, as a matter of form, glanced at her notebook and nodded. "Yes, Jules Duval's guess of ten minutes as to the time he waited for the girl would seem to be correct. He then opened and offered to serve the wine. Allow one minute approximately, certainly not more, as he stated that she ordered him to scram, which I understand means to leave quickly. Hmm. All of which checks with the fact that, at eleven-forty-three, we heard her request the band leader to perform a certain tune, after which apparently she went straight to the reception room. So—"

She jotted down on the schedule:

By well-substantiated statements we may now assume that Hero's death took place in the five minutes between 11:47 and 11:52.

"Now, as for the various persons who have been questioned con-cerning their whereabouts during the crucial period, or near it, I've put down the statements they made to Inspector Moore last night, as you related them to me. Please check them over carefully, Sister, and you too, Martha. You have a good memory for anything you have once really listened to. It may be very useful to us."

Blushing warmly at this uncommon praise, I turned my most careful attention to the following entries:

Bettine Greer: Says she went to sign married name in guest book, saw Hero in chair "looking horrible," screamed, ran from room. Seen by our man Walden, who places time inexactly, "several minutes" after waiter left. Screams heard at 11:52. Seems unlikely that Bettine was in room more than one minute, but this is not certain at all. No statement as to where she was before entering room.

Ted Greer: Hero asked him to play *Lament for a Dead Romance* at 11:43. He did so. Says he then went to pantry, was drinking milk when told Hero "had fainted, or something," went to reception room, saw Hero on couch, dead. Says did not hear wife's screams. Question: Did he go at once to pantry after leaving platform? Or did he leave platform, say, by window, climb up ladder and over roof into window of reception room, strangle Hero, return same route, repair to pantry? If music occupied two minutes (must check) and if he left reception room just before wife entered and screamed, we have an interval of approximately six minutes to accomplish trip over roof, and murder. Must question waiters on his presence in pantry, and if he was there, how long he remained. Seems improbable, but is possible, that he remained drinking milk in pantry for some eight to ten minutes.

"But, Cousin!" I exclaimed. "He may have stopped to chat on the way from the musician's platform to the pantry, which is way at the other end of the two big rooms, anyway."

"Certainly he may have, my dear Martha," said Amanda. "But I have had to put down certain items as they were stated. What may have happened is precisely what we still have to learn."

Which was, of course, true.

I returned to the foolscap page.

Sabina Brok: Was on terrace with party of four others, including Kate Kilgallon, when Hero and husband came out on terrace and when Hero left terrace, soon after which Sabina left also, with party, according to our man Jansen, and also Kate K. Says she went to powder room with K.K., and left with latter; K. substantiates this, waiter corroborates departure. Sabina says she then sat alone at table near dance room entrance for "a few minutes," before she heard screams and went at once to door of reception room where Bettine G. was screaming. Was evasive when asked if K. entered dance room with her; "saw" no one pass in and out of dance room. Question: Did she sit there alone for several minutes? Or did she recross hall to ladies' room, step out window to balcony and through reception room window, and strangle Hero?

"But—but why?" I stammered. For though it was true that I did not like Sabina Brok, when it came to a matter of murder—and set down, coolly, like that!

"The whys are something you have not yet reached, Cousin," replied Amanda. "But if you'll read on."

I read on:

Kate Kilgallon: On terrace with party, left with them, accompanied Sabina B. to powder room and left there with her. Says she then joined a gentleman, Harold Broderick, at bar, heard screams, went to reception room, found sister on couch dead. Question: Did she join friend at bar or return to powder room, slip out window and into reception room and kill sister?

This time I looked up, aghast. And this time Lutie caught my expression of dismay and protest; but before I could voice it she patted my arm quickly and murmured, "Now, now, Marthy dear. Don't you realize that Sister has simply listed the possibilities. And very, very cleverly, too! So just be a good girl and hold your horses."

I gulped, and went back to the sheet of notes before me:

Elinor Lynn: Says she was at bar, saw stepdaughter make request of band leader, then went out on terrace with a Mr. Baron Delacy, dismissed him, found Charles Leland sitting alone, talked with him "for a while," during which time she faintly heard screams. Presently left Charles still sitting on terrace, entered rooms, noticed "a commotion," met Ted G. who told her Hero had committed suicide (or words to that effect). Went toward reception room, near the door of which Charles L. ran up and into the room, she following, to find her stepdaughter dead. Question: Was she with Mr. Delacy continuously from 11:43 when Hero asked for the *Lament* to be played, until she appeared with him on the terrace?

If not, and if she had time to murder her stepdaughter, how did she get into the reception room to do so?

"But," I said, "why couldn't she have been in the powder room and slipped through the window and everything just as well as Kate could? Or even Sabina? Not that I have anything against Elinor, but if you're going to put the others in as suspects, especially Kate, I don't see why—"

"Dear Marthy!" Lutie shook her head at me. "Don't you understand that Sister is simply—"

Amanda interrupted, "Martha is quite right to examine the circumstances carefully. Obviously, what we must learn concerning Elinor's statement is, will Mr. Delacy support it?"

"Yes, Sister. That's what I meant," said Lutie meekly, and together we returned to Amanda's summary.

Charles Leland: Says he went out on terrace with his bride, they talked, she left terrace, telling him to wait for her, he did so, meanwhile Elinor "was there for a while." Statement vague in detail, but says he was on terrace "waiting" from time his wife went in until "someone" came out and told her she had fainted in reception room, when he hastened there to find her dead. He was seen coming out on terrace with his wife by Jansen and by Kate, who also saw Hero leave, and he was seen there sitting alone, by Elinor L., who joined him. And Jansen states positively that he was there from the time Hero left terrace until after Bettine screamed. If Jansen's statement is reliable Charles L. could not have killed his wife.

"But anyway, for heaven's sake, why should he have wanted to?" I cried. Then bit my lip. For why should any of those others—

"The possible whys, Martha, I have jotted down next. Or what little we yet know about them, which is very superficial. However, we must start with what we have. And please try to read them, Cousin, without— or at least before—throwing anymore conniption fits!" said Amanda.

So I went back to her "jottings," under the heading of:

POSSIBLE MOTIVES

Kate K.: The fortune she would inherit by her sister's death. Impelling factors: Anger at her father's will. The fact that she did not get on with her sister.

Elinor L.: The fortune she would inherit by her stepdaughter's death. Dislike for the girl with whom she was forced to live, and who "treated her like a stepmother."

Ted G.: Revenge, jealousy and hatred of the girl who may have jilted him. It is possible that he married Bettine to even the score, but found his emotions unappeased when confronted by Hero together with her husband. Or, it is possible that he planned to kill Hero as soon as she told him of her marriage, and himself married Bettine as a blind. (I believe this to be unlikely.)

Bettine G.: Jealousy, hatred and fear of the girl with whom, she may have believed, her husband was still in love, and who had, we know, claimed that to be the fact and threatened her with it. It is possible that she had been tormented for some time by gossip concerning Ted and Hero, and upon realizing that her own hasty marriage had immediately followed Hero's, was deeply wounded,and finally enraged by the girl's ruthless and boastful taunts to the point of insanity and murder.

Charles L.: Jealousy, anger. Possibly he overheard his bride make a rendezvous with the man whose name and hers had certainly been linked by gossip, or perhaps he merely overheard her order to the waiter, suspected that such a rendezvous had been arranged and was overcome by a sudden impulse of rage and wounded masculine vanity, which has frequently led to crime.

Sabina B.: Jealousy, of a rival whom she disliked,and who had as a crowning insult been chosen above herself to wear the badge of "glamour," the million-dollar necklace. (This seems a farfetched motive for murder; however, female vanity also has led to violent and fanatical acts.)

Unknown Person, male or female: Robbery. In which case the would-be thief, having strangled Hero so as not to be later exposed by her, was interrupted by hearing someone approaching the reception room, and being unable to unfasten the necklace quickly enough to make off with it, left the girl hanging by it in the chair.

"Oh!" I exclaimed excitedly, "I can just see the whole thing! This fellow strolling in through the window, perhaps someone that Hero knew, but anyway someone who was a guest and looked all right and didn't startle her. Probably he said hello or something and walked around behind the chair toward the door. And then, suddenly, he reached through the open carving of the chair back and grabbed the necklace and choked her! And then while he was trying to wrench it off, which wouldn't be easy— we saw Mr. Karkoff trying to tear it apart, too—he heard someone coming toward the reception room. So he just hooked that diamond strand around the scroll on the chair back and darted behind the window curtains and out onto the terrace! Oh, I'm sure that's what happened!"

Lutie said gravely, "That's very good, my dear Wat— Marthy."

Amanda said, "It may be so. However, there seem to me to be certain objections. Will you read my few remaining notes?"

These were on the last page, and read:

OPPORTUNITY TO COMMIT THE MURDER

Bettine G.: Complete opportunity.

Kate K. and Sabina B.: Excellent opportunity.

Ted G.: Opportunity, if he did not go at once to drink milk in pantry.

Elinor L.: Opportunity, unless her story of being with Mr. Delacy is convincingly supported.

Charles L.: No opportunity, according to our man Jansen's statement.

Unknown Robber: In this case we must assume one of several things. To present these in the most likely order: 1. The would-be thief had made up his mind to steal the diamond necklace when the best chance offered, had kept his eye on it and on its wearer, had overheard her order to the waiter to bring champagne to the reception room, or (possibly, but not probably) even heard her arrange a meeting with someone in that room. Had thereupon climbed over the roof, or slipped through the powder room, to the rear terrace, awaited her entrance into the reception room, etc. In the latter case, we must almost assume that the would-be robber was a female, which we must do also if: 2. Some person, stepping casually through the window of the powder room to stroll on the terrace, glanced through the adjoining window, saw the girl alone and was suddenly seized with the impulse to rob her of the necklace, etc. Or, 3. Some person (male or female) had casually climbed over the roof and was on the rear terrace, saw Hero alone and was suddenly tempted by the idea of robbing her of the diamonds she was wearing. Note: My opinion is that we must not entirely dismiss the hypothesis of an unknown having attempted robbery and committed murder. But I consider it improbable.

At this pronouncement on my favorite theory I burst out, "But why? Why isn't it probable? I don't see—"

"Because," said Amanda, slowly and regretfully, "though the first presumption, the premeditated robbery, is quite tenable, the would-be thief's escape is not. There were very thick carpets in the foyer, and I do not believe the footsteps of a single person approaching the reception room could have been heard by anyone inside, in time for him, or her, to disappear through the window. I believe he would either have accomplished his object or have been surprised in the attempt."

"Perhaps," I exclaimed, "he was!"

"What?" said Amanda sharply. "Who was?"

"Why, I don't know who. I was only thinking," I stammered rather lamely, and not liking what I was getting into, "that Bettine—well, she's a timid little thing, in a way. She might have seen the thief and be afraid to tell."

"Or," murmured Lutie, very slowly, "she might have seen someone there whom she wouldn't tell on to save her life."

It was my turn to say, "What? Who?" while Amanda merely gazed at her small sister, thoughtfully.

Lutie roused herself and said briskly, "Oh, nothing. I mean, I was just woolgathering. Anyway, what I was thinking had nothing to do with our unknown robber."

At this moment Jeff stuck his head through the door and said, "Inspector Moore, Boss. He says he was invited for tea."

"Ask him to come in," said Amanda brusquely.

The inspector was ushered in. "Hmm, a business conference!" he said.

Amanda said, "Yes. We have been retained, conditionally, in connection with the death of Hero Lynn Leland. Perhaps you would care to read our notes on the subject."

"I came in response to an invitation to tea," said the gentleman in gray, smiling, "but I would very much like to read your notes, Miss Beagle."

He put his soft gray felt hat on a corner of the desk and sat down opposite Amanda. She handed him the long sheets of blue-ruled paper.

He read them over carefully, laid them down, and picked up the crystal paperweight that had been Ezekiel's. Tipping it, so that a tiny snowstorm engulfed the little house and landscape within it, he said slowly, "Very complete, Miss Amanda. Very complete, indeed."

He set down the crystal globe.

"It's about where we've got ourselves. And I want to congratulate you on the men your agency had posted about the place to keep an eye on Karkoff's wares. They've been extremely helpful in this investigation. A very alert, intelligent bunch. Their sense of time, particularly, has been valuable."

"Hmmph!" snorted Amanda. "I consider their sense of time very wanting indeed! All this 'few minutes after' and 'a little while later' and 'pretty soon'! What had they to do but keep a most careful note of time, I'd like to know? Why doesn't everyone notice the time as a matter of course? What's more important? Moreover, my instructions were to be precise about everything, to the second. I declare, it's exasperating, especially since they are, as you say, more intelligent than the average male—or female, for that matter!"

Inspector Moore stroked his clipped gray mustache, covering a small smile at her uncompromising vehemence.

"Well, it was a piece of good fortune that they were where they were, and at least more observant and careful than the average male. Without them we'd have been still more at sea. Not that there's any promising shore yet in sight. The trouble is there's such a wide field. A big party like that— Good Lord, it's perfectly possible, even probable, that none of the people we've so far questioned is the murderer! Not only this unknown would-be jewel thief—and you've spotted the flaw in that theory, though of course we can't dismiss it entirely—but someone whose motive and identity we haven't even thought of."

The inspector's fingers tapped the desktop restlessly, then he said, "Well, meanwhile we've tried to fill the time gaps in the statements we have. The difficulty is, as I said before, the number of people, all intent on their own drinking, dancing, dining, and so forth. It's practically impossible to issue a questionnaire, for instance, as to whether Miss Brok was actually seen sitting alone at a table in the dance room near the entrance to the large hall for approximately four or five minutes, as she says she was, or whether Mrs. Kilgallon, after leaving the powder room, immediately joined Mr. Broderick at the bar or slipped back into and through the powder room, and so on, just as you've noted. That she did join Mr. Broderick I've ascertained, but exactly when? That Mr. Greer went into the pantry and drank milk we've also found out, but precisely how long he was there? According to your man Jansen, Leland didn't move from the terrace after his wife left it.

"As for Mrs. Lynn's statement that from the time when she saw her stepdaughter speak to the band leader she was with Mr. Delacy continuously, first at the bar, then dancing, then on the terrace—well, according to Jansen she came out on the terrace with a gentleman who answers to Delacy's description, but the gentleman's own statement is pretty vague. McGinnis questioned him and drew a complete blank. I gather that Delacy was considerably under the influence of Scotch and soda during Karkoff's party and also during the questioning. Which doesn't disprove Mrs. Lynn's story but doesn't entirely support it either. Of course," added the inspector a trifle grimly, "there are ways of sobering Delacy up, but even that might not revive his memory. Anyway, it's merely one small point among so many."

I surprised myself by bursting out, "Inspector Moore, did you find any fingerprints on those ladders?"

He smiled at me and shook his head.

"No, Miss Martha. Not any."

"You tested them the same night?" I insisted. "Right after—?"

He nodded gravely. "Yes."

Remembering the detective stories Lutie is so addicted to, a few of which I'd read, as well as bits I'd picked up during our first murder, I ventured, "But isn't that odd in itself? I mean, doesn't it look as if the murderer really had used those ladders and wiped them off?"

He smiled at me again. "Well, Miss Martha, the absence of fingerprints always does look suspicious, indoors. But, after all, those ladders are probably not in frequent use, and anyway there was a rather heavy April shower during the afternoon of the seventeenth. Remember?"

I did remember. I subsided.

Inspector Moore drew his pipe from a pocket. "As for fingerprints in the reception room, there were naturally so many as to be quite useless." He shrugged, then pulling out his tobacco pouch turned to Amanda.

"Haven't you omitted three rather obvious suspects from your list, Miss Amanda?"

She said, "What!"

He glanced toward Lutie. Her blue eyes were round, interested.

"'Three, inspector?" she asked meekly.

"May I smoke?" he asked, and as Amanda gruffly gave him permission he filled his pipe in a careful and leisurely fashion. Holding a match to the bowl and puffing, he remarked, "Yes, three, Miss Lutie. Jules Duval, the waiter, your man Walden, and your other man, Jansen."

"Oh," said Lutie. And into her face came a look I knew well. Clearly, to me, at least, she had half-expected the mention of another name. But whose name, she had no intention of revealing, that also I was sure of.

Amanda said, "Stuff and nonsense! Why should they be included?"

"I don't know. But each of them had a perfect opportunity. The waiter, there in the room alone with the girl. Walden, just across the foyer. And Jansen, who may have heard her order to the waiter, could have gone over the roof. After all, the girl was wearing a fortune around her neck." The inspector pointed with his pipestem at Amanda's neat foolscap pages. "I'm just suggesting, for the record."

Amanda glared at him. Then she reached for the record and grimly added the three names followed by brief notations. As she put down the pen Lutie asked rather absentmindedly, "I don't suppose the autopsy revealed anything we don't already know?"

"No. The girl died of strangulation, evidently from the chain of diamonds around her throat. There were no other marks on the neck nor any bruises on her body."

"Hmmph!" snapped Amanda. "That's hardly news, since there weren't any clothes to speak of on her body anyway, from the waist up."

Her high cheekbones reddened.

Lutie said hastily, "Dearie me! Inspector Moore really came to tea, and here we've been keeping him chatting about all sorts of gruesome things! Sister dear, I'm quite surprised at you!" she chided gently.

Amanda glanced at the big old-fashioned wall clock, which registered one minute past four-thirty.

"And rightly so," she admitted sternly, rising and leading the way through the narrow hallway to the apartment.

We followed. The inspector was placed in the seat of honor, Zeke's big worn leather chair, and Lutie soon had tea ready; with cheese biscuits and strawberry tarts as she had promised.

Our visitor appeared to relish the little meal very much. He consumed five biscuits, three tarts, and two cups of tea. Also he had what Lutie calls a soupçon of Uncle Abidiah's apple brandy. And we talked of all sorts of things: of the European situation, and the next election, and what flowers can be grown in a New York back yard, and How to Read Two Books, and the younger generation, and whether we preferred roast beef rare, medium, or well-done.

We didn't talk any more about last night's tragic event. And Lutie didn't talk at all.

After our caller had departed and Amanda had gone back to the office where, she said, she had routine business to see to, I turned to my little cousin and demanded, "Lutie, what's eating you?" I'm afraid my vocabulary is being terribly undermined by association with Jeff, or perhaps it's just sojourning in Gotham!

Lutie set down the tray she was carrying into the kitchenette, and gazed back at me.

"Lutie!" I exclaimed. "You don't think it was one of our own men, do you?"

She shook her head.

"Or that nice little waiter?"

Again she shook her head.

"Then, is it someone we haven't even thought of? Someone not on our list at all?"

I wasn't sure whether she heard this or not. Her eyes, fixed on me, were wide, solemn. There was a look in them I had seldom if ever seen before.

"Marthy," she said, "I'm frightened. I can't tell you why. But something horrible is going to happen, unless we can prevent it. And I don't know how to, or even what it will be. Only I'm scared!"

CHAPTER 19

YOU can imagine how her words scared me!

And not only her words, but her manner.

All through the terrible,and terrifying experiences in connection with our first murder, even during the awful time when we were on the trail of the murderer and he on ours—I can feel my scalp prickle at the memory— Lutie had been fearless, self-confident, blithe, even gay! And now—

I watched her face while I set the table and she stirred up a cake for supper, and while we ate supper. And afterward, while Jeff and Amanda discussed the case and my little cousin sat in her rocking chair crocheting Madame LaVelle's afghan, I kept watching her face.

From time to time she smiled, nodded, or put in a word or two, then a curious look of absorption would settle again on her small features. Finally Amanda, too, noticed that something was amiss.

"Lutie Beagle," she said, putting, her knitting abruptly down in her lean lap, "what's the matter with you? Aren't you feeling well?"

"Oh,"said Lutie, coming out of her abstraction, I'm perfectly well, Sister dear! But perhaps I'm a little sleepy." For Lutie to be sleepy before the rest of us was so unusual as to be alarming. Amanda rose sternly, dismissed Jeffy, and said sharply, "Hmmph. Well, then you'll have a cup of herb tea and go right to bed."

Lutie complied meekly. Amanda brewed the tea and saw that the last drop was swallowed. We put the cat out for his nightly airing, covered Rab's cage, and went to bed too.

But I was too tired to sleep right away, especially with Lutie's strange words and her even stranger manner to keep me awake. What had she meant? What was she scared of? What did she fear was going to happen? And to whom? Finally, of course, I dropped off to sleep, though only after deciding that, in the morning, I was going to maker her tell me.

But when morning came I didn't. Somehow there was no chance to broach the subject. Lutie was up very early and started on a violent bout of housecleaning. Immediately after breakfast she shooed Amanda off into the office, had up both our Swedish janitor and his wife who chores for us, and presently we were in the midst of an orgy of sweeping, scrubbing floors and woodwork, and washing windows, kitchen shelves and pots and pans. She sent me out to do the marketing alone, a pleasant task we'd taken over together in New York, since Amanda has been too busy with the business of the agency, and when I came back, and until supper time, the apartment was upside down and full of Mr. and Mrs. Jacobson.

We customarily forgo the ritual of tea during housecleaning days and have an early supper, at five-thirty instead of six o'clock as usual. Amanda, who had been out somewhere during the entire afternoon, arrived home only just in time for it, looking, I thought, somewhat tired and not very happy. But by that time I myself was so hungry and so fatigued by the day's exertions that I was interested in little besides the cold ham, hot biscuits, stewed tomatoes and apricot pie before me.

After the meal, however, the subject that had been almost driven from my mind by brooms, soapsuds and scrubbing brushes was revived by my older cousin's report of her afternoon mission.

She had, it seems, visited Mr. Karkoff's premises to examine them again in daylight and at leisure and with certain definite objects in view. For one thing, she had made the trip over the roof, from the ladder on the front terrace to the one on the rear. It had taken her precisely two and three-quarter minutes.

"But," she remarked, "undoubtedly it could have been accomplished in considerably less time by a younger and more agile person, particularly one unencumbered by petti—by skirts."

She had also traversed the distance from the dais at one end of the long room to the pantry, at the end of the other; which at an ordinary pace, took one minute, although this, she commented, proved nothing of value.

Also, finding that Mr. Karkoff happened to have a disk of the *Lament for a Dead Romance* recorded by Ted Greer's band, she had asked to have it played on his phonograph and had timed it. The piece took three minutes and one second from its opening bars to its closing.

After which, having obtained from the jeweler a list of the staff who had served at his party, she found that two of the waiters stationed that evening in the service pantry were regular employees of the Stuyvesant-Plaza. Telephoning downstairs she learned that they had just come on duty in the hotel. She sent for them and questioned them in Mr. Karkoff's office. Both recalled a gentleman coming into the pantry for a glass of milk. When Amanda had asked how long he stayed there, the older waiter said, "Too long."

Amanda asked if they knew this gentleman and the older waiter said no, he did not. He was a big young man with a beard. He stood in the passage, in everybody's way. And, added the old waiter sourly, all this the police had already asked, and been told. He would like to go now, he had duties—

Amanda dismissed him. The younger waiter was more cheerful and expansive. He said he knew the gentleman who had come to the pantry for a glass of milk. He was Mr. Ted Greer, the famous band leader. He listened to him often on the radio, he was a wonderful musician, he had seen him on the platform during the evening when he, Albert, had carried ice and so forth to the bar. But when Amanda tried to pin Albert down to exactly when and for precisely how long Mr. Greer had remained in the pantry, the best she could learn was that, "We were just serving supper, madame. Mr. Greer drank two glasses of milk, I think. I could not say just how long he took to drink them. We were very busy, I am sorry." and that was all.

Amanda added, with annoyance, "I had already questioned our man Ferrone on this subject. He is extremely vague about it. He recalls seeing the orchestra leader standing in the passage, but made no note of the time Mr. Greer came there or how long he stayed, on the ground that it seemed of no importance as he didn't go near the elevator, and there wasn't anything funny about him except that he asked for milk. I gathered," said Amanda grimly, "that Ferrone had been indulging in something stronger than milk himself! At any rate he was obviously negligent, and I reprimanded him strongly. Anyway, on that point I didn't find out any more than McGinnis already had, I daresay."

She added, "I have also interviewed Walden and Jansen again, merely to be on the safe side, not because I took the inspector's suggestion as to their possible guilt seriously. And my judgment was confirmed. I am satisfied they are both honest young men."

"I'm sure they are, Sister," murmured Lutie soothingly.

"As for the little waiter, Jules, Walden saw him leave the reception room and describes his manner as entirely unflustered, which it would hardly have been if he'd just tried to steal the necklace, been interrupted in the attempt, and strangled the girl."

"Hardly, Sister," agreed Lutie.

"But concerning other matters we know only a very little more than we did." Amanda looked bleak.

"Well, 'every little bit, added to what we've got, makes just a little bit more,' " said Lutie, quoting the old song brightly though rather mechanically.

We retired soon after that.

And the next day the orgy of housecleaning continued. Rugs were taken down to the back yard and beaten, carpets vacuumed, floors waxed, window curtains, quilts and blankets washed. The janitor and his wife were all over the apartment all day. Jeffy, too, was pressed into service. Lutie herself was a small tornado of activity.

By evening I was completely exhausted.

And during that whole day no mention whatsoever had been made of the tragic events of the night of April seventeenth, except that, after supper, Amanda had handed us the only newspaper she will allow in the house, the *Times-Tribune,* and in it we read the account of Hero Lynn's quiet funeral and interment in Greenwood Cemetery, in the "famous Lynn family's historic plot."

I happened to glance over Lutie's shoulder as she was perusing the paper. She had turned a page and was gazing at a column headed "Cafe Creme" by Percy Gotham, and a photograph of a heavy-jowled young man and a handsome young woman smiling arrogantly for the camera. I recognized the girl as Sabina Brok, though the picture didn't do justice to her beautifully colored skin and hair and eyes. Leaning closer I read that the man with her was Baron Delacy, "who has missed only two nights at El Tunisia for the past two years."

My thoughts of the party of three nights ago were revivified by the picture, by those names, as well as by the account of Hero's burial. Her death seemed to be accepted by the news journals as suicide, and although it had been heavily featured, with references to her "secret marriage," her father's will, the large fortune she had inherited, her friendship with the famous band leader who had also recently and secretly married, and so forth and so forth, the sensation was beginning to die out. As I drifted wearily off to sleep I wondered if Lutie too were dismissing it from her mind.

Next morning we polished silver and ironed the window curtains. I cooked pot roast and Lutie made an upside-down cake for dinner. She seemed quite cheerful again and even hummed as she worked. But there was a glitter in her blue eyes. What did it mean?

After dinner, when Amanda had gone to the office, I said, "Lutie, for the last two days you've been bustling about as if you were crazy! And you know the place didn't need it. Well, anyway, I haven't had a moment's chance to ask you what it is you were scared about. And don't deny it, for I remember what you said and how you said it! And I know now that you've suddenly got something up your sleeve, some idea."

She turned to me gravely. "I wish I had a really good one. But I've only got a theory, and it doesn't quite fit. I've not enough evidence to base it on. I haven't any evidence, really. And all the time we've been sweeping and dusting I've been trying to figure out something."

"Lutie," I said earnestly, "please tell Inspector Moore!" I shuddered, recalling how Lutie had taken—and kept—matters in her own hands during our first murder and what dangers it had led us into. "Please, please tell him what you're worried about!"

Lutie shook her head.

"It wouldn't do any good to tell him, because I don't know myself. What I'm thinking, I half-think is all wrong, you see. And my anxious feeling—well, I suppose that's because I know there's a murderer at large and I'm not really sure who it is."

She sighed, gave herself a little shake and then said briskly, "Listen, my dear. We all need a change of scene. So tonight we're stepping out, you and Sister and me and Jeff!"

I couldn't get a thing more out of her.

During the afternoon we pressed her black net evening frock and Amanda's satin gown and steamed my, black velvet. They were hanging in the wardrobe all spic and span by teatime, when Lutie said suddenly, "Sister dear, I've just remembered that tomorrow is the twenty-second of April!"

"Hmmph! Have you, indeed?" Amanda said, finishing a bite of Lutie's delicious devil's-food cake. "What an extraordinary memory you have, Sister!"

Her black eyes rested fondly on her little sister. There was in them a quizzical twinkle.

"Yes. Just think—tomorrow I'll be sixty-three years old! You know, I really can't believe it. Where have the years gone? I suppose everybody feels the same way. I mean, in my own mind, I'm still a little girl. Isn't that ridiculous?"

"Hmmph," said Amanda. I knew that in her eyes it was not ridiculous at all. Sister to her was still a very little girl. She added, brusquely, "As you know, I bought you that birdcage for your birthday. But as it is mostly for Rabelais—and Tabby," she admitted, with her usual sense of fairness, "I have another present for you that I hope you'll like."

"Oh, that's lovely, Sister!" exclaimed Lutie. Then she clasped her hands and said dreamily, "I was born at a little after midnight, wasn't I? Do you know, I've always wanted to stay up until then on my birthday, and have bright lights around, and people, and— Sister, could we do that tonight? Could we?"

So that's how it happened that at a little before twelve o'clock that evening we were seated in a crowded room with the tiny flames and shadowy curves of candelabras behind translucent panels in the walls and above a gleaming dance floor, while we leaned back against soft cushions and music throbbed in our ears and a solicitous waiter poured bubbly amber liquid into our long-stemmed goblets.

Our escort smoothed down his wiry red hair, and pulled his white tie straight.

"So this is El Tunisia!" He lifted his glass. "Many happy returns of the day. Here's to our Lutie, long may she wave!"

Amanda and I raised our glasses, clicked them, and sipped the toast, while Lutie blushed and beamed demurely.

"Isn't this fun?" Her eyes had sparkles in them like the champagne as she gazed about the softly lighted room.

Then they paused. Their expression sharpened, and I saw the flicker of a tiny satisfied smile touch her lips before she turned again to Amanda and said, "It is so sweet of you, Sister dear, to give me this wonderful party! Isn't it a charming place? All the gay faces, the pretty dresses."

"Hmm, pretty is as pretty does," said Amanda. "But I'm glad you're pleased, Sister. However, I hope—"

She broke off suddenly. She was facing toward the front of the nightclub and the bar, having seated herself with her back to the dance floor. We turned to see what had arrested her attention. A party of four young people had just entered.

Jeff whistled softly.

Lutie murmured, "How nice!"

Amanda made no comment, except for a certain wooden expression of disapproval which, I must say, I could not help sharing. For the party which, after a glance around the room, had ranged itself along the bar, consisted of Bettine and Ted Greer, Bill Cameron and Kate Kilgallon.

"Well!" I said tartly. "It seems to me Hero's sister might have shown a little more respect for the decencies! After all, even if she isn't grief-stricken she might at least—"

"Pretend to be?" said Lutie.

At this attempt to put me in the wrong I was momentarily quelled, then I retorted, "Well, why did she pretend to be so upset then, when she came to see us?"

"Now, Marthy! Of course she's upset, but do you really think she ought to mope instead of trying to snap out—I mean, not to brood? Anyway, you're not going to get upset and spoil my party, are you?"

My little cousin smiled at me placatingly and patted my hand. She added brightly, "Sabina Brok is here too, with a gentleman we have not yet met. Behind you, over there."

I craned my neck and became aware of the couple on whom, earlier, her alert glance had rested and paused: Sabina, in flame-red, and a heavy-jowled young man.

"With Baron Delacy!" I exclaimed, remembering the photograph heading the "Cafe Creme" society column I had noticed last evening, over Lutie's shoulder.

She nodded, with the trace of satisfaction I had observed before. And suddenly a suspicion struck me! This innocent birthday party that she'd finagled so demurely—was there something deeper behind it than she'd allowed us to guess? If so, what? Some sly little sleuthing scheme?

Jeff said blithely, "All the principals in our fine mur— in the tragic drama are here, except the fair Elinor and the widower."

"Jefferson, pray don't be flippant!" said Amanda.

The music struck up then, and under cover of its opening bars I caught the murmur of a small voice at my side: "I wish they were here, too."

Then the lights about the room were dimmed, a brilliant spot of illumination was centered on the dance floor, and a slender masculine figure in black and a feminine form in voluminous white stepped, bowing, into the circle and began to dance. As they glided and dipped and whirled and bounded, now swiftly, now slowly, the man a foil and pivot for the woman, whose draperies swirled and spread like the petals of a gigantic flower, Lutie clasped her gloved hands under her chin, leaning forward in rapturous absorption. When the dance ended she clapped delightedly. There were two encores before the couple, smiling gallantly above their heaving chests, bowed their exit.

As the lights around the room went up again Lutie sat back with a happy sigh. A waiter moved forward to replenish her glass, which I noticed, to my surprise, was empty. Also, her cheeks were very pink indeed. And suddenly she stood up, turned around toward the bar and waved to Kate Kilgallon.

"Hi!" she called. "Won't you join us?"

CHAPTER 20

KATE KILGALLON turned, waved back, and said something to her companions. A moment later they left the bar, threaded their way between the tables and were beside our own. Kate performed the introductions while waiters dashed up with chairs. Presently the party was seated and Lutie was beaming brightly around the circle.

"You know, I'm so h-happy to see you all! Sister's giving me this wonderful party, and it's so marvelous, your being here. What will you have, my dears?" She beckoned haughtily to our waiter, and without waiting for an answer, ordered more champagne and glasses to be brought. "You see, I'm c-celebrating. This is my birthday!"

"Ah!" Ted Greer rose, bowed to Lutie, then motioned to the musicians who were on the point of taking up their instruments again. Crossing to the leader of the orchestra he said, "May I borrow your fiddle, Paul? Just for a minute."

The young man called Paul grinned and handed over his violin with a bow. He stepped aside, and Ted Greer tucked the violin under his chin and began to play. It was the funny familiar little tune we've all heard so often, and as the piano and the horn followed, Ted Greer began to sing softly in his rich deep voice,

> "Happy birthday to you,
> Happy birthday to you,
> Happy birthday, dear Miss Lutie,
> Happy birthday to you!"

He bowed, smiling, toward my little cousin, returned the borrowed fiddle, and came back to our table, about which glasses were raised and the song carried on.

"Happy birthday, Miss Lutie, happy birthday to you!"

"Oh," breathed Lutie, "how terribly sweet of you! Oh, dear! Even if I never have another I shall always remember this b-birthday! Isn't it wonderful, Shister?"

Before Amanda could reply, the blond young horn player leaned across the table, shaking his head solemnly.

"Corny. Very corny, Miss Lutie," he said.

Lutie's blue eyes, round and reproachful, gazed back at him.

"Oh, Bill! Can't you forget and forgive? You know I really loved it when you were giving with those hot licksh—"

This was too much for Amanda.

"Lutie Beagle," she said, "what folderol are you talking now? And if you do have to talk gibberish, can't you pronounce your consonants correctly?"

"Oh, Sh—sister, s'cuse me—I'm afraid the ch-champagne's gone right to my head. But please don't be mad! I'm having sush a good time. P-please let me be jus' li'l silly—hic—"

She buried a delicate hiccup in her napkin, and above it fixed a melting glance on her sister's stern visage. Amanda said nothing. What could she say or do? Little Sister was tipsy; that was the long and the short of it.. But dignity forbade an adequate scolding before strangers, nor could she take the foolish child by the ear and lead her from the place and stand her in the corner, as I could see she felt like doing. Compressing her lips, her face stony, she held her tongue.

Lutie's tongue, however, was hung in the middle and wagging merrily at both ends. Presently she had the whole circle around our table smiling with her. Even little Bettine Greer, whose round childlike face had seemed grave and rather pale when I'd first seen her tonight, began to giggle and chatter with the others. Lutie kept commanding more champagne to be brought, and Amanda could do nothing about that. All she could do was to remove her little sister's glass, quietly, but Lutie had already had more than enough to go on, apparently, and did not even notice that it had been taken away.

She was cute, too, and even though she tripped over a word or slurred one now and then, she looked adorable with her blue eyes sparkling, her cheeks like cherries, and the tiny bouquet of violets and moss-rosebuds nodding above her silvery curls. Even Amanda gradually unbent and couldn't help a grudging smile or two. At the tale of Old Doolittle, our handyman back home in East Biddicutt, and Rabelais, she actually laughed.

"You see, Old Doolittle'd nev' seen Rab. I bought him from a sailor—

I mean Rab 'f course, not Old Dool'l—and he was pottering round the garden, I mean Old Dooli'l, not Rab. Rab was 'nside in his cage near the window, 'n' suddenly he shouted—well, I couldn' repeat what that naughty bird said, not before you young people. Poor dear Rabbie has a very seafaring vo-vocabulary. Anyway Old Doolittle jumped an' shimply ran! It 'mos' scared the pan—the ov'ralls right off him!"

"May we join the party?" asked a clear high voice, and we all turned to see Sabina Brok, making her way toward us, her escort, weaving slightly, trailing in her wake.

"Certain'y, certain'y!" cried Lutie gaily, and when chairs had been crowded together to make room for the newcomers and they were seated and introductions performed, she added, "I'm celebrating—thish my birthday—hic—" She giggled. "Maybe I'm c-celebrating li'l too mush—"

Mr. Delacy, who had declined champagne and ordered "scosh," grasped his glass of whiskey, drained it, shook his head as if to shake away an annoying fly, and drew his brows together in an attempt to focus his gaze on Lutie.

"Aren' you the femme dick 'at solved murder headless corpse 'n Johnny Bynam's bed? Or was't his gal's bed? Read 'bout you'n the papers, didn' I?"

Lutie looked modest, but before she had time to reply Sabina said with languid sweetness, "Shut up, Baron. Murders are too, too barbaric and boring. Suicide is much smarter, don't you think, Ted darling?"

Bettine clutched her husband's arm. He patted the small hand, smiling down at her. Sabina transferred her attention to the girl.

"Mrs. Greer—or mayn't I call you Bettine? After all, Ted and I know each other so well, it really seems too, too ridic to call you Missus. Anyway, Bettine, I do want to tell you that I think Ted was so wise. I mean, to choose a really nice girl, after Hero jilted—when she decided to marry Charley, I mean. Which was bright of her, too, even if it did seem rather startlingly sudden. Though of course it wasn't to me. I'd practically advised it, you see!"

Kate leaned forward and said sharply, "Saddie, what do you mean by that?"

Sabina's topaz eyes turned toward the other girl. She smiled.

"Darling, you are blooming tonight!"

She took an amber comb from her embroidered bag and drew it through the shining burnt-gold hair curling on bare shoulders that were thin and tawny and with a sheen like gold-dust.

"I only meant," she said, "that I had a talk with Hero, a heart-to-heart. I did think it was too, too ridic of her to throw away her fortune as she seemed simply bent on doing. And of course she agreed, after our little talk."

"When was this little talk?" said Kate, her voice low, her smoky gray eyes holding the other girl's.

"My pet, how too voracious you are!" drawled Sabina. "You're not annoyed with me, are you? After all, you shouldn't be. Everything has worked out so divinely. Oh, I forgot! You prefer rags to riches, don't you? But Hero didn't. She quite saw what I meant when I pointed it out, and married Charley the very next day. So right, wasn't it? Poor Charley might have been made to order, handpicked by her dear daddy; with all that gold in his coffers to mate up with hers, and wholly respectable as well as well-heeled. Not a garage hand or a six-day bicycle racer or— Of course it was rather sad-making that poor Hurry preferred a piccolo player in a— I mean, a fiddler. But that couldn't be helped."

Kate was sitting next to me, and I saw her hands, below the table, pressed together, the knuckles white. But her voice was steady, quiet.

"Sabina, what did you say to Hero the day before she married Charley?"

"Oh, that! Why, I merely suggested," Sabina shrugged, "that she really couldn't afford to take any more risks. You see, for instance, there was that night at Montauk, a dark and stormy night, a whole, long night, and such a cozy little out-of-the-way inn. Charming."

Her yellow eyes smiled sweetly at the band leader. "A dear little honeymoon inn, don't you think, Teddy darling?" Ted Greer's dark eyes narrowed.

"So you found out about that, did you? What a pleasant person you are, Sabina. And—not that it matters now, but I do have a slight curiosity—how did you unearth your information?"

"Why, Teddy dear, aren't you even going to play the little gentleman and deny it? My pet, I'm quite too, too shocked!" She widened her gleaming eyes reproachfully. "Not even try to protect poor Hero's memory? And besides, what will Mrs. Greer think?"

"Not," said the small girl sitting beside the band leader, "what you think, or want me to think. And anyway, if I did I wouldn't give a damn!"

Her delicate skin was aflame from the neck of her blue organdy frock to the round forehead under the baby-soft brown curls, but the shoulders under the puffed sleeves were straight and her chin was high.

"Bravo!" said Bill Cameron, and raised his glass.

Ted Greer smiled down at his wife. There was pride in his eyes and in his voice as he said gently, "That's my darling! But even if we don't give two damns, perhaps I should mention, to whom it may concern—"

He looked gravely across at Kate. After a moment he said slowly, "On that particular occasion our pleasant friend here has raked up"— he flicked a contemptuous glance toward Sabina—"your sister and I had sailed the *Betsy*, my sloop, from City Island, where I keep her, out to Montauk. It was a grand day, and probably Hero overdid the swimming. Also"—he smiled faintly—"one of the inn's attractions is cracked crabs, and she went in for them in rather a big way.

"Anyway, soon after dinner, which we ate early, at about five, we were on the point of starting back to town when I noticed she was looking green around the gills. She had to confess she was in pretty bad pain, and when Hero admitted that much there wasn't any question that it was bad, because she was a darn spunky kid. Truth is, she kicked like a little fiend when I said we weren't taking any boat trips that night, especially as it had turned suddenly squally. I was going to hire a car and drive back, but I decided against that too. She was sick as a pup for several hours. There was a nice little chambermaid at the inn who took care of her, and by midnight or so she was better, but too weak to move even if she'd wanted to, and by that time even she didn't want to. As a matter of fact I was pretty sure, later, that the attack was a preliminary bout of appendicitis.

"Well, that's that. And just for the record, we occupied separate rooms, though I took an adjoining one in case she got sick again during the night. It hardly seems necessary to add, though just to conclude the matter I'll mention it. There was no honeymoon."

Kate nodded. She said, "Thank you for telling me, Ted, though even if you hadn't I'd have known it. Hero had very definite ideas on certain subjects, wild and reckless as she was in most ways."

Sabina cut in, her voice slightly shrill, "A pretty good story, but as I remarked to Hero, she was stuck with it! It was simply too misfortune-making, Ted darling, that you hadn't called a doctor, for instance. And also, wasn't it rather rash of you to sign your very own names in the hotel register?"

Her voice was poisoned honey again as she added, "Especially as you hadn't made any secret of your find of Tuckaway Inn. Don't you remember the day last summer you sailed a whole crowd of us out there? Quite too, too bad you gave it away."

"So it seems," said Ted, rather wearily. "However, that was before the night we've been talking about. So you didn't do your snooping then."

A mocking gleam shone in Sabina's yellow eyes, and her flame-red lips curled in an amused smile.

"The fact is, my friend," she said, watching Kate, "it was your boy-friend here who sailed us out to Montauk on his li'l sailboat a couple of weeks ago. Don't you remember that divine day, Bill? Just like summer, it was, though the water was rather too cool for a swim. Mmm, those cracked crabs, and that chowder! But of course Katy, the poor little working girl, had declined to join the party. Or so I heard. I took it for granted she'd been asked."

Kate, her eyes on Sabina, said, "So you threatened Hero, did you? When you knew very well the poor kid was telling the truth. She did have an operation for appendicitis last summer."

"So she said," drawled Sabina, "but, my pet, that was six weeks later, and after all, these appendicitis operations—" She shrugged.

Kate's eyes flamed.

"You—are—a—brutal—little—beast," she said, each word coming slowly, like a measured blow. "But why? What did you do it for? Was it just nasty, petty spite?"

"Why, darling! I told you I was simply advising your sister, for her very own good. I knew how old Holmesy would have absolutely pounced on that hotel register. He's our family lawyer too, and he's told Daddy that he thought your papa's will was unfair, that he shouldn't have cut you off like that and that Hero would have been much better off depending on Kate's bounty. Yes, sweet, those were his very words. He's so old-fashioned and quaint! But naturally Hero didn't care for the idea."

"So that's why she married so suddenly!" Kate's voice was molten lava. She stood up, gripping the table and leaning across it. "Oh, how could you! You—"

"Shall we dance?" said Bill Cameron. He sprang up, linking his arm in Kate's. Under the folds of white chiffon draping her breast the breath came fast. Her gray gaze clung to Sabina in anger, and contempt, and a kind of wonder. Then Bill drew her away.

"Come on, Betts," said Ted Greer, taking his wife's hand.

Sabina Brok's eyes followed them onto the dance floor. As the big bearded young man put his arm around the childish figure in pale blue organdy I heard a sharp cracking sound. Sabina's amber comb had snapped in two. Thin golden-fleshed fingers, tipped with flaming red enamel, thrust the fragments of the comb into her embroidered evening bag. I thought, what strong fingers they were.

Lutie was saying, brightly, "Mr. Delacy, why don't you dansh?" She nodded toward Sabina.

"Nev' do it," said Mr. Delacy, reaching for his third scotch, that is, the third since he'd been at our table. "Don' like bein' bumped by lotsh shtupid people. Silly business—int'feres m' drinkin'." He drained his glass.

"What, never? You mean you nev' dansh?" said Lutie, seemingly astounded. 'B-but tha's too, too ridic! I shaw you at Sandro's party—danshin' Elinor Lynn."

"Nope. t'Gainsh my princ'ples. I'm phil—philosh'pher—shtay in m'iv'ry tower—wash worl' g'by—let other people make fools 'emself. Not me. Zat's my philosh'phy."

Sabina stood up and yanked the philosopher to his feet, on which he tottered slightly.

She said abruptly, and her voice was like a heel striking gravel, with all the treacle quality forgotten and forgone, "Of course Baron never dances! He never learned. He's a look-oner and sit-downer, and he's sitting pretty on a thousand oil wells. Come on, Baron darling, let's go back where we came from. Good night, Miss Loopy, and Miss Boggle, and Miss Whosit, and Mister M'Goofy."

She left, with Mr. Delacy weaving after her.

"Creeps," said Jeff, yanking his tie straight, "what a bit— I mean a sti— Excuse me, what a nize little piece of drek."

Lutie was watching the "little piece of drek" and her escort sweeping back to their table. That is, the girl swept, scattering photogenic smiles, while her escort stumbled after.

"Dear me. He isn't very sprightly, is he?" murmured Lutie. "I wonder what a girl like that, a glamour girl and all, sees in him?"

"A thousand oil wells!" said Jeff. "And she'll probably marry him too. The Broks," he added somewhat smugly, showing off his New York society lore, "aren't very well heeled. Delacy's a good catch, a young Lochinvar come out of the west. Except he's pretty much a washout as a Lochinvar, as you've observed, Miss Lutie. But what can a pore gal do? A pore little Glamour Gal Number Two? Or would you say she's become Glamour Gal Number One now?"

"She's very much enamored of Ted, isn't she?" murmured Lutie thoughtfully. I didn't realize until later that she was no longer slurring her words. "That performance tonight was all for Bettine's benefit. Pure spite. Of course I noticed at Mr. Karkoff's party that Sabina was—well, interested in Mr. Greer, but I thought then it was mostly a matter of girlish rivalry for his attention. So she threatened Hero and practically told her to drop him! Dear me. Well, we've learned quite a number of things tonight."

I said quickly, "Lutie, do you think Sabina wanted to marry Ted? Do you suppose she hated Hero enough to kill her?"

Amanda snorted, and Lutie looked at me with an amused twinkle.

"You don't like the girl, do you, my dear?"

"Who could?" I returned shortly. "Not," I added, "that I want her to be a murderess, exactly."

"But if we can't stick to an unknown thief, she's your choice, isn't she?"

This was so true that I replied, defensively, "Well, I don't want to choose anybody."

But the music stopped just then, and Kate and Bill, Bettine and Ted returned to the table, for which I was thankful.

Nor did anyone else mention Sabina, or the matter she had raked up, except for a brief question that Lutie put to Kate in an undertone: "Kate, why did you call Sabina Saddie?"

Kate frowned and answered: "Oh, that was Hurry's name for her. Short for sadistic."

"I see. And very apt," remarked Lutie, dropping the subject and turning to give her rapt attention to the conversation between Bill Cameron and Ted Greer, who were talking about the sailboats they both kept, it seemed, off City Island.

"I simply adore sailing!" she said brightly, with an ecstatic sigh.

"And when," asked Amanda, "have you ever had a chance to decide that, Lutie Beagle? I doubt if you've ever been on a sailboat in all your born days!"

"Why, Sister, no more I have! But do you know, I've imagined it so often that I thought I had," said Lutie with such a funny little air of surprise at herself that we all laughed, including Amanda. Bill Cameron said something must and certainly would be done about that, and couldn't we all go sailing with him this Sunday? He explained that the band didn't broadcast on Sundays, so he and Ted had the whole day free. And Ted Greer said that his own sloop wasn't quite yet in commission, but it would be in a week or so. He was going out to the Island this weekend to see how the scraping and painting and so on were getting on, and we must all go sailing with him and he hoped Miss Lutie would find it everything her fancy'd painted it.

Lutie thanked them prettily and said she was sure she would.

And then she said, unexpectedly, "And now, Sister dear, it's getting rather late, isn't it? We've seen the New Year in—I mean, my new year! I've had the most beautiful birthday party, and I thank you all for making it so gay! But there's no use stretching things out, is there? I think I'd like to go now. I hope you won't mind our leaving, my dears?" she added to the young people.

One person who undoubtedly didn't mind our leaving was Amanda, even though, when the check was laid before her, she stared at it for a second with something like horror. But a moment later she'd placed a hundred-dollar bill and four tens on the waiter's tray. She didn't even wait for the change, but stood up, her lean shoulders erect, and said, "Come, Marthy, Sister. Good night." She bowed graciously to our guests.

Lutie murmured to them, "You don't think I'm a sissy for leaving?"

They said no, that they were leaving too. Perhaps it was my fancy, but it seemed to me that a quick glance of understanding passed between Kate and my little cousin.

A few minutes later we were in a taxi, and Amanda had said, "Forty-fourth Street."

She leaned back as the cab started off. Thank goodness, we were going home.

But Lutie leaned forward.

"East Sixty-eighth, please, driver," she said.

Then she turned to Amanda. "Sister, I couldn't help it! We must go there. To the house where Hero lived, where Elinor lives now."

Amanda said sharply, "What? Are you still in your cups, Lutie Beagle? At this hour? What are you thinking of?"

There was no slightest trace of hiccups or hilarity in Lutie's voice now. Indeed it was quite dreadfully sober as she replied, "Sister, I don't know. Truly I don't. I've got an idea, two ideas, and they're all mixed up. Only, don't you see? We found out tonight that Elinor lied. She said she was at the bar with Baron Delacy and that then they danced, and then they went out on the terrace. But Baron Delacy doesn't dance. Not ever. He said so, Sabina said so. And I think we ought to talk to Elinor right away. After all, it isn't quite two o'clock, that's not really late for New York."

Her voice sank to an undertone. She added, in a whisper, "Though perhaps it is too late—"

Amanda stared at her. Then she leaned forward and said to the cabby: "Driver, please hurry."

As for me, I wanted to go home. That oddly troubled, portentous tone of Lutie's left me quite dull and unaffected. Perhaps I'd been keyed up too long. For three days I'd been on tenterhooks, wondering, mulling over my little cousin's queer uncertainty and moodiness, and moreover worn out with violent housecleaning. And to cap it all there had been the birthday party, apparently so innocent and actually so connived, and the noise, and the bright lights, and the champagne.

Anyway, all I knew was that I wanted to go home.

But we weren't going home. Up Fifth Avenue, past the Plaza and along Central Park sped the cab. I think if I had known then what was in store for us I'd have stopped it firmly, opened the door, and jumped out.

CHAPTER 21

OUR taxicab drew up in front of a tall residence built of brick and stone, the latter engraved with the horrible wormlike decoration that mark many pretentious edifices of the late nineteenth century.

This solid, wide and tall house was unconditionally ugly. An ostentatious overhanging cornice topped it. Its broad stone steps were guarded by a brace of badly modeled stone lions. Its plate-glass windows were forbidding.

They were also completely dark. Only through the fanlight and the heavy glass panels in the entrance doors could a dim light be seen.

As we got out of the taxi I protested, "Lutie, Elinor's not home or else she's gone to bed."

But neither of my cousins answered. Amanda paid the taxi driver. We mounted the five wide broad shallow steps to the door. Amanda pulled the old-fashioned bronze bell handle beside it. Away inside we heard a thin, reverberating, jangling peal.

We waited.

Then Amanda yanked the bell-handle again. Again we waited.

I expected my older cousin to say, "You see, Sister? This is all stuff and nonsense!" But she didn't. She seemed, now, even more resolute than Lutie was herself.

In the white glare from a nearby street lamp her lips were grim. She reached for the bell the third time and kept her long, gloved hand on it. Deep within that dark, forbidding-looking house we could hear the muffled shrillness of the bell.

But no one answered. And a wind came through the lonely street from the East River. A chill wind. I shivered, there on the stoop between those grinning stone lions.

Then we heard padding footsteps, a key turned, and the oak door opened a few inches. A voice, dull with sleep, said, "Who is it? If you're from the press, kindly go away. Mrs. Lynn has retired."

"We are not from the press," said Amanda.

Lutie pushed gently but firmly against the door.

As we entered the dim hall, hung with dark crimson brocatelle, the person who had answered the door stepped back, then closed and bolted it behind us. He was a stocky, elderly man in an elegant but shabby dressing gown over pajamas. His thin gray hair stuck up like wisps of withered straw from a left parting; it was meant to cover the bald scalp on top of his narrow head, but it was sadly disarranged. He put up a bony hand to smooth it in place as he repeated, "Mrs. Lynn has retired. I am sorry."

Amanda said, "You are the butler, I suppose. What's your name?"

He said, "Banks, madame." He blinked. "May I ask—"

Lutie had stepped farther into the hall. She had parted the drapery of a wide doorway at the right, and now she was staring up the dark staircase with its newel post supporting a discreetly half-draped bronze figure holding aloft a cluster of grapes. From within their frosted knobs glowed the dim effulgence illuminating the hall.

Amanda replied to the servant, "We are acquaintances of Mrs. Lynn's, Banks. Of course, if she has gone out—"

The butler said, "She has not gone out, madame. She has retired."

I don't know what had gotten into Amanda, though if it had been anyone else I should have thought it was alarm. She started up the staircase at once. Lutie and I followed. Banks brought up the rear.

There was a light in the upper hall, too, shining dimly from the stomach of an alabaster Venus.

Amanda said, "Which is Mrs. Lynn's room?"

"That one, madame," said the butler, and pointed toward a door at the rear of the hall. Then he indicated one toward the front, and gulped. "That was Miss Hero's, before—"

Amanda strode toward the rear door and knocked. There was no answer. She knocked again. Then she opened the door and pressed a light switch beside it.

The room was empty. The heavily carved walnut bed, in Louis Philippe style, had not been slept in. The dark green satin coverlet was folded back, the linen sheets turned neatly down. The stiffly lace-edged pillows were untouched.

Amanda said, "Mrs. Lynn did not retire."

"No, it seems she did not," said the butler. In the whitish light from the electric bulbs set in the old-fashioned gasolier in the middle of the ceiling his face looked pasty. Presently, however, he pulled himself together. "She told me to close the house, since she intended to retire. She must have changed her mind and gone out, madame."

"Perhaps so," said Amanda. She added, "Had she any visitors this evening?"

The man shook his head. "No, madame. She had dinner as usual at eight o'clock. Afterwards she read for a while in the library. During that time there was a telephone call. She answered it herself, before I could do so. A little later, at about nine-thirty, she told me she was retiring. I was to close the house and go to bed. Then she went upstairs. I saw her go, and turned out the main lights. The ones on the stairs are always left burning. I went to my room, which is in the rear on the top floor, and went to sleep."

The man looked at the untouched bed, around at the large room with its heavy furniture and wallpaper strewn with garlands of writhing vines and hideous fullblown roses.

"It's odd, madame, isn't it? She must have gone out. But she hasn't gone out of nights since Miss Hero died."

He drew his frayed brocade robe closer around his chest and shivered. "It seems peculiar, also, that she has not returned at this hour."

I shivered myself. The room seemed cold.

Amanda said, "Yes, it seems somewhat peculiar. It is now three minutes before two o'clock. Was she given to late hours?"

"No, madame. On the contrary."

"She's not here," said Lutie, who had been opening closet doors and peering into a white-tiled bathroom. "Let's just glance into Hero's room. Perhaps she decided to move in there."

"Oh, no, ma'am, she never would have done that. Never in the world!" said the butler.

But Lutie was already trotting through the hall, opening the door, touching the light button.

Soft radiance from amber-shaded lamps filled a room all pale gold and clear green. The thick soft carpet was green and there were vases of jade with twisted flowers of jade and rose-quartz. The Empire canopy over the bed and its coverlet were the white-green of water. The woodwork was blond and the walls were hung with pale gold lamé looped up with small emerald plumes. It was a luxurious room, expensive and pretty and somehow quite hideous.

There was no one in it, nor in the elaborate dressing room and the adjoining green-tiled bath.

Jeff whispered, "Gosh! Have you ever seen anything like that, even in the movies? It isn't real, is it?" He craned his neck but didn't venture to step inside.

The butler didn't follow us into the apartment, either, but stood in the doorway clutching his robe and peering around, not intently, but as if his watery light-blue gaze beheld the ghost of a slender figure with pale gilt hair and brilliant ice-green eyes.

He was muttering, half to himself and half to Jeff and to me, who stood nearest to him. "This used to be the master's. Miss Hero had the bedroom just above—" he jerked his head toward the ceiling. "Then she moved down here and had it all done over. It looks just like she did, doesn't it? I haven't been in here since she—"

He didn't finish the sentence, but added, "Nor would Mrs. Lynn. She must have gone out."

Then he blinked and said abruptly, in a different tone, "Of course she went out! I've just remembered—"

Amanda turned and regarded him sharply. "Yes?"

"The door was unbolted! I mean, madame, when I let you ladies in. And I had bolted it, with the chain in place and all, as usual, before I went upstairs to my room. So—"

"You are quite sure of that?" Lutie, who had concluded her tour of inspection, asked quickly.

The servant, now wide awake and more alert than he had been, said positively, "Yes, madame. I am certain."

"Und dot iss so!" spoke up another voice from the hall behind him.

We all turned, rather startled, to see a stout woman standing at the foot of the staircase leading to the floor above. She had yellow hair set in rigid water-waves and metal curlers under a net and was wearing a kimono covered with a design of gigantic cornflowers, transparent gloves of what looked like cellophane, and felt bedroom slippers which, with the thick stair carpet, had muffled her footsteps.

"This is Mrs. Haug, madame. Bertha Haug; our cook," explained the butler.

Giving us a perfunctory and sullen nod, the cook turned a fat face, shiny with cold cream, on her fellow servant.

"Vot iss all diss? Vy at sooch an hour are you Miss Hero's room herein? Dis verboten iss."

Amanda said sternly, "We came to see your mistress, Mrs. Lynn. Banks thought she had retired. But she is not in her room."

"Vell, herein she vould not be. Dis Miss Hero's room iss!"

The cook looked around it. In her beady black eyes, as they rested on the silken walls, the canopied bed with its lace and satin spread, there was a fierce possessiveness. As we left the chamber she stepped into it, smoothed a cushion, snapped off the lights, shut the door firmly and faced us.

"Nobody herein comes no more. Nobody but me! Der utter servants I don't allow to set deir cloomsy feet inside door, efer. Miss Hero's room I tend, myself. Und Mrs. Lynn nefer steps herein. Nefer! Vot right—?"

The butler stiffened his narrow shoulders. "That will do, Mrs. Haug!" he interrupted. "Kindly remember I am in charge of the household. Now, as I was just telling these ladies, I bolted the front door on my way to retire, and I understood you to say you can corroborate that. Apparently you came up from the kitchen by the front stairs instead of the rear."

"Ya. Und I look to see iss chain on door. Dot's vy I come by front vay."

"At what time was that?" asked Amanda quickly.

"About ten o'clock. Ven I come up from my kitchen I look to see iss door fastened, efery night since vot happen to Miss Hero."

Again Amanda cut in, "On your way upstairs tonight did you see your mistress?"

The woman shook her head. "She vass in her room."

"How do you know that if you didn't see her?" inquired Amanda sharply.

"Her door iss liddle open, I see her light. Downstairs iss dark." The cook hesitated, then added, "But aftervards she go downstairs to parlor. Dot I know because ven I go to bed I put vindow up and I see light from parlor vindow shining."

"Let's go down to the parlor now, shall we?" said Lutie, starting ahead.

We trooped after. In the wide, dismal lower hall Banks stepped past us through the draped double doorway, switching on the light. We followed into a high-ceilinged drawing room, crowded with ornate furniture and statuary in a style that was undoubtedly rich and fashionable in the early years of the century but was heavy and tasteless now. The dark green brocatelle walls and mahogany woodwork absorbed the cheerless light from the huge brass chandelier. The parquet floor and its thick oriental rugs held pools of black shadows. Shadows lurked, too, in the far corners of the long room, in which there was no sign of a living occupant, which looked, indeed, as if no one had really lived in it for a long time. True, there were two vases holding flowers, pink gladioli on the ebony grand piano, American Beauty roses in the exact center of the pretentious onyx and mahogany mantelpiece, but they looked like artificial flowers, stiffly arranged. There were no books, no music on the piano. It was a room without a soul. Or one in which the soul had died.

Lutie said, "The window curtains are all drawn now," and nodded toward the drapes of maroon plush through which no ray of light could possibly escape.

"Vell, maybe she look out vindow. Maybe she expect a caller, maybe she vait for taxi. Anyvay, my vindow iss in attic front, I see light from here!" the cook declared angrily. "I am not liar."

"Where does this lead to?" Lutie, calmly ignoring the woman, trotted toward a wide archway at the rear of the room, where sliding double doors framed pitch darkness.

"That is the library, madame," replied the butler.

He turned on lights, showing a room much like the first, except that the walls were almost lined to the ceiling with glassed bookcases. As Amanda and I started to follow Banks and Lutie, the cook placed herself in our path. Eying us very rudely she demanded, "I like to know vot business you got here mit der mistress out at sooch hours uff night?"

Amanda looked the woman up and down with cold disfavor.

"We are here to ask questions, not to answer them!" she snapped. "What brought you downstairs at this hour?" At Amanda's tone Mrs. Haug recoiled. My cousin repeated the question even more sternly.

"Vell, ven I hear bells going like fire alarms and Banks going downstairs und not coming up again—"

"I see." Amanda accepted the explanation and stepped firmly past the cook.

Lutie, at the door to the next room, was asking, "And this, Mr. Banks?"

"The dining room, madame," replied the butler.

He opened the door and pressed the light switch. He and Lutie went into the room.

Banks said, "Beyond is the conservatory. Which, I might add, Mrs. Lynn never enters."

Then he screamed.

It was a horrible sound, shrill yet hoarse, rising to a pitch of terror and breaking into a choked sob.

Jeff, who had been at my shoulder, dashed forward. I caught at Amanda's arm, and together we ran into the dining room, near the middle of which stood Lutie and the butler. They stood rooted, staring toward an open glass doorway flanked by palms in enormous jardinieres. I glimpsed a dim space, glass-walled, and the shadows of more palms, tall ferns, and spidery vines drooping from hanging baskets.

And another shadow. Suspended, too, but from a narrow archway, a long slender shadow, silhouetted against the dim light filtering through the vine-laced windows of the conservatory. A figure in trailing black chiffon like moss dripping from a tree in a dank swamp. The figure of woman.

There was a squeal just behind, a voice muttering, "Gott! Ach! Gott im Himmel!" and small fat fingers in crackly gloves clutching my arm. I shook them off, stumbling dazedly forward.

Amanda and Jeff and Lutie were already lifting the slim limp form in their arms. And my older cousin's voice said crisply, "Cut the scarf. Don't pull at it, Jefferson. Cut the damn thing! Banks, get a knife."

But the butler was sagging against the wall. Before he could move, Jeff had grabbed a penknife out of his pocket. An instant later he'd slashed through the long black chiffon handkerchief that was knotted around the woman's throat and looped over a hook in the center of the narrow archway in which her body hung. A moment later they were carrying her into the dining room. There was no couch there, so they laid her on the long mahogany table, thrusting aside the mirrored centerpiece and the runner of thick ecru lace.

White light from the bronze ceiling fixture shone down on the dead face of Elinor Lynn.

CHAPTER 22

LUTIE said slowly, "This is what I was afraid of. But I didn't—I couldn't believe it would happen before I could stop it."

Her cheeks were pale and her blue eyes held a look I'd never seen in them before. A devastated look.

Amanda drew a fold of heavy ecru lace over the stark staring features that had been beautiful.

She said, "Jefferson, telephone the authorities at once. Banks, show Mr. Mahoney to the telephone. Don't stand there like Stoughton bottles. Be quick!"

Jeff grabbed the dazed butler, and they left the room.

The cook stood, staring at the slender, rigid figure on the gleaming mahogany of the long table. Her little black eyes, like raisins in rice pudding, held a kind of sly, greedy excitement. She trembled, and as her tongue slid out, licking her thin, grease-coated lips, I felt a sudden repugnance so acute that it was almost nauseating. I backed and sat down abruptly in the nearest chair as the woman moved closer to the table, her yellow head in the tight hairnet pushed forward. Her pudgy hand in the cellophane glove slipped out of the folds of her kimono sleeve, hovering as if to draw the concealing lace from the dead face

"Stop that!" said Amanda.

The cook jerked herself upright and turned. Her sullen eyes met Amanda's and slid from my cousin's commanding face to her regal black satin frock, the chinchilla cape. Then her thick little eyelids dropped.

"Get over there and stay there!" Amanda pointed to a chair against the wall, and the woman backed away and obeyed.

"Sister, Marthy, please come here!" called Lutie softly. I hadn't noticed till then that she had left the dining room. But her voice came from the room beyond, the room where we had found the body of Elinor Lynn.

I didn't want to go back in there. But I didn't want to stay in the room with the dead, black-robed form on the table and the stout woman so avidly watching it again, either.

So I followed Amanda into the conservatory.

How dank the place was, with the smell of moist earth, sometimes so lovely, deepening the odor of some rank plant and the cloying sweetishness of a large vaseful of tuberoses. It was shadowy in there, too, with only the dim light from the garden beyond and the light that came from the dining room through the open door and one leaded window. The window was set with colored glass, and lozenges of green and purple lay on the marble floor.

Lutie stood before an iron table that supported several large potted plants. She held a tiny pocket-flash in her hand, and as we approached she pressed it, turning a thin beam on a flat white oblong on the tiled tabletop. It was a sheet of note paper, with one corner slipped beneath a majolica jardinière.

"I haven't touched it," she said, virtuously. "Read it." Amanda reached in her satin evening purse for her steel-rimmed specs. I leaned closer and read:

I can't face it through. What I am going to do frightens me terribly. I don't want to do it. I wanted to be happy. But when there is nothing to live for, how can I bear this burden? Why should I? I am so dreadfully alone, you see.

ELINOR

There was an embossed address at the top of the sheet of thick cream-colored paper, the address of the house we were now in; with a monogram *E DeB L* above it.

When Amanda, too, had read the note, Lutie clicked off her flashlight and slipped it back into her reticule. We looked at each other for a long moment of silence. Then we turned almost with one motion, our eyes going to the figure of the dead woman in the next room, so quiet now, past whatever agony of unhappiness and remorse she had suffered.

We left the conservatory. As I followed my cousins from the dim, dank-smelling place I stumbled over the leg of an iron table. Something brushed my neck. I gasped at the touch of cold, gloved fingers. I cowered. But it was only the thick, clammy leaves of a gigantic rubber plant

I jumped again as a discordant jangling peal ripped through the quiet of the house. But of course that was only the bell announcing the arrival of the police.

Two precinct patrolmen tramped into the dining room, followed almost immediately by two officers from radio cars. The ambulance reached the house soon after them. We left the ambulance surgeon with the body of Elinor Lynn. He was, as it happened, the same young fellow who had been on duty that other night, April seventeenth. It was just four nights ago, but how much longer it seemed! He went into the drawing room. Amanda and Lutie and Jeff and I seated ourselves together. The cook and the butler stood stiffly at opposite ends of the long room, while a blue-coated policeman stationed himself at the hall doorway.

I don't know how long we sat there, waiting for Inspector Moore. None of us spoke. Amanda looked tired and grim, and Lutie's blue gaze was withdrawn and intensely thoughtful. I wondered what she was thinking about, but only vaguely. I was too weary and shocked to speculate or feel more than a dull horror and pity. So Elinor Lynn had killed her stepdaughter. Surely it must have been in a moment of half-mad rage that she had done it. No cold-blooded murderess, greedy for money, would have felt such swift and anguished remorse.

The light from the chandelier beat down on my eyeballs. I must have closed my eyes, for the next thing I knew they flew open and I jerked my head upright. The bell had pealed again, and a moment later Inspector Moore had entered the parlor, followed by his squad. He paused only for a brief word with Amanda before he proceeded with his men to the room where we had laid the dead body of Elinor Lynn.

Again we waited

But the waiting did not seem so very long. Perhaps my catnap had refreshed me. And besides, it was such a relief to feel that this time we had done nothing for which we might be held at fault! Even Lutie's behavior had been exemplary. She had left the suicide note in its place without even touching it or anything else. And we had lost no time in calling the police. So far as I could see our conduct was above reproach!

And Amanda's account to the inspector, when he rejoined us, was complete but admirably concise, from our arrival at the house to our discovery of the body hanging in the archway of the conservatory.

"And," she added at this point, "although it was obvious that the girl had been dead for some time, for several hours, I believe, it was not seemly to allow her to remain where she was. So we carried the body into the next room and laid it down. But I did not allow the scarf around her neck to be unfastened. It was cut. Therefore you will be able to examine the knot and learn how it was tied around her neck and over the hook; from which you may be able to decide whether it was tied by her own hand or someone else's.

"Of course, we had not then seen the note slipped under the pot of ferns. Sister discovered that later. I suppose if the note proves to have been written by her, and not a forgery, we must conclude that death was self-inflicted."

Though Amanda spoke formally, controlling any emotion, her face was pale, and as her own words recalled the ghastly scene in the conservatory she could not quite keep her voice from shaking.

Inspector Moore did not comment when she had finished her report.

But instead of the complimentary, or at least not disapproving, attitude I had expected, and thought we deserved, his manner was definitely cold. As the silence lengthened, I wondered dismally what was wrong. What *faux pas* had we been guilty of this time?

Suddenly he said, and his tone was sharp, "Miss Beagle, you haven't told me how you happened to think of calling on Mrs. Lynn at such a peculiar hour. I would like to have your explanation, if you please!"

Amanda's cheekbones reddened. Obviously she resented the gentleman's tone, and a retort to that effect was on the tip of her tongue. But for a wonder she did not make it, and after a moment she replied, though stiffly, "It was Sister's idea."

She then explained that we had been "at a place called El Tunisia, where Sister had expressed a wish to spend the early hours of her birthday. How she had conceived this whim and why she selected such a particularly garish and expensive place, I do not know." She mentioned the young people who had joined us there but did not go into the various conversations that had ensued. She said nothing of Lutie's slight overindulgence in the cup that cheers, though at this point her flush deepened and the glance she shot at her little sister was eloquent.

After a brief pause she continued, "When we had left, which was at one-forty-one A.M., we took a taxicab and I gave the driver our home address. But Sister, without informing me of her intention or her reasons, substituted the address of this house, where we now are. She then explained to me that she thought we ought to talk to Elinor Lynn without delay. Frankly, the notion seemed to me preposterous. At first I believed that Sister was still inebri— that she was off on one of her wild-goose chases and letting her imagination run away with her, as there's no wonder it frequently does, considering the kind of fiction with which she stimulates it! However, she pointed out to me that we had learned during the evening that Mr. Delacy never dances, and therefore that Elinor Lynn had told a falsehood in her statement concerning her activities during the time when her stepdaughter was murdered. This convinced me that her reason for wishing to talk with Elinor as soon as possible was not without sense. But—"

Amanda cleared her throat. She added slowly, "But I must admit it was not so much what Sister said as her manner of saying it, that persuaded me, or, I should say, alarmed me. She murmured something about it perhaps being too late. What she actually meant when she said that, or how she knew what she was talking about, if she did, I don't yet know. Unfortunately, she was right."

While Amanda spoke the inspector had turned to Lutie. When she concluded he said curtly, "Well, Miss Lutie? What did you learn tonight besides the interesting fact that Mrs. Lynn had probably stretched the truth when she said she had danced with Mr. Delacy?"

"Why," said Lutie, "I didn't really learn anything else I hadn't known before. I've had a feeling for days that something dreadful was going to happen. But truly it was just a feeling. It was quite illogical. And so—"

"Yes?" he said. And added sternly, "There has been a tragedy here tonight. Couldn't you have prevented it?"

"I don't know, Inspector. I'm sorry."

She looked up at him. She looked sorry. "I simply didn't know what to do."

"This feeling you had," said the inspector sternly, "why didn't you communicate it to me?"

"Because," murmured Lutie, "I hadn't the slightest proof to base it on. So I didn't believe you would pay any attention—"

"Nevertheless," interrupted the inspector, "I would appreciate it if you would tell me now, even though it is a little late, why you felt that Elinor Lynn was about to kill herself tonight."

"Oh," said Lutie, "but I didn't think that!"

"No?" Inspector Moore said, and his tone was edged with sarcasm. "What about this?"

And he drew from his pocket what looked to me at first glance like a small passe-partout picture. Then I recognized it as the note we had read in the conservatory, now placed between two pieces of glass held together by strips of adhesive tape.

Amanda leaned forward, peering at the exhibit. When she saw what it was she snapped, "Well, what about it? It's the letter we found. I told you about it. I told you where we found it."

"You did," said the inspector, but without taking his eyes from Lutie. "And," he went on quietly, very quietly, "I suggest that your sister put it there."

"What?" said Amanda.

Lutie didn't reply for several moments. But into her blue eyes had crept a spark.

"And where," she asked gently, "did I get it?"

"That," said Inspector Moore, "I would like you to tell me. Perhaps Elinor Lynn sent it to you, but my guess is that she sent it to Kate Kilgallon, who gave it to you tonight at El Tunisia. That it was the reason why you were afraid that something was going to happen."

Lutie regarded thoughtfully the man who stood facing her.

Was he right? I wondered. I dismissed the notion that the note had been sent to my cousin as most unlikely. I knew she had received no letters during the day just past. But that Kate had, and slipped it to her during the evening, at El Tunisia—was that possible?

But why should Kate have done just that? With this testimony that her stepmother had killed her sister, surely she would have communicated with the police. Or hastened to Elinor herself.

Or would she? Perhaps she preferred to let Elinor take her own way out rather than turn her over to a harsher justice.

"Lutie Beagle," said Amanda sternly, after we had waited for what seemed like minutes for Lutie to speak, "is this true?"

Lutie said quietly, "No, Sister. I did not see that note, or know anything about it, until I found it exactly where I left it, there in the conservatory where we found Elinor's body."

She looked, very gravely and directly, at the inspector. "I expect you to believe that, it is a matter of fact. And I will tell you something that I am sure of. Elinor Lynn did not kill herself, nor did she kill her stepdaughter. That, however, is only conjecture. So naturally I do not expect you to believe that."

I could see that her manner had impressed Inspector Moore. Yet as he glanced again at the glass-framed note in his hand his tone was skeptical.

"You do not believe Mrs. Lynn wrote this?"

"Oh, yes, I believe she wrote it! I think her murderer, and Hero's murderer, is much too clever to attempt forgery in these days of handwriting experts. And I'm sure you've already tested it for fingerprints and found hers on it, and no others."

"You are correct. And can you interpret this note as anything but an admission of guilt for Hero's death and a resolve on the writer's part to take her own life?"

"I think," said Lutie slowly, "that it is part of a letter, perhaps to the person who killed Hero."

"And who is this person, Miss Lutie?" queried the inspector. But he had made the mistake of veneering his irritation and sarcasm a little too thinly. Bright color, like battle flags, rose in Lutie's cheeks.

"That," said Lutie, very sweetly, "would be very silly for me to say. It is only a notion, built on foolish little surmises which I do not think would impress your much more logical, masculine mind, Inspector."

"Nevertheless," cut in the inspector impatiently, "I would like to be the judge of the value of these so-called surmises."

"I'm sorry. I don't think it would be wise or fair for me to bother you with my fanciful little guesses. But I promise," Lutie raised her small right hand solemnly, "that if I am lucky enough to find any proof of my notion, or against it, I'll be only too happy to let you judge its value. That's all I think I'd better say right now."

"And," said Amanda shortly, "I consider that a very sensible attitude. Anyway, there is nothing you can do about it, Inspector, for when Sister has once made up her mind to keep her mouth shut, which isn't often, she can be as stubborn as a little jackass!"

"Thank you, Sister," said Lutie demurely. "Only wouldn't jenny-mule be more ladylike?"

Amanda snorted. Ignoring this flippancy she said, "Meanwhile, we are wasting time. If Sister is right, and there are times when she has been, the murderer is still at large, and still dangerous."

"If your sister is right," interrupted the inspector coldly, "she is protecting the murderer."

"You flatter me, sir," said Lutie.

Then her tone changed. She rose to her full height of five feet. "But you are mistaken. I do not like murderers!"

Her eyes flashed. I wanted to cry, "Bravo!"

And so, I think, did Amanda. But what she said, gruffly, was, "Sister is quite right. Murderers are not likable people. And another stupid mistake too often made is in thinking that likable people can be murderers." She added, grimly, "I think the cook should be questioned."

Inspector Moore continued to fix Lutie with an inimical gaze. It was obvious that he believed she had something up her sleeve but that he realized the futility of pressing her further for the moment. Controlling his annoyance, he sent for the cook.

The woman looked somewhat less repulsive than she had appeared before. She had wiped the cold cream from her face and removed her transparent gloves. Her manner was respectful, her expression phlegmatic. I realized that her sly little eyes were quite unfrightened and shrewdly intelligent. She answered questions calmly, without hesitation.

She said she had sent the maids, Mamie and Millie, to their rooms by the rear stairs. Soon after, at about ten o'clock, she had left the kitchen. She had come up the front stairway to make sure the chain was on the front door, as she had done ever since Miss Hero's death. Since that death, the mistress, Mrs. Lynn, had retired early to her room, every evening. She had not gone out of the house and had received no visitors.

When questioned on this point the cook admitted that she could not, of course, swear to it.

"But nefer until tonight haff I seen a light from der parlor shining, like tonight."

She explained about that, and the inspector asked what time it was when she noticed the light. She replied that it was eleven o'clock. She knew because she had just set her alarm clock.

"And what were you doing during that hour, after you had gone to your room?"

"I prepare for bed. I fix mine hair." She touched the rigid waves and metal curlers under the tight hairnet. "Und I put cream on my hands. Und gloves." She drew the gloves from the pocket of her kimono. "Miss Hero tells me I haff so preddy hands, so I take goot care of dem. Und my face I cream too. I haff t'in skin."

The inspector interrupted, cutting short these complacent remarks. The cook recounted what she had already told us and what we knew of her being awakened by several loud peals of the front doorbell, of coming downstairs, of our finally finding the body of her mistress.

"And what did you think then?"

"I t'ink she haff kill herself because she haff kill Miss Hero." The woman made the statement stolidly.

"You did not believe Miss Hero had committed suicide "

"Nefer. Nefer."

"Why are you so certain of that?"

"Miss Hero? Gott im Himmel! You don't know her. Nefer, nefer she hurt herself. Vy should she?"

"Why should your mistress—why should Mrs. Lynn kill her?"

"Ach, she vill be rich. If Miss Hero dies, she iss rich. Und also, she does not know how to submit. Miss Hero iss princess, she iss beautiful, she iss boss. But stepmutter iss not goot, meek. She vants Miss Hero's money und her yoong men she vants also."

The inspector eyed the cook unpleasantly. I was sure he didn't like her any more than I did, which was not at all. But he merely said, smoothly, "Were you on good terms with your mistress?"

The woman had no eyebrows, but the plump flesh lifted where eyebrows would have been if she'd had any.

"Goot terms? She vass goot mistress. If servants stay out after ten o'clock on nights out, if dey break a dish or don't sweep der beds under, out dey go! Sure, she runs house goot. Ve get on fine. Ya."

"But it was Miss Hero you were fond of?" the inspector asked quickly.

The woman blinked. If I hadn't taken such a hearty dislike to her I'd have thought there was the moisture of tears in the corners of her small eyes. And probably there was. But her voice was an unemotional monotone.

"Miss Hero iss two years old ven I come here. I vass her nurse. I read to her fairy tales from Grimm. She hass hair like Rapunzel. Alvayss she iss liddle princess. Ven I tell her do dis, not do dot, she kick me in stomach. Ach, she iss vonderbar."

The pig-eyes gazed into the past. Then the woman sighed and brought herself back.

"Ven she iss twelf, t'irteen, too big for nurse, I become cook. Miss Kate vants me to go avay. But Miss Hero makes fuss. Und ven Miss Hero makes fuss Miss Kate alvayss gifs in." The cook's tone was tinged with contempt. "So I stay. Und ven Miss Kate goes and der master gets married, also I stay."

"I see. Why do you believe Mrs. Lynn killed herself?"

"Someone find out she kill Miss Hero. She iss afraid."

"Did you come downstairs tonight and kill your mistress?" asked Inspector Moore quietly.

For a moment the woman looked frightened. But only for a moment.

"Dot iss crazy," she said phlegmatically. "Vy should I? Now I haff anutter job to find. Mrs. Lynn, she vould keep me. But Miss Kate—nicht!"

The inspector asked a number of other questions, but nothing else transpired from the cook's answers. I was relieved when he dismissed her and sent for the butler.

Banks was what Amanda might have called another kettle of fish. He was upset, nervous; though evidently trying to conform to the pattern of an efficient servant, he was too distraught to do so. He either answered questions too eagerly, or hesitated and stammered. Before the interrogation was over I was sitting on the edge of my chair, wishing that I could prompt him. He seemed, I thought, a very human, nice little fellow.

But nothing in particular developed from the interview. He told the inspector what we already knew: about bolting the door, going to bed, being aroused by the bell, letting us into the house, and remembering, later, that when he did so the bolt and its chain had been unfastened.

When Inspector Moore sounded him out on his relations toward the family for whom he worked—he had been butler in the house for seven years, and second man for three years before that—he drew forth the timid pronouncement that Miss Hero had been "a very pretty young creature, perhaps wilful at times," that Mrs. Lynn had been a good mistress, "stern, maybe a little harsh, but proper and just," and that "Miss Kate" was his idol.

"Miss Kate never wanted to boss anybody," he said, his nearsighted watery eyes actually glowing. "But nobody could boss her either! She is a great lady."

It was at this moment that the doorbell rang and Kate walked in.

CHAPTER 23

KATE was there, we learned, because Inspector Moore had telephoned her apartment and told her to come. He hadn't said why. He told her, now, simply that Elinor Lynn was dead. She sat down quickly as if her knees had given way, and turned very white.

After a moment she said, "What happened?"

Inspector Moore handed her the glass-framed sheet of paper we had found in the conservatory.

"Is that Mrs. Lynn's handwriting?" he asked.

She looked at it and read it. "Yes, it's her writing." She gave him back the note, and asked, "How did she die? Who found her?"

The inspector told her, briefly, and added, "And I would like you to tell me, Mrs. Kilgallon, just how you have spent the evening."

The girl's gray eyes stared at him as if she were dragging her mind forcibly to his question. Finally she nodded and said, "Yes, of course. Well, I had dinner at the Lafayette, alone. Then I went home, at about eight-thirty, I suppose. I had some captions to write. I worked for about an hour. Then I dressed. It was around ten when Bill arrived. I mean Bill Cameron. I'd asked him to go with me to El Tunisia. You know, of course, that Miss Lutie had asked me to meet her there."

Of course none of us had known it, though I recalled, with a flutter of excitement at my own perspicuity, that I'd almost guessed it. Amanda, who apparently hadn't, looked grimly noncommittal. Inspector Moore eyed Lutie but said nothing.

"She'd asked me to bring Bill if I liked, and Ted and Bettine, and Elinor and Charles, if they would come. That was in the late afternoon. I phoned the Greers. Bettine said she couldn't possibly, she's been terribly upset, naturally, since— Well, then Ted got on the phone and said they would come with me. He asked would we stop by for them, and I said yes, between eleven and twelve. But neither Charles nor Elinor would come. I reached him at his office and Elinor at home. I tried to persuade them, without telling them, of course, what it was all about."

"And just what was it all about?" asked Inspector Moore.

"Why—" Kate looked at Lutie. I gathered she'd thought all this ground had been covered before. Lutie merely nodded quietly and Kate resumed, "Well, I don't know exactly, of course. But I'd asked Miss Lutie and Miss Beagle to find out what they could about my sister's death. And when Miss Lutie phoned she said that was why she wanted us all to come to El Tunisia. She said she might learn something if we were all there, just casually. And we certainly did learn something!" Her deep gray eyes flamed. "We learned how that little brute Sabina had threatened Hero."

"Please tell me about that, Mrs. Kilgallon," said the inspector.

She described the incident. When she had finished he said, "That is very interesting. And now, if you'll tell me about the rest of your evening?"

"Where was I? Oh, yes. Bill got to my apartment a little after ten. We talked for a few minutes, then we took a cab and started uptown. But we were quite early, earlier than I'd told the Greers we'd stop for them. They're staying at the Waldorf, and we'd got to the door when I thought I'd have another try, to see if Elinor would come with us. Besides, I wanted to see her anyway. I didn't like her much, but she's been so alone in that big house. Well, anyway we went there. Bill waited in the cab while I went in."

"What time was that, Mrs. Kilgallon?" asked the inspector.

"I've told you, sometime between ten and eleven," she answered rather impatiently.

"How did you get in? Have you a key?"

"No, I haven't. Elinor let me in herself. I'd hardly touched the door-bell, as a matter of fact, before she answered it. But I couldn't persuade her to come with us. She said it was an outrageous idea, that to go to a nightclub right after Hero's death was shameful. What would people think? I said I didn't give a damn what people thought, and that she couldn't shut herself up forever. I argued with her for ten minutes. But I don't suppose I was very convincing. After all, I didn't really feel like nightclubs either, but I couldn't tell her why I was going. Miss Lutie had said not to.

" Anyhow, finally she almost pushed me out of the door. So then we went to the Greers' and waited for Ted, who wasn't home yet. He came in at about eleven-thirty, and then we went to El Tunisia. And that's all, I guess. We left right after Miss Lutie did and dropped off Ted and Bettine, and Bill took me home and went home himself. I'd just got to bed when you phoned me to come here. So I did."

"Did you kill your stepmother, Mrs. Kilgallon?" asked Inspector Moore.

Kate looked back at him. There was disgust and exasperation in her look. Then she drew a long breath, like a child who has counted to ten before venting a wrathful answer.

"I suppose you have to ask questions like that. No, I didn't."

He said, slowly and significantly, "You are a very rich woman now, Mrs. Kilgallon. You are heir not only to your sister's fortune but to your stepmother's."

"So what?" said Kate rudely. Then she shrugged. "I beg your pardon. That sounded like an ill-mannered brat, and childish, besides. I know perfectly well that money is a strong motive for crime and I daresay the most common one. As it happens, I want no part of this fortune." She controlled a shudder. Her firm jaw was set. "I loathe it. But you can't be expected to believe that."

"Mrs. Kilgallon, you said you spent about ten minutes trying to persuade your stepmother to go with you to El Tunisia. I'd like you to tell me just what you talked about and to describe her manner, everything about the interview that you can recall, as carefully as possible."

"Well, as I said, she answered the door herself, and very promptly. She seemed annoyed when she saw me. She asked me what in the world I wanted. I said, 'Come on, Elinor, come along with us. You've cooped yourself up in this mausoleum long enough.' She said, 'Kate, are you insane? Haven't you any sense of decency? With Hero's funeral only yesterday. Why, it's the most outrageous idea I ever heard of. I should think you'd be ashamed of yourself!'

"That made me mad. I'm afraid I get mad pretty easily, but I held onto my temper. I pushed past her—she was standing holding onto the door—and went on into the drawing room. She followed me in quickly. I said, 'Look here, are you going to shut yourself up for another long drawn-out period of retirement? I think you're a chump!' She said she'd rather I'd think her a chump than to have other people think her a cold-blooded etcetera and so on. I said for heaven's sake to quit worrying about what people would think. For my part I didn't care a hoot, and she told me all right, if I wanted to make a show of myself in night clubs, to go ahead. But for goodness sake to go, since she was tired and wanted to go to bed.

"As a matter of fact she looked frightfully tired. She looked awful, strained and white, like a ghost with a bad case of the jitters. I told her so, and she said that was her own business. Which of course it was, and anyway, I realized I couldn't budge her, so I left."

"I believe you said a while ago that she almost pushed you out of the door," said the inspector. "Did you mean that literally, Mrs. Kilgallon?"

Kate smiled, though wanly. "No, not literally. Elinor was much too reserved and proper to do anything like that. But I had the feeling that she wanted to! I suppose I irritated her. We had a way of getting on each other's nerves rather. She thought me a barbarian and I thought she was bending over backwards trying to live up to some ideal of how the young widow of an older man should act, or something like that. Not that we saw much of each other, even after Dad died. But when we did I always started feeling sorry for her and ended by being annoyed. I told her once that suttee had gone out, even in the best Indian circles, and that the role didn't suit her. She really—"

Kate stopped herself. She flushed.

"Yes?" prompted the inspector. "'She was really—?"

"I only meant that Elinor seemed to me— I had the feeling that she was a woman of an intensely passionate nature, under that carefully cool manner," Kate answered.

"Did you believe that her devotion to your father was genuine?" asked the inspector slowly.

"Oh, yes, I'm sure it was! Even before they were married, and before I was, when Elinor and I were girls together—we came out the same year, you know—I knew she was crazy about him. In those days she wasn't all lacquered with reserve as she is now, she showed her feelings. But it's since Dad's death that I've felt she was, well, not putting on an act, but—oh, I'm not saying what I mean well enough. Only, after all, she's young and it's unnatural to pretend that she has no interest in men any more. Don't you see what I mean?"

"I think I do," said the inspector. Then he reverted to a former point. "Did Mrs. Lynn go with you to the door, Mrs. Kilgallon, when you left the house?"

"Did she come with me?" Kate frowned as though she were puzzled at his insistence on the question, then, as if trying to remember precisely, she said, "Why, she came out into the hall. But when I started to leave I left quickly. I reached the door before she did and opened it. I'm afraid I slammed it after me, too."

"Mrs. Kilgallon, I'd like to have Mr. Cameron's phone number, please."

"Bill's phone number?" She gazed back at the inspector, and then understanding flashed in her gray eyes. She smiled, though wryly. "I get it. You want to find out whether I left Elinor alive. Well, I doubt if Bill can swear to it. I don't think he saw her, unless perhaps she came to the door immediately to put the chain on and he saw her through the curtains. That would be possible. They're net curtains. Anyway, Bill's phone is Sylvester 9-2281."

Inspector Moore spoke in an undertone to one of his men, who left the room.

The inspector turned back to Kate. "Mrs. Kilgallon, you told me you had asked Miss Beagle and her sister to find out what they could about your sister's death. Why did you do that?"

"Because I wanted to know!" answered the girl.

"You didn't trust the police?"

She blushed. "Well, I didn't distrust them. But I'd noticed Miss Lutie's face that night when you were questioning me. She looked so acute! And I'd heard from John Bynam how clever she was. So I went to her on an impulse."

"I see. Just one more thing. You have said that you did not believe that your sister committed suicide. Do you believe her stepmother killed her?"

It was several moments before Kate answered.

"I don't know. I don't believe it, but I don't find it impossible to disbelieve." She paused, then asked, "May I see Elinor now?"

Inspector Moore said, "Yes," and went with her.

They'd only just left the room when the doorbell rang again and one of the inspector's men brought Charles Leland into the parlor where we were sitting.

He said, "What's happened? The police phoned me to come here."

Amanda started to reply, but the officer standing at the doorway said, "No conversation, please. Chief's orders."

Amanda said, "Hmmph," but she didn't dispute the orders or try to overrule them.

Charles Leland sat down, holding his Homburg hat in his hand between his knees and staring at it. His heavy-jawed young face looked blank. I thought he seemed like a man walking in a nightmare. He was an extremely handsome man, though. Blond as a Viking, heavy-shouldered yet taut and slim-waisted. And he had handsome hands, I observed as he turned the gray felt hat in them, long, square-tipped fingers, sensitive and strong. Oddly enough he'd impressed me rather as a mediocrity when I'd seen him on that tragic evening four nights ago. He didn't seem so now.

Inspector Moore came back without Kate. She had gone upstairs to her stepmother's room to lie down, he said. Then he told Charles Leland why he had been called to the house, that Elinor Lynn had been found dead, hanging from the archway in the conservatory. He showed Charles the note that had been left on the tile-topped table and asked if he could identify the handwriting.

Charles Leland said, "It's Elinor's. " His voice was thick and dull.

Inspector Moore asked him the routine questions about where he had been during the evening. He said he had been at home at his apartment on Park Avenue. He had dined there at eight o'clock, dismissed his servants, and gone to bed a little after ten. He'd read for an hour, gone to sleep, been awakened by the inspector's phone call, called his chauffeur and driven at once to the Sixty-eighth Street house.

"You didn't leave your apartment at all during the evening?"

"No."

"Can you prove that?"

The young man raised his weary-looking eyes. He said, "No, I don't suppose I can. I sleep alone. You're asking me in effect if I killed Elinor, aren't you? I didn't. I suppose you have to check up on everything and everybody, even if the whole story's there." He gestured toward the glass-framed note the inspector still held in his hands.

And that was all that transpired from the interview.

When asked, Charles Leland said, yes, Kate had phoned him that afternoon to go to some nightclub. He had not wanted to. Did he believe Elinor Lynn had killed his wife and then herself? He said, "You read that note. What else can anyone think?" His tone was indifferent.

Inspector Moore commented on that fact, and the young man said, "What do you want me to do, yell? Elinor's dead, isn't she? And so is Hero. That's all that matters to me."

"Did you know Mrs. Lynn well? You seem to accept the fact of her guilt very readily."

"Oh, for God's sake!" said Charles Leland. The stiff felt hat was crushed in his fingers. He stood up, running his hands through his straight thick blond hair.

"Look, Hero's dead. I don't care about anything else. Of course I think her stepmother did it. She hated her and she wanted her money. But what does it matter what I think? She's dead now, so I can't— If there's nothing more to do, Inspector, I'd like to go home, unless you want to arrest me. Which doesn't make any difference to me either. Hero is dead."

Inspector Moore told Charles Leland he could go. And he left.

The two maids were sent for then. But neither Mamie nor Millie knew anything. They had gone up to bed at about ten o'clock, as usual. Their room was at the back of the house on the top floor. They had gone to sleep and had slept until they were called downstairs. That was all. Millie, who was thin and trim with a reddish nose, was frightened. Mamie, Irish, compact and inclined to be bellicose, was not. Millie said, "Miss Hero was a beautiful young lady, and how would anyone like that want to—oh, dear, she had everything to live for, hadn't she?" And as for the mistress, she was kind. Millie had nothing against her. Mamie said pertly that Miss Hurry was—well, Mamie wasn't a bit surprised at what had happened. And the mistress was nice enough, there were lots worse, or she would have given notice. She could get plenty of good places!

Bill Cameron arrived then, and Inspector Moore dismissed the maids.

Bill was asked how he had spent his evening. The young man, it seemed, had a family, a mother, father, three younger sisters and a kid brother. They lived in an old house on Thirteenth Street, and Bill lived with them, unless the band was playing somewhere outside of New York. But as it wasn't playing anywhere now except on a seven o'clock radio program, he had dined at home at eight-thirty and left there at ten o'clock to go to Kate's place. After that his story followed Kate's.

When Inspector Moore asked how long he had waited for her outside the Sixty-eighth Street house he said, "Gosh, it seemed ages. I suppose it was about fifteen minutes. I didn't see what they could be gabbing about. I knew Elinor wouldn't step out with us, she was bound to mourn a while."

"Did Mrs. Lynn come to the door with Mrs. Kilgallon when she left?"

"I don't know. I didn't see her. Kate came slamming out of the door the way she often does. Say, should I have seen Elinor? What's this all about?"

The inspector told him then. Bill Cameron turned pale. He dropped the cigarette he'd been smoking, and as it fell on the Persian rug he pushed a long foot in a cordovan leather shoe over the glowing ash.

He said, "My God, that puts Katy on a spot, doesn't it? Until you find out— Lord, why didn't Elinor come to the door? Or why didn't I say she had, anyway! Damn."

He picked up the crushed cigarette butt. The bell rang again, and Bettine and Ted Greer came in.

CHAPTER 24

INSPECTOR MOORE sent Bill into another room and told the newcomers that Elinor Lynn was dead, "either by her own hand or someone else's," and that he would like to know how they had spent the evening. He'd like Mrs. Greer's account first, and would Mr. Greer please wait in the hall?

Bettine looked about fifteen years old in her short blue suit and a small halo hat, her soft light-brown curls tied at the back of her neck with a ribbon. She had apparently a moment of panic and her lips trembled as her husband left her, but she rallied gallantly as he turned and smiled at her from the hall doorway.

"Just tell the truth, Betts, the whole truth, and nothing but the truth," he said lightly. "Don't get rattled. After all, you've nothing to get rattled about."

"I know. I'll be all right, Ted. I'm not frightened this time." She couldn't help a slight shudder as her words recalled that other time, but she controlled it quickly. I found myself hoping intensely that she would prove to have a complete alibi that would clear her positively of this murder and thus, by inference at least, of the first one.

Her account of her evening was simple. She and Ted had had dinner in their rooms at the Waldorf. Then they'd talked and listened to the radio news, Ted had played the piano, and she had sung for a little while.

"I can still sing a little, you know, and I like to, just for Ted." She blushed. "Well, at about ten o'clock Ted said, 'What about taking a walk?' But I said I'd better not, because Mrs. Kilgallon had asked us to go out with her that evening and I had to dress. So Ted said if I didn't mind he'd like to stretch his legs, and he wanted to see a man about a dog.

"That's not joking, it's true!" she assured us earnestly. "One of Ted's friends is giving us a puppy! You see, we've bought a little place in Connecticut. At least we've almost bought it. It's a place Ted's seen and we've talked about it. We're going to have dogs and flowers and books and children, of course. Then I'll have plenty to do when Ted's working, and he won't be restless when he isn't."

Anyway Ted had gone out soon after ten, and then she'd dressed. Mrs. Kilgallon and Mr. Cameron had arrived at a little after eleven. Ted hadn't come in yet, so they had a drink, and then he came in, and soon after they'd all gone to El Tunisia.

"And we had a very lovely time!" said Bettine valiantly, her round cheeks pink, though I knew quite well that Sabina Brok had spoiled the evening for her, and her memory of it was anything but lovely.

Then Ted Greer was asked to come back into the drawing room. His story corroborated his wife's.

"And where were you, Mr. Greer, between about ten and a little after eleven?" asked Inspector Moore.

"I wasn't killing Elinor Lynn, Inspector," answered the band leader in his slow, rich voice. He smiled. "But I'm afraid I can't prove it. I set out, mostly out of a feeling of restlessness, to call on Joe Nicholls, a friend of mine who is giving us a Kerry Blue pup. We're to have second choice of the litter, which is just back from the vet's. Of course we can't take the pup for several weeks, but I wanted a look. Have you ever seen a week-old Kerry? They're cute little devils, just like baked potatoes in sealskin jackets. I walked to Joe's house, he lives in Sutton Place, but he wasn't home. His man let me have a look at the pups. I only stayed a few minutes, strolled along the river, and had a beer on the way home. That leaves a couple of half-hours, split by my short stop at Joe's house, quite unaccounted for. Do they happen to coincide with the time of Elinor's death? And how, by the way, did she die? Or mayn't I know?"

Inspector Moore said curtly, "She was found hanging in the conservatory. A scarf was wound around her neck and looped over a hook in the middle of the archway there. Miss Beagle and her sister and cousin and Mr. Mahoney and the butler and cook found her. The butler saw her alive at about nine-thirty. Mrs. Kilgallon saw her sometime between ten and eleven, here. She was trying to persuade her to join the El Tunisia party, she says, and failing to do so, left her here alone and went to your hotel."

Ted Greer took this in.

After a short silence he said, "So that leaves Kate on the spot, doesn't it? As well as myself. Of course, you're pretty well convinced it was murder, not suicide, or you wouldn't be having us on the carpet, would you?"

Inspector Moore said, "Frankly, we don't know. Do you know Mrs. Lynn's handwriting?" He drew forth the glass-framed note.

Ted Greer scrutinized it.

"That's Elinor's writing, of course, or a damned good forgery."

"You knew Mrs. Lynn well? You know her handwriting?"

"Well, we never exchanged any billet-doux, that I remember. But yes, I've seen her handwriting. As for knowing her well, that's different. I saw something of her, you know. I used to be here at this house pretty often. That was when I was supposed to be intrigued with Hero Lynn. As a matter of fact her stepmother was a much more subtle and exciting person."

Bettine's face paled at her husband's calm, rather reflective statement. I thought, the child is certainly going to have her task cut out for her. To be married to this popular, sophisticated young gentleman wasn't going to be simple! I also thought there was something Machiavellian about Ted Greer's casualness.

Whether or not Inspector Moore shared this fleeting notion of mine, I couldn't tell. He merely asked for the address of Mr. Greer's friend in Sutton Place and then said that the Greers were free to go. "Of course I'll expect you to stay where I can find you."

The band leader answered, "Of course, Inspector." Then he and Bettine said good night and left.

"That seems to be all. Get anything from it?" said the inspector, turning to my cousins.

They didn't reply at once. Then Amanda said, "I'd like to go home, Inspector. But I think you would do well to question the cook further."

Jeff said unexpectedly, "That's right! I think the old biddy did it!"

He subsided, his freckled face red, as the inspector turned to regard him thoughtfully.

Lutie said gently, "May we speak to Kate Kilgallon before we leave?"

Inspector Moore looked at her rather curiously. But he made no comment as he nodded consent. We went upstairs to Elinor Lynn's bedroom, where we'd been told Kate had gone.

Amanda knocked on the door, and after only a second Kate called, "Come in." She was standing in the center of the room when we entered. When she saw who it was she said, "Oh! Come here, please. I've just noticed something. Look."

We followed her to a walnut desk in one corner of the room. It was open, and the pigeonholes showed neat arrays of note paper, envelopes, what looked like filed bills, and a few letters. But Kate was pointing to the large square of light gray blotting-paper in a leather-cornered pad on the hinged desk flap.

"That was clean yesterday. I stopped in to see Elinor in the late afternoon, and she was up here. I don't know why I noticed it particularly. Oh, yes, I wanted a stamp and she told me to help myself, they were in the drawer." Kate pulled open a small drawer containing a large stamp book, some pens, erasers, and paper clips. "Anyway, the picture of that blotter is perfectly clear in my mind. There wasn't a mark on it. And look at it now."

The blotter was certainly crisscrossed with lines. I leaned forward excitedly. But there were no words that seemed to be distinctly imprinted, even if—

"Oh, I've held it up to the mirror," said Kate. "And I can't decipher a thing. But just the same, don't you see, she was writing a letter. A long letter. And on the same shaped note paper on which that suicide note was written. Look."

She drew several sheets of paper from the pigeonholes. There were three sizes. The marks on the blotter would all appear to fit the medium-sized sheets, it was true. But that didn't seem to me very significant.

Jeff grabbed up the blotter and held it before the mirror over the bureau. A few letters stood out, one or two words, and parts of words, were distinguishable. "I . . .wh. . .ecr. . .know. . .lo. . ."

We all stared at the reflection in the mirror for several minutes. But the lines were imposed and superimposed on each other, some faint, all blurred. I certainly could make nothing intelligible of the inky mess. And presently Jeff laid it back in its place on the desk with a long sigh.

"Gosh, what's the use in that? It doesn't make any sense!" he said, gloomily.

And oddly enough I, too, felt a certain disappointment, until I realized that as a matter of fact that was an insane reaction. Because, dreadful though it was to think that Elinor Lynn had committed suicide, it was surely far more terrible to believe that she might have been murdered, and that the murderer was still alive, at large, a coldly dangerous creature, capable not only of one crime of violence, but of a second, perhaps a third

As this terrifying thought struck me I shuddered.

I was still staring dumbly, unseeingly, into the mirror before which I stood. And at that moment my vague gaze chanced to focus on the reflected faces of Lutie and of Kate. They were behind me. My little cousin had been looking into the glass, past my shoulder. Now she had turned, and her blue eyes, narrowed and thoughtful, were fixed on the girl.

Kate's lips were set and there was a faint white line rimming them. Her eyes were hard.

As they encountered Lutie's it seemed to me that a curious defiance blazed in them, to be replaced in the space of an instant by an even stranger wariness. Then she turned away.

"Sister, I see nothing further to be learned at the moment, and as it is nearly dawn I am leaving," said Amanda, who was at the door. "Kate, are you coming with us?"

"The inspector said that he'd inform me when I was free to go home," Kate answered. "That is, if I still am free to go home."

She shrugged, and her stiff lips stretched in the parody of a smile. Again, and it seemed against her will, she glanced at my small cousin. A peculiar look passed between them. Lutie's, I felt sure, held some kind of warning. She started to speak, then changed her mind. As we followed Amanda, however, my younger cousin paused in the doorway.

"I'll phone you early tomorrow, Kate," she said.

"Not too early. I intend to sleep until noon, or later if I get a chance," said Kate.

We went downstairs then and bade good night to Inspector Moore. But as we stood in the vestibule waiting for Jeff to fetch a taxicab, I overheard an exchange between Lutie, who was behind me, and the inspector, who had stepped to the door with us.

He said quietly, "Anything new?"

Lutie shook her head.

"You're still determined to keep still about what you know?"

She said, slowly, "I don't know anything. Honestly!"

And then, as if suddenly making a decision, she put her small gloved hand on his arm.

"But I'll tell you something I wish you'd do," she whispered quickly. "I can't tell you why, because it's just another hunch. Inspector Moore. Keep an eye—if you'll take my advice you'll keep a very close eye—on Kate Kilgallon."

I heard him draw a sharp, surprised breath. But I couldn't see his expression, for just then Jeff arrived with a taxi and Lutie thrust her arm through mine and hurried me down the wide stone steps and into the waiting cab.

CHAPTER 25

DAWN was breaking and the city sparrows were beginning to burst into their loud chirping chorus as we left that tall gloomy house. We ourselves were silent almost all the way home.

Then Amanda said, brusquely, "If you are right, Sister, and Elinor Lynn was murdered, Kate Kilgallon is the natural suspect. She inherits her stepmother's share of her father's wealth, and she visited her this evening; after which, so far as we know, Elinor was not seen alive."

She paused, eying Lutie grimly. Lutie didn't reply.

"Had you thought of that, Sister?" said Amanda.

Lutie had apparently been thinking hard about something else. Now she shook off her abstraction and answered, "Yes, Sister. Do you believe Kate did it?"

I burst out, "But any of the others could have. Even Charles Leland hasn't any real alibi this time. He said so himself! And Ted Greer was wandering about between ten and eleven o'clock. Bettine might not have stayed home,while he was out, not that I think the child could be guilty, of course, but— And then there's Sabina Brok, who wasn't even questioned! And that cook—"

Jeff exclaimed, "Kate never did it! She's the swellest gal I've ever seen in my life. Why, she'd never sneak up on anybody and strangle 'em and then try to cover up her tracks! She might pop off somebody, shoot 'em—but then she'd slap the gun right down in front of the police and say, 'Here I am. I killed that so-and-so and I had a darned good reason.' "

"But," Lutie looked at Jeff thoughtfully, "the police might not agree with her, Jeffy dear. You were saying, Sister?"

"I was pointing out that you've probably set the police on Kate's trail," Amanda said, "that is, if they take any stock in your notion that her step-mother did not commit suicide."

"Ah. Then you think it would have been wiser to keep my little notions to myself?" asked Lutie, gently. "Well, perhaps it would."

"I didn't say that!" snapped Amanda. "I was merely trying to say that it's now quite likely the police will leap to the most obvious conclusion, in their usual fashion. And that unless we can do something about it they'll probably arrest Kate tomorrow, or, I should say, today."

Our cab turned into Forty-fourth Street then and in a moment drew up before our house. Jeff jumped out and Amanda paid the fare.

I'm sure that only I caught Lutie's murmur, "I almost wish they would."

I had no chance to ask her what she meant. But those strange words and what I'd overheard her say to the inspector just before we'd left him-lingered in my ears as I prepared for bed and repeated themselves miserably in my tired head as I laid it on the pillow. Nevertheless I was too exhausted to stay awake long, and I slept like a log.

I was startled awake sometime later by a loud crash, to find the curtains at my window blowing wildly into the room, whipped by wind and driving rain. The pot of ivy had been swept from the sill and lay smashed on the floor. I stumbled out of bed and slammed the window shut, wondering dazedly what time it was, and reaching under my pillow for my watch I found that it was after ten o'clock!

A few minutes later, having hastily brushed my hair and slipped on a dressing gown and slippers, I hurried into the living room to find as I expected that my cousins had already breakfasted. Amanda had repaired to the office. Lutie, in her lilac-sprigged percale house dress, rocked in her small chair, her fingers flying busily among a heap of bright green wool squares.

"Why didn't you wake me?" I exclaimed, as she got up to bring me coffee, cereal and muffins. I hadn't slept past seven for years, except, yes, one morning after our very first murder.

"Well, my dear, you don't stay up as late as five, as a rule. There was no reason why you shouldn't catch a few hours sleep," replied Lutie, trotting in from the kitchenette.

I said that I didn't want anything but coffee. But I had three cups and I did eat a muffin or two, and felt slightly better. Lutie went back to her crocheting. We didn't talk while I ate, nor while I was clearing up my breakfast dishes. I didn't feel like talking, my brain was too weary and muddled, and Lutie seemed absorbed in her own thoughts.

But after I'd dressed and swept up the heap of spilled earth and broken pottery in my room, I rejoined her, and by that time my head had cleared a little. The events of the night before came crowding back. I had to know what that strange interchange of glances meant last night between Kate Kilgallon and my cousin. And also, and even more especially, why had she warned Inspector Moore to keep an eye on our client?

Should I ask her outright or try to find out by indirection whether she suspected Kate? I doubted that I was clever enough to trap her into any admissions. If she didn't want to tell me anything she wouldn't, no matter how anxious I was to know.

But she, too, was anxious about something. Seldom, if ever, had I seen her so solemn. Her small face was actually pinched and pale, which it might be, naturally, from lack of sleep and after such a night. Yet Lutie had come through other nights as disturbing without that look of troubled tenseness.

"Lutie," I blurted out, "what is it? What's the matter?"

Rain beat against the windows and wind slashed through the branches of the ailanthus tree. It was cold, more like a wild March day than a day in April. I pulled a shawl around me.

Lutie put down her bone crochet needle, but she didn't reply. She was staring at the mantel clock.

"Lutie—" My voice stuck in my throat. I didn't want to ask this question, but I had to. I swallowed.

"Lutie, you don't believe Kate could kill?"

She was still gazing at the clock, and it ticked several seconds away before she answered slowly, "If she were driven I don't know."

She saw the expression of horror on my face, and gave herself a little shake.

"Don't look like that, Marthy. I didn't mean to scare you. Only—" She bit her lip. She'd been on the verge of confiding something, then changed her mind.

"Let's talk," she said, cheerily. "There are several possibilities. Let's go over them, shall we? We'll take things in order. First"—she checked it off on a forefinger—"there's the possibility that Elinor Lynn may have murdered her stepdaughter, and later, out of remorse or fear or both, may have killed herself."

"Of course!" I interrupted. "That's what I think! Or I did. It was so obvious. Only you told us last night you didn't believe it!"

"Still, it is a possibility," said Lutie. "The other is that Elinor was killed by someone who wanted her death to look like suicide."

"But that letter!" I exclaimed. "Do you mean that someone forced her to write it at the point of a gun, or something?"

Lutie's lips twitched. "Why, Marthy, you haven't been dipping into my thrillers, have you?" Then she sobered. "Do you remember that note, precisely?"

"Why—" My mind struggled back. But only one line was sharp in my mind.

I repeated it, " 'When there is nothing to live for, how can I bear this burden?' I remember that and the gist of the rest of it."

Lutie took a slip of paper from beneath the oddments in her sweet-grass sewing-basket and handed it to me. In her small Spencerian script I read the words of the note we had found last night:

> I can't face it through. What I am going to do frightens me terri-bly. I don't want to do it. I wanted to be happy. But when there is nothing to live for, how can I bear this burden? Why should I? I am so dreadfully alone, you see.
>
>   ELINOR

"I copied it last night before I called to you and Sister," Lutie explained. She leaned forward, pointing. "It doesn't say anything about murder and suicide, not a thing, actually, though it seems to. Don't you see?"

She watched my face as I studied the note. Suddenly I did see.

"Why, of course!" I exclaimed excitedly. "This might have been written about just anything." I felt myself turn hot with embarrassment at certain youthful memories but I went on. "I mean I used to write wild silly things almost like that when I was young. About not being able to bear it all, and going away, far away. I used to write bitter farewell letters some-times, when life seemed harsh and unfair and lonely. Of course," I stammered, "I never did go away, and after a while I'd tear up the letters."

"Of course," Lutie murmured, and it seemed to me there was a faintly sad little introspective smile in her blue eyes. "All young people feel desperate at times, I guess."

"And Elinor was young! And she told us she'd felt pretty desperate at times!" I said.

I looked at the note again, and suddenly a further idea struck me. "Why, perhaps she wrote this while her husband was living! In a mood of feeling that he didn't love her as much as she loved him. You remember what Karkoff said about Mr. Lynn not caring for anyone but himself and his older daughter? And Kate virtually told us the same thing."

"Yes, I remember," said Lutie. But her voice had a rather absent tone. Then she brought her attention back to me. "You agree, then, that

the note needn't have been written under coercion, and that it isn't neces-
sarily a confession of murder and a farewell to life?"

I nodded. But the momentary thrill of catching her meaning had
passed, and depression engulfed me. A great gust of rain lashed the
windows. Rabelais croaked, not with his usual gusto but in a dismal
raucous mutter.

I shivered and said dully, "I suppose so. Yes. Well, go on, Lutie. "

"We'll go on the assumption that Elinor Lynn was murdered, and for
one of three motives—money, fear, or hatred. So far as we know Kate is
the only person who gains materially by Elinor's death. If Kate killed her
own sister it would be easy to believe that she also murdered her stepmother."

As I started to speak Lutie said quickly, "I said 'if,' my dear. I didn't
say I believed it."

"But you deliberately warned the inspector to watch Kate!" I cried.

Lutie ignored my interruption. "Another strong motive for Elinor's
death would be fear, I mean fear on the murderer's part, if Elinor knew or
guessed who had strangled Hero. This letter—"

She checked herself, took the note from my flaccid fingers and tucked
it away in her sewing basket.

I was thinking of something else.

"As for hatred," I exclaimed, "it's certainly obvious that Sabina hated
Hero! And as for the cook, she hated Elinor, I'll swear she did!"

"Unpleasing personalities, both of them, aren't they?" agreed Lutie.
"But unfortunately the Haug couldn't have murdered Hero, since she
wasn't at the party, though she might have known or guessed or believed
that her mistress had killed her nursling and idol."

"And she would have known all about Elinor's letters and so on, even
if they were kept in some secret drawer. That woman's a snooper if ever
I saw one! Lutie," I said excitedly, and clutched her arm, "I do believe she
did it! Listen—"

But Lutie wasn't listening.

And suddenly I realized that she'd hardly been thinking during our
whole conversation. She'd been talking merely to pass the time! Her eyes
were on the clock, which read eleven-thirty, and abruptly she rose.

The crochet needle and the squares and ball of green wool scattered
from her lap to the floor.

"Marthy," she said, "I can't stand it any longer! I can't wait."

She was across the room and at the telephone, dialing rapidly.

I gaped at her, and then I got down on my knees and began mechanically to gather up her belongings. The ball of wool had rolled under the

davenport. As. I reached for it I heard Lutie say tensely, "Keep on ringing, Operator."

Scrambling to my feet I saw my small cousin, her face tensely waiting as she held the phone to her ear. I too stood waiting, watching her, holding the bone needle, the tangled wool, the brilliant bit of afghan against my bosom.

At last she put down the phone and turned to me.

"Marthy, Kate's not there!"

"Where?" I said inanely.

"Where she lives," she said shortly, and dialed the phone again. This time I watched her over her shoulder, and saw her pick out the letters "S, P," and the numbers "7, 3, 1, 0, 0." With a sinking heart I realized that she was calling police headquarters.

Sitting abruptly, and still ridiculously clutching my armful of wool and feeling that my head was bursting with the same fuzzy stuff, I listened. Lutie was asking to speak to Inspector Moore. Presently she took the phone from her ear and murmured dully, "He's not there. They can't say just where he is." Into the mouthpiece she said earnestly, "When you locate him, ask him to call the Beagle Agency. At once, please tell him."

She hung up then.

But to my anxious questions I could get no satisfactory answers. And as it was nearing dinnertime the next half hour was spent in setting the table, baking biscuits, whipping up mashed potatoes, making sauce for the asparagus and gravy for the roast chicken, and stirring ice cream, which despite her preoccupation Lutie had not forgotten during our conversation.

The chicken and ice cream reminded me that it was Lutie's birthday, because we always have roast chicken and ice cream on birthdays. The bird was done to a turn, tender yet beautifully crisp and brown, when Amanda and Jeff came in from the office at noon, their arms full of packages.

It is our custom to open gifts right after dinner on birthdays and Christmas, so in due course Lutie unwrapped her presents and exclaimed and smiled over gloves, sachets, handkerchiefs, doilies and tidies from friends in East Biddicutt, including a new silk bandana for Rab's cage from Old Doolittle. The new cage itself was a very large and handsome one. It had to be hung up at once.

Then Lutie had to try on Jeff's gift, a resplendent Chinese coat and pajamas to match! She fastened the neck with the beautiful brooch which was Amanda's extra present and put on the tiny blue slippers with high silver heels, my offering. Looking very cute and gay in her finery, she thanked us all prettily for her lovely birthday. No one would have thought there was anything on her mind, except myself, once, as I saw her eyes stray toward the clock.

It was nearly two by that time, and soon afterward Amanda and Jeff departed for the office. The instant they'd gone Lutie said quickly, "Marthy, you won't mind redding up?"

She was already at the phone. And as I went back and forth from the living room to the kitchenette, clearing the table, I could hear her dialing, speaking into the instrument, dialing, talking again.

I caught only the barest scraps of what she was saying. But I did not miss the tenseness of her tone. When I finally came in, having hurried with the dishes and given the kitchen a lick and a promise, she was sitting very straight in her little rocking chair.

She was not rocking. Her hands were tightly clasped together, her soft lips set.

"Marthy," she said, "Kate has disappeared."

CHAPTER 26

"WHAT? Where? How do you mean disappeared?" I said.

There was a vertical crease between my cousin's silvery brows.

She said, "Just that. I've phoned her house, twice. I've phoned the magazine office where she works. I've phoned the Sixty-eighth Street house. She was at none of those places. I've left word that she's to call me if she comes in, but—"

Her tone frightened me.

Yet just for that reason, perhaps, I said stoutly, "Well, for goodness' sake, there are certainly plenty of other places where she might be! What do you know of her various friends and her habits? Maybe she didn't feel like going home and staying there alone. Have you phoned Bill Cameron? He lives with his family. Maybe she went there."

"She didn't. I called there. Bill's mother talked with me. She says Bill came home in the early morning, went to bed and then went out just before lunch. He didn't say where he was going. She mentioned that he often goes out on his boat and fools around all day, especially on weekends. And this is a Friday."

I glanced at the dark sky. The rain was still falling, and though it was by now a straight heavy drizzle and the wind had dropped, it seemed like no day for boating.

I said so, and Lutie nodded.

"However, there's no knowing what boat lovers will do. Well, any-way, Bill isn't at home. And neither are the Greers. Nor Charles Leland, not that I expected Kate would be visiting him at his apartment, of course. And they still can't locate Inspector Moore."

She looked again at the clock.

"But it's perfectly silly to worry, Lutie!" I said feebly. "Kate might be anywhere!"

"I know," said Lutie.

That was at three o'clock.

At three-thirty, watching her tense face, I said, "What are you going to do?"

She said, "I don't know."

At four she phoned Kate's apartment again. There was no answer.

Again she phoned police headquarters. Inspector Moore was still out.

At four-fifteen she went into her bedroom and changed from the gaudy Chinese pajamas into her oldest black serge street dress.

"Well, this is the last shot," she said, and took up the phone and dialed. After at least five minutes of waiting and listening, during which she told the operator to keep on ringing, she hung up. Her little jaw was set. I knew she had given up that attack.

But her eyes were determined. I watched with foreboding when she went into the coat closet, which is off the passage that leads through to the offices. When she came back with her old wool jacket and her bonnet, her last year's bonnet with the jet butterfly, I knew that she had decided on action.

"Lutie," I quavered, "where are you going?"

She answered, "I just phoned Kate's apartment again. There's still no reply. But she may be there. Something may have happened to her. I'm going there, of course. I shouldn't have waited as long as this."

"But what could have happened?" I stammered, and then felt myself growing pale. "Lutie, you don't mean?"

Lutie had put on her little coat and was tying her bonnet strings. She didn't answer me.

"Lutie," I cried, "I'm going with you!"

And I dashed for my own coat and hat and purse.

Lutie was gathering up her glove and transferring her belongings from her spangled evening reticule to her rainy day one of crocheted black wool, while I fumbled in the bottom of the closet for my rubbers. It was at that moment the phone rang.

My little cousin jumped to answer it. Forgetting my rubbers and ev-erything else I ran back into the living room.

Just then Amanda opened the office door, saying cheerfully, "Well, Sister, it's teatime! And a good hot cup of tea will be very nice on this cold wet day."

She paused in the doorway.

Lutie, at the phone, was saying breathlessly: "Yes, yes, this is Miss Lutie Beagle. Yes, Inspector, I asked you to phone me. I've been rather anxious. . .Oh. . .Oh, she did?. . .Where did they lose her?. . .I see. Thank you, Inspector. No, I haven't heard from her. . .Yes, I know I told you to watch her. . .Yes, if I do I will. . .Yes. Thank you. Goodbye."

She placed the phone in its cradle with a sharp little click and sat down abruptly.

Amanda, standing in the doorway, said sharply, "What was that all about?"

Lutie said, "Come in, Sister dear. Well, that was Inspector Moore, at last!" She sighed. "And it seems Kate isn't dead or anything. You see, I've been phoning her, and finally I became nervous. Silly of me, wasn't it? Sorry, I was just letting my imagination run away wish me, as usual."

She untied her bonnet strings. "And after all, Inspector Moore has been keeping an eye on her all the time. That is, not his own, he's had two men watching her house. And when she went out they followed her, but it seems they lost her taxicab in the traffic somewhere. Quite like a policeman, isn't it? Or some of them. I'll bet it was that McGinnis. I really think he isn't very bright."

She rose, took off her bonnet and unbuttoned her jacket. Then in sudden contrition she said, "Sister! I've been so worried about Kate I forgot to fix tea! Marthy, do you mind putting the kettle on? Dear me, I was flustered, wasn't I?"

Giving me an apologetic little smile she trotted into the passage, swinging her bonnet by its velvet strings. But she had also taken with her her gloves and her reticule! And she had closed the living-room door softly behind her.

"Amanda!" I said, and clutched my older cousin's arm. "She's off! I don't know why, I don't know where, but—"

"Martha Meecham, what in the world are you gibbering about?" She stared at me. "And where ever were you both going on a day like this?"

Of course, I'd forgotten that she didn't know, as I did, how uneasy— yes, alarmed Lutie had been all day! Not that even I knew what she'd been afraid of, except that Kate might have disappeared and—anyway there was no time now for explanations. All I knew was that Lutie was up to something. She was slipping out on us

I said hurriedly, "Amanda, Lutie's going somewhere. After Kate, I think. I don't know. But I'm going with her!"

I had on my hat and coat and one rubber. I couldn't bother about the other. Nor even about Amanda, if she was simply going to stand there staring at me!

Pushing past her I ran through the passage, following Lutie. As I yanked open the door to the inner office I heard the outer door click to, softly.

As I stumbled through the office—it was dark, Jeff had evidently been dismissed for the day—I realized that Amanda was right behind me. And as she'd gone through the hallway she'd snatched her fur cape and her pancake hat from their hooks. She was jamming the latter on her head, poking the long black hatpins into her scalp, or so it seemed! Then she was at the desk, Ezekiel's big desk, pulling open a drawer.

I ran through the outer office and flung wide the hall door.

"Are you coming, Amanda? Or aren't you?" I called, and started for the head of the stairs. Four long flights below I caught the patter of quick light feet.

As I began the descent of the top stairs the office door slammed. When I was half a dozen steps down Amanda was beside me. Before we'd reached the bottom of the flight she had passed me. The thud of the street door closing, away below, came up to us then, and there were still three long flights to go.

I've never been very fast at getting downstairs and by the time I reached the street door Amanda was holding it open for me impatiently. I tottered out onto the stoop, panting. And there were still the high stone steps, slick with rain, to get down. Well, I grabbed the iron banisters. And then, I think, my feet fairly slid out from under me. But I managed to cling to the railing, though I shut my eyes.

When I opened them, at the bottom, I stood in a deep puddle. And Lutie was nowhere in sight.

"She's gone! She's disappeared! She's vanished!" I gasped despairingly, feeling ready to weep.

"Nonsense," said Amanda, taking my arm and hustling me across the sidewalk. "There she is!" She pointed.

"Where?" I cried.

But Amanda didn't answer.

Leaving me gawping on the curb in the direction she had indicated, she stepped out into the street. At that moment I caught sight of a little figure halfway down the block. It was Lutie, and she was hopping into a cab.

As I spied her I heard a loud screeching of brakes and turned my head to see my older cousin practically in the path of an oncoming taxi, which managed to stop, by a miracle, just before it reached her. Calmly ignoring the stream of extremely annoyed expletives with which the cabman was relieving his feelings, Amanda called, "Come, Marthy, don't stand there like a bump on a log. Hurry!"

She opened the door of the vehicle. I tottered weakly across the pavement, and she pushed me in, climbed in behind me and slammed the door after us.

"Driver," she said, leaning forward and pointing to Lutie's taxi which had just started up, "do you see that car?"

The driver grunted.

Amanda said, "Well, follow it! If you catch it quickly I'll give you five dollars. If we have a long ride I'll give you a tip of five times your fare, provided you don't lose sight of that cab. Now, hurry!"

"Okay, lady!" said the man, and the cab jerked forward.

I fell back in my seat but struggled up in time to see Lutie's car turn the corner. We lurched after it.

As we veered around the corner ourselves and into the avenue I toppled sidewise. Righting myself again with some difficulty I searched wildly through the rain for Lutie's cab. Had we already lost it? How could we keep track of it? It was a yellow cab. But that was all I knew about it. There were many yellow cabs. There were three just ahead of us right now!

"Amanda," I panted, "how can we tell which cab she's in? How can we follow—?"

"The license number," snapped Amanda, "is MNX seven-seven-four-oh. Besides, the car has a dented fender. A rear fender, fortunately, and badly dented."

"Oh!" I cried excitedly, for just then I spotted the damaged fender. The car was only half a block in front of us. "There she is."

At that instant the lights changed from green to red. Lutie's car had just shot across the street.

Ours stopped short.

"Oh, mercy, do we have to stop?" I groaned. "This is important! We can't waste time on signals."

Ignoring my absurd outburst Amanda leaned forward and said quietly, "Driver, you got their license number?"

"Yup, MNX seven-seven-forty. Besides, they've got a bumped tail!" said the man. He was a wiry little fellow with an underslung jaw, and the jaw was set.

"Good," said my cousin. "I'm making your tip twenty times the fare. Or nothing! Does that suit you?"

"Yup," said the driver. His tone was laconic, but the excitement of the chase gleamed in his sharp gimlet eyes as he turned them on us for a second, evidently sizing us, up. He grinned slightly as he added, "If you can take it, lady, but it's a slippery night. Okay?"

Amanda, gripping the vertical bar on her side of the cab, sat stiffly upright.

"Okay," she said, firmly.

The lights changed then and we bounced forward.

I was flung backward again and my hat went over my eyes. By the time I'd got them uncovered and regained my seat on the slithery leather cushions Lutie's cab was nowhere in sight. At least I'd lost it!

"Can you still see it?" I gasped.

Amanda's eagle eyes were fixed ahead. She nodded.

And on we went, sometimes skidding over the wet pavements, now and then our fenders grazing other fenders, spinning around corners, stopped by red lights, and caught, once, in a tangle of other vehicles.

That time I did catch a glimpse of Lutie's cab! It was just four cars ahead of us. And as the snarl broke and the line jerked and crawled forward, our driver crowded a tiny Austin into the curb and nosed past. We were now only three cars in the rear of our quarry.

But we couldn't seem to gain much on it after that. The blocks went past, then as we reached less crowded uptown streets, the miles. And clinging with all my might to whatever I could catch hold of, bracing my feet against the creaky floorboards, I strained my eyes through the darkening twilight and the thin curtain of the rain. It was only a misty drizzle by now, but it was hard to see through. However, I managed to keep that yellow car with the dented fender in sight as we sped through Harlem, then through wide ugly avenues lined with warehouses, across a river, and on again.

Finally we were held up by another traffic signal and I lost the car again. Blocks and blocks passed as I peered vainly into the mist.

At last I said, "Cousin, can you see Lutie's cab? I can't!" Amanda was still sitting up very straight.

"Yes," she said. "It's way ahead. But we're gaining on it a little. Now they're turning a corner."

A moment later we careened around the corner ourselves, and at the same time we went over a great gully in the road. My head hit the top of the cab . . .

And that's all I knew until I felt my shoulder being shaken and from what seemed a long distance Amanda's voice was saying: "Martha, pull yourself together! What's the matter with you?"

"My head— Oh, my head!" I groaned weakly.

"Cousin, we've no time to worry about your head! Come, now, sit up. We're stopping here."

And so we were. In fact as my stunned senses returned I realized that Amanda was already out of our taxicab. Taking my elbow firmly she helped me onto terra firma. Only it didn't seem very firma.

"Have we caught Lutie?" I mumbled. "Where is she?"

"She's right ahead of us. Marthy," said Amanda impatiently, "have you any money?"

It seemed an irrelevant question. I always have about five dollars in my purse, and some change.

I said, "Why, of course I have. What for?"

"Let me have it, please!" snapped Amanda. "I didn't stop for mine."

Our little chauffeur picked a dripping object out of the gutter.

"Is this yours, lady?" he asked.

It was my purse. I must have dropped it as I scrambled from the cab. I nodded and motioned for Amanda to take it.

She opened the bag and poked hurriedly through it. "Fiddlesticks!" she said. "There's not enough. Here, driver."

She stripped off her chinchilla cape. "This would cover your tip, I daresay. You can hold it and wait here until we come back!"

Swiftly she drew from the inner pocket of the cloak a long dark object. Faintly the dim fading light gleamed on metal. Amanda thrust the cloak at the cabman. Holding it in his arms as if it were a large furry animal, he stared, open-mouthed and goggle-eyed, at Amanda.

"Jeez, lady, what you got there?"

She didn't reply.

But as she shoved the object she'd removed from her wrap into the pocket of her bombazine skirt, I too gasped. For I saw now that it was a gun, and I realized it was what she'd stopped for in the inner office, what she'd grabbed from the drawer of the big desk.

It was Ezekiel's big, ancient revolver.

I had no time to comment. She had grasped my arm and was hurrying me down a muddy slope toward—

Toward nothingness, apparently.

Then I saw that what I hadn't seen was water. Dark gray water and sky, mingling, at the end of the rutty street along which we were plodding.

"But where are we? Where's Lutie?" I quavered.

My eyes focused then. A yellow taxicab was backing, turning around, coming toward us. It passed us

But except for the driver it was empty.

I moaned feebly, "She's gone!"

"She's out there!" said Amanda, and pointed.

I looked where she was pointing and made out, just beyond the end of a long narrow dock, a rowboat. There was a figure in the rowboat. In each of its hands was an oar. The oars dipped in and out of the water. The small boat was moving slowly away from us. And on top of the tiny creature propelling the oars quivered two tiny wings, the wings of a jet butterfly.

CHAPTER 27

"HURRY, Martha. Don't stumble!" said Amanda sharply as my feet slid on the slimy surface of the dock over which she was dragging me. She let go my arm then, and knelt down. She was unknotting the rope of one of the several rowboats that were tied to the dock. In another moment she was swinging herself down from the wet rickety pier. She was standing in the bottom of the wide stubby boat and reaching her arms up to me.

"Quick. Come on, if you're coming!" she commanded.

I was coming if it killed me.

And it pretty nearly did. Because although I lay flat down on the slippery boards and slowly edged myself over, I hadn't gaged quite where the boat was.

As I landed one of my feet went into the water. It was the foot with the rubber on, but much good that did me. And besides I am no featherweight. The rowboat tipped precariously.

But Amanda yanked me back to safety.

"Now just sit still, for goodness' sake!" she commanded, grasping the oars from the bottom of the boat and pushing them into place.

The heavy paddles grated in the oarlocks, wobbled and splashed.

But there is a little lake in East Biddicutt on which Lutie and Amanda had picnicked when they were girls, and Amanda had learned how to row then. As I sat up in the sloshy bottom of the boat, having shipped a great deal of water when I'd come aboard, I realized that she hadn't forgotten how. Rhythmically the oars lifted, fell, cut through the water. And her long arms were not only surprisingly skilful, they were strong and she was resolute.

We were gaining on the small figure in the other rowboat, but not very rapidly. She too was making good progress over the smooth rain-dimpled water.

"Where is she going?" I said.

"Sshh. Not so loud, Marthy. She is headed toward that sailboat out there."

Amanda was slightly out of breath. Resting for a moment, she craned her neck. Then she bent to the oars again. Presently she asked, "Has she reached it yet?"

I was seated so that I could look forward, and as Amanda spoke I saw Lutie's rowboat some twenty yards or so in front of us glide into the shadow of a small sloop, a slender shape about forty feet long, with a single mast silhouetted against the sky. The beautiful little boat had flush decks, and two portholes glowed along the side like enormous eyes watching us. It was only by the light from these reflected on the water that I could now see Lutie's tiny craft nose up to the larger boat.

I whispered, "Yes. Yes, she's tying up alongside, Amanda! Oh, she's going up a ladder or something. Now she's on deck. I can see her. Now I can't! Amanda, she's on the boat, but she's disappeared, I can't see her any more!"

Amanda grunted, bent to her oars, and we shot forward. In a moment or two we also were within the shadow of the small sloop over whose gunwales Lutie had vanished. Within a few yards of us was the ladder ascending from the water to the deck.

I whispered, "Amanda, it's right there—the ladder—just a little pull on your right oar."

"Hush," said Amanda, softly but sharply. I hushed.

And then I heard what her sharper ears had caught sooner than mine. A voice, someone within the yacht, was speaking in measured tones, not loudly but so distinctly that the words struck the surrounding silence like smooth pebbles dropped one by one into the water.

The unseen speaker was very near us. The voice issued from the open porthole just above our heads. It was saying, "It wasn't clever of you to follow me here. Why in the name of the devil couldn't you mind your own business? Did you really think you could trap me, with your naive questions and your silly little gun?

"So you guessed that Elinor hadn't committed suicide, did you? Bright woman! Perhaps you can guess what will be said about your own disappearance? No, don't answer. Keep your mouth shut, darling. Remember I have your gun now. I shall use it if I need to, though I have other plans.

"As a matter of fact Elinor did commit suicide. When she sent me that letter, whose last page you so brilliantly deduced was not meant for a suicide note, she cut her own pretty throat."

There was a short, unpleasant laugh.

"More accurately, she put it into a noose. Anyway, she threw her life away. Just as you've done, little one."

There was a pause. I clutched Amanda's arm, which was shaking, yet tense under its wet sleeve.

"Amanda!" I moaned in a whisper. "Amanda, we've got to do something. We've got to get up there. We've got to!"

For though I could not place that voice with its deep, unnatural timbre, its manner unhurried, without vehemence, yet all the more awful for that, I knew it must be speaking to my little cousin. Lutie, who we knew was on the yacht, Lutie, who had doubted Elinor's suicide, Lutie, who in her mad recklessness had tracked the murderer to this remote, unlikely spot and had been trapped by him instead.

Amanda looked at me. There was terror in her face, and a fierce caution to keep silent.

And slowly, quietly, she stood up in the rowboat, her fingers grasping the edge of the porthole until, rising to her full height, she could look through it. Her eyes narrowed as the light struck them, then widened. She stared.

Grabbing at Amanda, and at some sort of knobby thingumbob on the yacht's side, and finally at the rim of the porthole, I raised myself until I too could see, though just barely, what she was staring at.

Which was not what I had expected, for Lutie was nowhere in sight.

And neither was the owner of the voice we had heard, were still hearing, in fact, though what it was saying I cannot remember. My mind was too dazed with astonishment to function at all.

Amanda and I were gazing into a small cabin, and across from us, lying on a narrow berth, was a girl. She was bound around the shoulders, wrists and ankles with rope. Her hair, spread on the ultramarine-blue cushions, was like dark flames, and her gray eyes blazed fearlessly from her pale face.

"It's Kate!" I breathed.

Amanda's hand went across my mouth.

Below us the water lapped softly. Around us wrapped the misty rain, with the light from the porthole cutting across it. Inside the cabin the unseen speaker went on:

"Poor Elinor. She was in love with me and I was in love with you! Funny, isn't it? Damn funny. But what I didn't know was that I was crazy about you because you were like your sister. Just the same, and this may surprise you, Elinor and I were going to be married next summer! That, you see, would be just two years after C.V.'s death. And Elinor was very discreet, at least since her marriage to your father. She'd been criticized and misjudged enough, she said, for marrying an older man for his money. Poor fool. Actually she didn't give a damn about money. She loved your father, and she loved me. But she was nuts to wait. 'We're young,' she said, 'we have all our lives before us. Why feed the gossip-mongers?' "

There was a short mirthless laugh.

"Well, she waited too long."

There was the sound of a match striking, and a thin stream of cigarette smoke floated past the porthole.

"She might have known, any girl should have known, that compared to Hero she was simply nothing."

After a pause, the voice resumed thoughtfully: "I guess she thought of Hero as a child. A beautiful, irresponsible, sometimes gay and sometimes moody, often annoying kid. That's the way I thought of her myself until a week or two ago. But that isn't what she was. She was a woman. A witch-woman, fiery, tender, sorrowful and funny. When she looked at you, when she really looked at you, as if you meant something to her—"

There was the sound of an indrawn breath. Then a cloud of blue smoke was expelled and drifted past us.

The voice went on, "Well, Elinor waited. If she hadn't, if she'd announced our engagement, she wouldn't have lost me to her stepdaughter. I wouldn't have gone back on my word, after that. But she was stupid. Stupidly cautious, and then, after she'd lost me, stupidly hasty. After I'd killed Hero, if she'd waited, if she'd never told me that she knew what I had done—but do you know what she actually wrote me?"

The stub of a cigarette was flung on the cabin floor just within our range of vision. The toe of a cordovan leather shoe crushed out the smoking tip, then retreated again. We heard the scrape of a match. Then the voice continued:

"Elinor wrote, 'I know you killed Hero. I saw you climb over the roof. I didn't know then, of course, what you'd done. When I did know, I didn't blame you. I love you, and if you loved me I would keep the secret forever. Neither of us would ever speak of it. Because I know why you killed her. She didn't love you. She never had loved you.' "

The voice rose. "And Elinor imagined that after that I would let her live! My God, even if she hadn't known what I'd done, even if she hadn't threatened me, I never would have let her live after she had said that! The fool. The utter fool. And then, not that it greatly mattered, I should have killed her, anyway. The last page of her letter furnished me with a perfect suicide note."

The girl lying bound in that narrow berth smiled. It was a twisted smile, rueful and ironical. A grim comment on the fact that the suicide note hadn't been quite perfect, or she might not have been where she was!

But the man who was speaking to her followed his own train of thought.

"I took the note with me when I went to see Elinor last night. She'd asked me to come at ten-thirty. And do you know, priceless, I actually watched you visit the Sixty-eighth Street house? I was across the street when you drove up and went in. I waited until you'd left.

"And then Elinor, who was waiting for me, let me in. We talked. And I told her that I loved her, as I always had, that my infatuation for Hero had been a crazy mistake, that I'd discovered that and killed her. And Elinor cried then on my shoulder. So I took her long soft black scarf out of her hand, and dried her tears, and then I wrapped it very swiftly and tightly around her throat. Then I put on my gloves and carried her into the little dark room with the palms and the ferns and the tuberoses, and I hung her up by her neck. Just as Hero had once pretended to hang herself in a doorway."

Kate said, "You petty, puny, spiteful, vicious brute. I know exactly why you killed Elinor. It wasn't because she knew that you were a murderer. It was because she realized, just as I do, and as you should have done, that Hero was only using you. It was a devilish thing to do, and if you had slapped her down then and walked out on her, I could forgive you. Yet you should have known it. You should have known that she despised you and would tell you so."

From the man we still could not see came a kind of choking growl. And then words, hardly intelligible, as though forced through clenched teeth.

"I . . . do not like . . . what you have said. It is . . . a lie. I killed Hero because I did not like her any more. And I do not like you. I have changed my mind. I do not think I shall wait to throw you overboard. That will come later. But I shall kill you first. I shall kill you . . . now."

And then we saw the man's outstretched hands. And then his figure, the back toward us, moving toward the helpless girl on the berth. The shoulders were forward, hiding the head. The outstretched fingers were long, strong, curved. They were just above her throat

Amanda swiftly drew Ezekiel's revolver from the pocket of her black bombazine skirt. She raised it and gripped it tightly in her strong lean fingers. But the fingers were shaking.

I thought even I could do better. I remembered that Amanda had never shot a gun in her life. Not only that but she'd never killed anything.

She'd never set a mousetrap or hooked a fish. As Lutie had once said, she could hardly kill a fly.

But she was steadying the revolver on the rim of the porthole. And I heard the click of the trigger as her finger pulled it back, just as the man within the cabin heard it too and turned and we saw his face

At that moment the narrow door behind him opened and a small hand in a puce-colored glove showed in the narrow space. Then something flashed—the pearl butt of a tiny pistol.

It struck neatly on the top of a smooth blond cranium, and Charles Leland crumpled to the floor.

CHAPTER 28

AS the tall body went down in a sprawling heap on the cabin floor Amanda said gruffly, "Well, Sister's done it again." I almost lost my grip on the edge of the porthole, and our rowboat nearly capsized. It didn't, quite, and, with one dripping shoe desperately scrabbling for another foothold, I saw the door to the cabin open wide as a small figure stepped inside. It was a very damp figure, with a row of drenched curls under a sopping bonnet. But the jet butterfly atop the bonnet was jaunty and none the worse for wear, and neither was Lutie.

Her cheeks were bright pink, and her blue eyes were brilliant but calm as she gazed at the limp form at her feet. Then they rose to the porthole through which we were peering.

Both of us were spellbound, agape, me with my hat over one ear and Amanda still grimly clutching the big old revolver. No doubt we made an odd picture, framed in the circle of the porthole against the background of the misty sky. Comic, I daresay. But I am afraid I shall never properly appreciate the humor of it.

My little cousin did, however. Even now it makes me indignant to recall the slight involuntary upquirk of her lips as she nodded at us.

"My dears, you'd better come in now," she suggested fondly.

And somehow we did, though I practically collapsed back into the rowboat, which almost went over again. I lost my hat, which went drifting away. How I ever got up the ladder, even with Amanda steadying our boat and shoving me, I'll never know. When we finally gained the deck of the sloop I stumbled over something and almost pitched down the hatchway, too.

However, we made our way through the small saloon and reached the cabin at last, to find that Lutie had loosened the bonds around Kate's wrists and was now keeping a weather eye, and a steady little pistol, trained on the inert form of the man on the floor.

Kate said, "Hello!" with a rather wan grin.

Lutie greeted us affectionately. "My dears, I'm so glad you've come! I really would have waited for you only I was so afraid you'd tell me I mustn't follow my hunch. I mean, that my notion was foolish, Sister, and you know I've never disobeyed you. Of course I did wait for you once or twice, after that first red light, and then when we crossed the Harlem River and turned east, remember? That time I almost feared I had lost you."

Sister vouchsafed no reply. She was too busy untying Kate, for one thing. For another, I'm sure from her expression that words would have failed her.

When Amanda had unfastened the last knot in the rope around Kate's ankles Lutie said, "But you've arrived right in the nick o' time! While you tie Mr. Leland up I can keep him covered, just in case he comes to. But," she added, "I don't think he will, for a bit. There's plenty of time to do a good job. So don't hurry."

We did a very good job. That is, Amanda did. I tried to help but my hands were shaking too badly to be of much use, and Kate's were swollen and helpless from the ropes that had bound them. The girl's lips twisted with pain as the blood rushed back into her hands and feet, but she managed a smile at us as she said, shakily, "I should say you did arrive in the nick of time, all of you! But however in the world did you get here, Miss Lutie? I mean, how did you know?"

"My dear, I've been worried about you all day. I realized last night that you'd guessed who the murderer was. So I asked the inspector to have you watched. He did, but his men lost you somewhere up in Pelham. When I learned that I put one and one together. Knowing that Leland wasn't at home either, and that he kept his boat off City Island, and usually spent weekends on it—"

"And I never knew I was being trailed!" said Kate. "I simply went home, plugged the clappers on my phone and my doorbell, and had a good sleep. I knew what I meant to do, and that I'd never get to do it if I wasn't careful. Bill wouldn't have let me—ouch! Charles certainly tied those ropes tight."

She looked at the ugly red marks bitten deep into the purpling flesh of her slender wrists. So did Amanda, and her face grew even bleaker than it had been. The ropes binding the man on the floor were very efficiently fastened indeed.

During the process he lay motionless. And when finally the last firm knot was finished he was still so utterly quiet that I stammered, "Is he dead?"

"No," Amanda replied shortly, rising from her knees.

She gazed distastefully down at our prisoner and wiped her palms on her damp skirt. "And now that you've got him, just what are you going to do with him, Sister?"

Her tone implied that he was entirely Lutie's affair.

Lutie considered.

"Dear me," she murmured thoughtfully, "that is rather a problem, isn't it? Probably he'd keep just as he is, right there, until we could send the inspector for him. But I'd hate to risk it. If he should manage to do a Houdini—I mean if he got loose somehow, we'd never forgive ourselves. But I suppose it would be pretty difficult for us to get him ashore. I'm afraid we might accidentally drop him overboard if we attempted it, and that would be a pity, wouldn't it? After all our bother."

I had no doubt whatever that we might drop that trussed, heavy bundle overboard if we attempted the appalling feat of getting it to shore. I was perfectly sure we should. Not that I cared. What concerned me was, how were we going to get back ourselves? Have you ever climbed to the top of some great height, and looked down, and realized with absolute conviction that you were never going to be able to make that trip back to earth again, never in the world, not possibly? Well, that was the way I felt about the trip back to shore in a rowboat, with or without any encumbrance.

But I said nothing, for a very good reason. I was feeling, with rising apprehension, that faint but to me very disturbing motion that even a boat riding at anchor keeps up, and I did not care to open my lips.

In fact I had my handkerchief pressed to them and was wondering miserably how anyone could possibly like boats, except in pictures, which oddly enough are rather a hobby with me, when Lutie suddenly exclaimed, "What's that?"

She said it so vehemently that I jumped, thinking first that some new danger threatened. Then realizing that the danger lay trussed at our feet, I felt a moment's wild hope that her ears had caught the sound of some approaching craft that perhaps we were going to be rescued!

But the hope was doomed to disappointment. She had not heard anything; she had spied something

"That isn't a phone, is it? Do they have phones on boats?"

Kate, who was gingerly rubbing her swollen ankles, said through gritted teeth, "It's a radio. I didn't notice it before, but I should have thought of it. You call W O X and tell them this is the sloop *Paradise* and where we are. They'll connect us—"

Before Kate had finished Lutie had the receiver off and was calling into it. "W O X . . .W O X, this is the sloop *Paradise* calling W O X. Hello, W O X. This is the *Paradise,* anchored at City Island. Please connect me with Manhattan Police Headquarters, Spring seven, three one-hundred. Immediately. I'll hold the line."

And presently she was saying eagerly, "Police headquarters? I'd like to speak with Inspector Moore. Is he there? Yes, yes, it's quite important. Tell him it's the Beagle Investigating Bureau. Yes. Hello, Inspector Moore? Oh, I am so pleased to hear your voice! Yes, it's Miss Lutie. We've found Kate . . . yes, she's all right . . . No, of course she isn't the murderer, but we've got him too, only we don't quite know what to do with him. We're on a sloop, the *Paradise,* off City Island. What?. . . I'd better wait to tell you all about it when you get here. You'll get here as quickly as possible, won't you? Oh, of course I know you will! Thank you, Inspector. Good-bye."

She hung up firmly.

"Well, he'll be here soon. He wanted to know whom we'd caught, but I thought that could wait. Sister, there's a tumbler over there, and will you get Kate some water? We've neglected her dreadfully. Perhaps cool compresses on her ankles and wrists would feel nice. There must be towels, or we can tear up a sheet. And I'm sure this will help."

She took her small flask of apple brandy from her reticule and handed it to Amanda, who was already ministering to Kate's raw bruises. But Lutie herself kept the little pistol in a firm grip and her eye on our captive, who was beginning to moan weakly.

But when he came to, or what, if any, his comments were on the situation, I don't know. So far as I am concerned what happened for the next few hours is very much of a blur.

I recall realizing none too soon that I was going to be worse than useless below, and crawling up the hatchway, and gaining the deck. I was still there, quite flat with my head in the scuppers, when the inspector and his men reached us. And I remember only vaguely the motorboat journey back to shore, and being bundled into our still waiting taxi while Inspector Moore departed, remarking that he'd see us later, in another vehicle with the murderer, now conscious but still dazed, and manacled to two large policemen.

Anyway, we reached home at last, bringing Kate with us. She, naturally, made a beeline for the phone and after calling Bill's house located him at the Waldorf with the Greers.

Amanda was putting arnica on the egg-sized lump on my head, but we could hear excited masculine shouts coming over the wire and Kate's answer: "Darling, I can't tell you everything right now! Yes, yes, I'm perfectly all right, only cold and kind of tired and hungry."

She hung up then, and we got her into a hot bath, and afterwards wrapped her in a warm woolen robe of Amanda's with icepacks on her bruised spots. By the time Lutie and Amanda and I had changed into dry clothes Jeff arrived, wanting to know where in heck we'd been. And then Bill burst in with Bettine and Ted and three huge steaks and similar demands for information.

But Amanda absolutely set her foot down.

"We will not go into the matter until we've had supper!" she stated. "Kate found the murderer, who proved to be Charles Leland. Sister found Kate, and we managed to follow Sister," was the most she would vouchsafe.

So Bill broiled the steaks while Lutie made biscuits and Ted mixed a salad and Bettine hulled strawberries and Jeff fixed a fire in the grate and Amanda fed Tabby and the parrot and I set the table.

Presently supper was ready, and Bill cut up steak for his Kate and practically fed it to her bite by bite, meanwhile tenderly calling her the most uncomplimentary names imaginable. "Crackpot" and "dam' little fool" and "blithering idiot" were the mildest of these. The others I shan't quote.

We'd only just finished clearing away the dishes when Inspector Moore arrived, and Lutie brought him coffee and a soupcon of brandy and offered him her rocking chair. The latter he declined and disposed himself on the rug beside Bettine and Ted and Bill. We'd tucked Kate up on the davenport much against her will, so there weren't quite enough seats to go round.

And then the questions broke out in such a flood that Amanda had to call a halt again.

"If," she said, "you're all going to get in a dither I'll send everyone home at once! Kate ought to be in bed and asleep. She's had enough upset for one day."

"But I couldn't sleep, honestly!" protested Kate. "I should just keep going over things in my mind. I want to know—"

"Please," said Bill, "I've got to know. Just how did you get these service stripes?"

So Kate told him.

"Well, you see," she said slowly, "last night, in Elinor's room, I noticed the blotter on her desk. She'd been writing a letter on the same-sized paper as the note that was found near her body. And all of a sudden it came to me, that note wasn't a suicide note, it was the last page of a letter, and the murderer had used it. And then, in a flash, I felt sure that letter was to Charles! I can't explain that. It was a pure hunch. But I knew that if I talked with him somehow I'd know if it were true or not. And perhaps I could even get him to confess if I were right and if we were alone together and he thought I was unprotected. Well—"

She drew a long breath. "I phoned his apartment this afternoon and found he'd gone out to the *Paradise,* as I'd expected. So I followed. And the minute I saw him and he saw me, I knew he'd killed Hero and Elinor. I told him so. I said I had proof, that Elinor'd told me. And that's all. I had a gun, and I had my hand on it. Perhaps he thought I meant to kill him right then. Anyway he was quicker than I was. He knocked the gun out of my hand and kicked it across the cabin and then he hit me, I guess. Anyway when I came to I was on the bunk all tied up so I couldn't move. And he pointed the gun at me while he confessed the whole horrible thing. Both murders."

Her voice trailed off.

Bill's fists were clenched. He groaned. "The swine! And to think I left you there on your doorstep at five this morning, instead of dragging you home to my ma by the hair of your crazy red head. I felt in my bones you'd a bee in your bonnet and I was sure of it when you didn't answer your phone or your doorbell."

"Plugged," explained Kate, sweetly, and added, "I'm surprised you didn't break down the door, my good man."

"Well, you'll be interested to hear that I did, my good woman, after phoning every darn place in town where I thought you might be."

Ted said, "We've been walking the floor with him for hours. He even shook the show—"

"Heavens!" said Kate. She looked down at Bill, shaking her head. "What devotion! And now, horn tooter, please keep your mouth shut for a minute or two." She placed her palm softly over the lips she'd admonished. Catching her fingers, he held them against his face. "Please, Miss Lutie, you know all the things we want to know. Tell us!" urged Kate.

"Why," said Lutie, "there's really not much to tell."

"Then begin telling it, Sister," suggested Amanda, glancing at the clock.

"Yes, Sister," said Lutie meekly. She had put on Jeff's birthday gift; and now, folding her hands within the long satin sleeves of the embroidered coat, she looked like a tiny brilliant doll. "Well," she reflected, "the beginning was a very intangible thing among the number of striking happenings at Mr. Karkoff's party.

"Of these, there was, first, Hero's announcement of her marriage.

Second, Ted's, of his. It seemed natural to guess at some connection between the two, even without reading columnist's gossip. I mean there was an undercurrent. And then there was a scene in the powder room between Hero and Bettine."

"What was that?" interrupted Ted sharply.

Bettine's cheeks were flushed but her chin firm. "I didn't tell you about it," she said to her husband, "because I knew it wasn't true. I was in the powder room when Hero came in. She said, 'So you're the other woman!' Then she said you'd only married me because she'd married someone else, but that I was a sap if I didn't know she 'had ways of keeping what she really wanted.' "

"And"—Ted's voice was quiet —"what did you say?"

"I left. I was too mad to say anything. Except"—Bettine's blush deepened—"I did say I was *your* woman!"

Ted reached for her hand and held it tightly.

"Well," Lutie continued, "I know this sounds sentimental but in spite of other appearances I'd seen Ted look at Bettine when he said they were married and I was sure he loved her truly. So I didn't believe he was still in love with Hero, even if he ever had been. Therefore I didn't think he'd killed her. However, evidently Hero was in love with Ted and not with Charley, it seemed.

"And there was Sabina, who liked Ted too and didn't like Hero at all. Dear me, it's embarrassing, but I really tried to persuade myself Sabina was the guilty person! But of course I knew that was simply because I didn't like her. After all, the motive was pretty thin. If she'd killed anyone it should have been Bettine, shouldn't it?"

She smiled at Bettine. "And then, of course, my dear, there was you to consider. You had found Hero's body, and after that scene in the powder room—"

Bettine nodded thoughtfully. "If I'd really believed what she said, I'm not sure what I might have done."

"Well," said Lutie, "I didn't believe you believed it."

She turned toward Kate. "Then, we considered Kate, who had a great deal to gain, materially, by her sister's death. But, though anyone can see Kate has a reckless temper and an uncompromising temperament, it's practically impossible to imagine her killing anyone for money, isn't it?

"And Charles Leland? If he thought his bride was still fond of another man? To tell the truth, my suspicions lingered on Charles, but mostly because I did not like him. And I told myself that was silly, that he was only a somewhat dull but innocuous young man. Besides, he had a very strong alibi."

Lutie explained about his alibi.

Then she resumed. "And that brought me, finally, to Elinor. And I found that I'd been almost certain of her guilt, all along. Why? Because of that intangible thing I mentioned, the expression on her face when Hero announced her marriage to Charles. That was the real beginning."

Lutie drew in her breath and her hands tightened in her lap.

"It was a terrible expression. Stunned, stricken, devastated. I couldn't get it out of my mind. And when we learned of the provisions of her late husband's will, I seemed to have the answer to that look. Quite likely she'd expected her reckless young stepdaughter to forfeit C.V.'s fortune, but by her sudden and timely marriage to unobjectionable Charles Leland, Elinor had lost it.

"Yet, her face had registered a deeper, a different loss. And all at once I knew. She had lost not only money but a man she wanted even more than money. Charles Leland.

"After that, everything fitted. Or almost. Yet there was some sort of odd doubt nagging at me. I couldn't put my finger on it and I couldn't decide what to do next. I had nothing to go on."

"But," I put in, "what about Elinor's fingernail?"

Lutie gave me an annoyed glance. "Skip it. I mean, Marthy, that was of no importance, as I told you! Anyway," she went on hurriedly, "I felt worried. There was a dangerous creature loose, and I couldn't do anything about it. So we cleaned house. And then I read in a gossip column that Baron Delacy spent practically all his evenings at El Tunisia. And it was on Mr. Delacy that Elinor's alibi hung.

"So—" she stole a glance at Amanda, "I thought it would be a nice idea to go to El Tunisia for my birthday. And if various people were there, who could tell how many birds we might kill with one stone? I mean, when people talk, especially if they have a little drink or two, things are apt to transpire, aren't they? So I phoned Kate. Well, we did learn several things, as you know; but the most important was that Baron Delacy never danced. So then we knew Elinor had lied. Which gave us the handle we needed— I mean, I decided we should talk to her at once. And yet—"

Lutie sat up very straight, and her eyes were brilliant yet slightly puzzled.

"The curious thing was this. All at once I knew what had bothered me in thinking Elinor guilty of murder. Suddenly I knew she wasn't, that she was shielding someone.

"It was while we were in the taxi on our way to Elinor's house that I saw what might have happened. I visualized that shallow jog in the terrace where Charles had sat and knew that if he stood on the arm of the settee he could reach the coping of the penthouse and, helped by the nearby window ledge, draw himself up and over the roof.

"And if someone had stepped from the French window and sat down in Charles' place? Someone who had been standing at the bar and had seen him scramble over the roof? Someone in a black dress, someone smoking a cigarette? Would Jansen have noticed the change? I was sure he wouldn't. I was certain that was what had happened!

"The only question was, had Elinor gone back through the window on some sudden impulse as she heard Charles' returning steps on the roof just above? Or had she been there when he returned? In either case she held his life in her hands. And her own was in danger.

"Well," Lutie sighed, "that's really all. When Elinor's body was found it was clear what had happened. Charles had killed his wife in a mad rage of jealousy and frustrated love. Elinor held the proof of his crime and had protected him. Then in an insane attempt to get him back and bind him to her forever, she had told him what she knew. It's not surprising that he killed her. But it was an ironical twist of fate that the last page of her crazy, threatening, pleading letter furnished him with an almost perfect suicide note to explain her death.

"As Kate guessed," said Lutie, "and she proceeded to do just what I meant to. Which," she added, frowning, "I should have prevented somehow. I mean, we are professionals. Kate isn't. I should have realized the truth before I did and saved Elinor. But when I didn't do that I should certainly have got to the murderer before Kate did and made him confess, which had to be done somehow, since there wasn't a shred of proof against him.

"Only, I couldn't do it with everyone around last night. It would have to be a special sort of attack. I knew I'd have to be alone with him, to threaten him, and make him show his hand. To threaten me, probably, or—

"Well, Kate got just what we needed. And I guessed last night she was going to try to. So all I could think of was to warn you, Inspector, to look after her. And today when I couldn't get in touch with her or with you I was scared out of my wits."

"Hmm, not quite,." said Inspector Moore. "When I told you my men had lost her in Pelham you made a very shrewd deduction as to her destination. But wouldn't it have been better if you'd confided in me last night, or even today, and let me send my men on that very dangerous job?"

"Well, you see, Inspector," said Lutie demurely, "Sister brought me up. And she always says, 'When you want anything done do it yourself.' Or is it 'Never send a boy to do a man's work.' And besides, what if it had been a wild-goose chase and I'd been crying 'Wolf!' and you'd never have trusted me again? No, I couldn't afford it. Moreover," she murmured, "I had to earn my necklace."

But, thank goodness, only I heard that last utterance.

Because little Bettine was saying, "There's one thing I still don't understand. How did you all know that Hero hadn't committed suicide? That was what I was afraid of. I thought that was what she meant when she'd told me she had ways of keeping what she wanted. That she died so that Ted would never get over her. And when I learned what she'd written in the guest book, I was sure she meant it for him always to remember her by."

Ted Greer said slowly, "I thought so, too."

"But," said Lutie, "you see, Hero had really written the words as they were composed. Another hand had added that deludedly inspired touch that makes the plans o' mice and murderers aft gang aglay. He'd blotted out the 'We' and made the line read 'Now you will never forget' and underlined it for good measure. Or so I guessed," added Lutie modestly. "But there was more definite evidence, almost incontrovertible, against the idea that Hero had taken her own life, which Elinor demonstrated while trying to prove the contrary."

She told of Elinor's experiment with my necklace and how, when she'd let herself slip down into the chair, the folds of her frock had rucked up, whereas Hero's had hung straight, showing that she must have been pulled backwards and up.

I said hurriedly, to break in on that picture, and also because it was something I'd been wondering about, "How did Charles Leland know Hero would be there in the reception room alone just at that time?"

There was a short silence. Then Kate said, "She told him. He let that slip while he was talking to me, there on his boat. He didn't mean to, his pride wouldn't admit his awful jealousy, but—"

She stopped abruptly.

"But what did she tell him?" blurted Jeff. "What was she doing there? What was the idea of the champagne and everything?"

No one said anything for several moments.

Then Ted Greer said, slowly, "Well, I may as well tell you. Hero asked me to meet her there when she asked me to play the *Lament* thing. I suppose she chose that place because it was comparatively the quietest. And she must have scribbled that foolish stuff while she waited. I thought she just wanted to prove I'd come when she called. I didn't go. Perhaps if I had she wouldn't have been killed. I've been blaming myself ever since."

"Well, then stop it!" said Amanda unexpectedly. "If you'd seen Charles

Leland's face today you'd know that sooner or later he meant Hero to
die. She married him and then told him she never intended to be his wife,
which was a very wicked thing to do, and I'm sure that it sent the man
quite mad. Not," added Amanda, "that he was a good kind of person,
under the best of circumstances. And now—"

She glanced significantly at the clock, which read very nearly midnight.

But Ted Greer, holding his wife's hand very tightly, said, "Listen, please.
Just for the record, and between us, I want to say something. It's true I
never knew I was in love with Hero, and I never thought she cared a
damn about me, except that we liked each other and had fun together. As
for that stuff about our 'blazing' and so on, we used to laugh about it.

"But"—a slow red painfully rose in his face—"this is the something I
haven't told, even Bettine. Hero came to see me and told me she'd married Charles Leland that morning. And I called her all sorts of a fool. You
see I'd never liked Charley, and I knew she didn't either. But maybe that
made her think I was jealous, and maybe I was, and perhaps it gave her
the idea that she was crazy about me. I don't know. She was given to
sudden impulses, emotions too.

"Anyway–this is pretty ghastly. Suddenly she laughed and told me not
to worry, that she hadn't the slightest intention of staying married to Charley. She said she meant to get her money, not only because she wanted it
but because she wasn't going to be bossed, even from the grave! So I—
when she said that, I—well, I felt sunk. Because I liked her. I thought she
was a good kid. And then she topped it. She said, 'Don't be ridic, presh.
I'll divorce Charley and then I'll be your li'l bride. As good as new, and
much richer!"

Ted Greer's jaw was set, his voice low.

"I'm not proud of my reaction. And it's pretty low to spill the whole
thing. But you know most of it, and I'm damned if I want you to think I just
married Betts in a fit of jealousy, which seems to be the way it looked.
The truth is bad enough. I did ask Betts to marry me right away instead of
in June as we'd planned because I was mad as the devil at Hero. I ought
to be kicked. I made an unholy mess and dragged Betts into it."

"Nonsense!" said Bettine. "You didn't drag me anywhere I didn't
want to be drug. I don't like white satin and—and fuss. And why should
we waste time when time is so short?" She looked about ten years old as
she uttered this solemn dictum. Then her face broke into a blissful smile.
"We've bought our house in Connecticut—that's where we were today!
It's sweet."

"I know," said Bill, "just an itsy-bitsy made-over farmhouse with six bathrooms, no doubt." He turned to Kate. "As for you, you . . . screw-ball, I suppose you realize that nice little boy you grew up with, that poor sap I never did like and you used to say you were sorry for, I daresay you understand that he meant to dump you into the Sound with sandbags or something around your silly neck. And that if it hadn't been for Miss Lutie and Miss Amanda and Miss Martha arriving just in time you'd be a goner."

"Well," said Kate, "they did and I'm not. It's all their laurel wreath and I'm lucky. But we got the confession we wanted to get and Charles Leland isn't going to get away with murder and he isn't going to murder anyone else. So what, my fine-feathered friend!"

Bill swallowed. He exercised great control before he answered." So what? so tomorrow, so help me, I'm taking you to Elkton, Maryland, and tying you to my apron strings! And if you don't like it—"

"I'm sure I'll like it, darling," said Kate gravely.

And he did. And she does, very evidently.

They've bought a house in Connecticut near the Greers'. Bill describes it as a "mere shack with only four bathrooms,"and Kate has given up her magazine job, and she and Bettine exchange recipes and seeds and patchwork quilt patterns. Their only difficulty is that the Greers have a Kerry Blue named Mike and the Camerons have a Kerry Blue named Pat and never the twain must meet. They did once, and two very nearly dead dogs marked the spot. But aside from that all is gay and peaceful, and we visit them frequently, and a good time is had by all. But I do not accompany my cousins on the occasional weekend sailing trips they take with our young friends.

Perhaps I should mention that Kate gave all her inherited money to Babytown. Every cent of it.

She even paid the Beagle Detective Agency's fee from her own funds that she'd been saving for a rainy day. "But," remarked Kate, "now that I've got Bill hogtied there ain't gonna be any rainy days."

Of course the fee, though a goodly sum, didn't quite pay for Lutie's summer ermine and my silver fox and Amanda's chinchilla, which our nice little cabbie returned, very thankfully receiving his tip of one hundred and thirty-eight dollars and twenty cents in exchange.

Ezekiel's old revolver, however, is gone. Amanda lost it overboard while she was helping me up the ladder onto the *Paradise*. She felt quite badly about it. "But," said Lutie, just to me, "perhaps it's as well. You see, Marthy, Zekie was just like Sister, too tenderhearted to shoot a fly. Now she'll never know that gun of his she was poking so gallantly through the porthole hadn't had a bullet in it in all its life!"

Oh, yes—there's just one thing I forgot to mention. Lutie has her little necklace from Karkoff, Inc.

She wears it only on special occasions; and it is very pretty and becoming. But I always shiver when she does wear it; Lutie declares I like to shiver. Certainly she is never fazed by the reflection that her charming little platinum strand with its tiny diamond pendant is a souvenir of Our Second Murder.

THE END

Torrey Chanslor's first Beagle Sister mystery, *Our First Murder* (0-915230-50-X, $14.95) is available wherever books are sold. A catalog of other Rue Morgue Press books may be found in the back of this volume.

About The Rue Morgue Press

The Rue Morgue vintage mystery line is designed to bring back into print those books that were favorites of readers between the turn of the century and the 1960s. The editors welcome suggests for reprints. To receive our catalog or make suggestions, write The Rue Morgue Press, P.O. Box 4119, Boulder, Colorado (1-800-699-6214).

Catalog of Rue Morgue Press titles
as of February 2004

Titles are listed by author. All books are quality trade paperbacks measuring 9 by 6 inches, usually with full-color covers and printed on paper designed not to yellow or deteriorate. These are permanent books.

Joanna Cannan. This English writer's books are among our most popular titles. Modern reviewers favorably compared them with the best books of the Golden Age of detective fiction. "Worthy of being discussed in the same breath with an Agatha Christie or a Josephine Tey."—Sally Fellows, *Mystery News.* "First-rate Golden Age detection with a likeable detective, a complex and believable murderer, and a level of style and craft that bears comparison with Sayers, Allingham, and Marsh."—Jon L. Breen, *Ellery Queen's Mystery Magazine.* Set in the late 1930s in a village that was a fictionalized version of Oxfordshire, both titles feature young Scotland Yard inspector Guy Northeast. *They Rang Up the Police* (0-915230-27-5, $14.00) and *Death at The Dog* (0-915230-23-2, $14.00).

Glyn Carr. The author is really Showell Styles, one of the foremost English mountain climbers of his era as well as one of that sport's most celebrated historians. Carr turned to crime fiction when he realized that mountains provided a ideal setting for committing murders. The 15 books featuring Shakespearean actor Abercrombie "Filthy" Lewker are set on peaks scattered around the globe, although the author returned again and again to his favorite climbs in Wales, where his first mystery, published in 1951, *Death on Milestone Buttress* (0-915230-29-1, $14.00), is set. Lewker is a marvelous Falstaffian character whose exploits have been praised by such discerning critics as Jacques Barzun and Wendell Hertig Taylor in *A Catalogue of Crime.*

Torrey Chanslor. *Our First Murder* (0-915230-50-X, $14.95). When a headless corpse is discovered in a Manhattan theatrical lodging house, who better to call in than the Beagle sisters? Sixty-five-year-old Amanda employs good old East Biddicut common sense to run the agency, while her younger sister Lutie prowls the streets and nightclubs of 1940 Manhattan looking for clues. It's their first murder case since inheriting the Beagle Private Detective Agency from their older brother, but you'd never know the sisters had spent all of their lives knitting and tending to their garden in a small, sleepy upstate New York town. Lutie is a real charmer, who learned her craft by reading scores of lurid detective novels borrowed from the East Biddicut Circulating Library. With her younger cousin Marthy in tow, Lutie is totally at ease as she questions suspects and orders vintage champagne. Of course, if trouble pops up, there's always that pearl-handled revolver tucked away in her purse. *Our First Murder* is a charming hybrid of the private eye, traditional, and cozy mystery, written in 1940 by a woman who earned two Caldecott nominations for her illustrations of children's books. *Our Second Murder* (0-915230-64-X, $14.95) is the only other book in the series.

Clyde B. Clason. Clason has been praised not only for his elaborate plots and skillful use of the locked room gambit but also for his scholarship. He may be one of the few mystery authors—and no doubt the first—to provide a full bibliography of his sources. *The Man from Tibet* (0-915230-17-8, $14.00) is one of his best (selected in 2001 in *The History of Mystery* as one of the 25 great amateur detective novels of all time) and highly recommended by the dean of locked room mystery scholars, Robert Adey, as "highly original." It's also one of the first popular novels to make use of Tibetan culture. *Murder Gone Minoan* (0-915230-60-7, $14.95) is set on a channel island off the coast of Southern California where a Greek department store magnate has recreated a Minoan palace.

Joan Coggin. *Who Killed the Curate?* Meet Lady Lupin Lorrimer Hastings, the young, lovely, scatterbrained and kindhearted daughter of an earl, now the newlywed wife of the vicar of St. Marks Parish in Glanville, Sussex. When it comes to matters clerical, she literally doesn't know Jews from Jesuits and she's hopelessly at sea at meetings of the Mothers' Union, Girl Guides, or Temperance Society, but she's determined to make husband Andrew proud of her—or, at least, not to embarrass him too badly. So when Andrew's curate is poisoned, Lady Lupin enlists the help of her old society pals, Duds and Tommy Lethbridge, as well as Andrew's nephew, a British secret service agent, to get at the truth. Lupin refuses to believe Diana Lloyd, the 38-year-old author of children's and detective stories, could have done the deed, and casts her net out over the other parishioners. All the suspects seem so nice, much more so than the victim, and Lupin announces she'll help the killer escape if only he or she confesses. Set at Christmas 1937 and first published in England in 1944, this is the first American appearance of *Who Killed the Curate?* "Marvelous."—*Deadly Pleasures.* "A complete delight."—*Reviewing the Evidence.* (0-915230-44-5, $14.00). The comic antics continue unabated in *The Mystery at Orchard House* (0-915230-54-2, $14.95), *Penelope Passes or Why Did She Die?* (0-915230-61-5, $14.95), and *Dancing with Death* (0-915230-62-3, $14.95), the fourth and final book in the series.

Manning Coles. The two English writers who collaborated as Coles are best known for those witty spy novels featuring Tommy Hambledon, but they also wrote four delightful—and funny—ghost novels. *The Far Traveller* (0-915230-35-6, $14.00) is a stand-alone novel in which a film company unknowingly hires the ghost of a long-dead German graf to play himself in a movie. "I laughed until I hurt. I liked it so much, I went back to page 1 and read it a second time."—Peggy Itzen, *Cozies, Capers & Crimes.* The other three books feature two cousins, one

English, one American, and their spectral pet monkey who got a little drunk and tried to stop—futilely and fatally—a German advance outside a small French village during the 1870 Franco-Prussian War. Flash forward to the 1950s where this comic trio of friendly ghosts rematerialize to aid relatives in danger in *Brief Candles* (0-915230-24-0, 156 pages, $14.00), *Happy Returns* (0-915230-31-3, $14.00) and *Come and Go* (0-915230-34-8, $14.00).

Norbert Davis. There have been a lot of dogs in mystery fiction, from Baynard Kendrick's guide dog to Virginia Lanier's bloodhounds, but there's never been one quite like Carstairs. Doan, a short, chubby Los Angeles private eye, won Carstairs in a crap game, but there never is any question as to who the boss is in this relationship. Carstairs isn't just any Great Dane. He is so big that Doan figures he really ought to be considered another species. He scorns baby talk and belly rubs—unless administered by a pretty girl—and growls whenever Doan has a drink. His full name is Dougal's Laird Carstairs and as a sleuth he rarely barks up the wrong tree. He's down in Mexico with Doan, ostensibly to convince a missing fugitive that he would do well to stay put, in *The Mouse in the Mountain* (0-915230-41-0, $14.00), first published in 1943 and followed by two other Doan and Carstairs novels. A staff pick at The Sleuth of Baker Street in Toronto, Murder by the Book in Houston and The Poisoned Pen in Scottsdale. Four star review in *Romantic Times*. "A laugh a minute romp…hilarious dialogue and descriptions…utterly engaging, downright fun read…fetch this one! Highly recommended."—Michele A. Reed, *I Love a Mystery*. "Deft, charming…unique…one of my top ten all time favorite novels."—Ed Gorman, *Mystery Scene*. The second book, *Sally's in the Alley* (0-915230-46-1, $14.00), was equally well-received. *Publishers Weekly*: "Norbert Davis committed suicide in 1949, but his incomparable crime-fighting duo, Doan, the tippling private eye, and Carstairs, the huge and preternaturally clever Great Dane, march on in a re-release of the 1943 *Sally's in the Alley*. Doan's on a government-sponsored mission to find an ore deposit in the Mojave Desert…in an old-fashioned romp that matches its bloody crimes with belly laughs." The editor of *Mystery Scene* chimed in: "I love Craig Rice. Davis is her equal." "The funniest P.I. novel ever written."—*The Drood Review*. The raves continued for final book in the trilogy, *Oh, Murderer Mine* (0-915230-57-7, $14.00). "He touches the hardboiled markers but manages to run amok in a genre known for confinement. . .This book is just plain funny."—Ed Lin, *Forbes.com*.

Elizabeth Dean. In Emma Marsh Dean created one of the first independent female sleuths in the genre. Written in the screwball style of the 1930s, the Marsh books were described in a review in *Deadly Pleasures* by award-winning mystery writer Sujata Massey as a series that "froths over with the same effervescent humor as the best Hepburn-Grant films." *Murder is a Serious Business* (0-915230-28-3, $14.95), is set in a Boston antique store just as the Great Depression is drawing to a close. *Murder a Mile High* (0-915230-39-9, $14.00) moves to the Central City Opera House in the Colorado mountains, where Emma has been summoned by an old chum, the opera's reigning diva. Emma not only has to find a murderer, she may also have to catch a Nazi spy. "Fascinating."—*Romantic Times*.

Constance & Gwenyth Little. These two Australian-born sisters from New Jersey have developed almost a cult following among mystery readers. Critic Diane Plumley, writing in *Dastardly Deeds*, called their 21 mysteries "celluloid comedy written on paper." Each book, published between 1938 and 1953, was a stand-alone, but there was no mistaking a Little heroine. She hated housework, wasn't averse to a little gold-digging (so long as she called the shots), and couldn't help antagonizing cops and potential beaux. The result is one of the oddest mixtures in all of crime fiction. It's what might happen if P.G. Wodehouse and Cornell Woolrich had collaborated on a crime novel. The Rue Morgue Press intends to reprint all of their books. Currently available are: *The Black Thumb* (0-915230-48-8, $14.00), *The Black Coat* (0-915230-40-2, $14.00), *Black Corridors* (0-915230-33-X, $14.00), *The Black Gloves* (0-915230-20-8, $14.00), *Black-Headed Pins* (0-915230-25-9, $14.00), *The Black Honeymoon* (0-915230-21-6, $14.00), *The Black Paw* (0-915230-37-2, $14.00), *The Black Stocking* (0-915230-30-5, $14.00), *Great Black Kanba* (0-915230-22-4, $14.00), *The Grey Mist Murders* (0-915230-26-7, $14.00), *The Black Eye* (0-915230-45-3, $14.00), *The Black Shrouds* (0-915230-52-6, $14.00), *The Black Rustle* (0-915230-58-5, $14.00) and *The Black Goatee* (0-915230-63-1, $14.00). *The Black Piano* (0-915230-65-8) is due to be published in March 2004.

Marlys Millhiser. Our only non-vintage mystery, *The Mirror* (0-915230-15-1, $17.95) is our all-time bestselling book, now in a seventh printing. How could you not be intrigued by a novel in which "you find the main character marrying her own grand-father and giving birth to her own mother," as one reviewer put it of this supernatural, time-travel (sort of) piece of wonderful make-believe set both in the mountains above Boulder, Colorado, at the turn of the century and in the city itself in 1978. Internet book services list scores of rave reviews from readers who often call it the "best book I've ever read."

James Norman. The marvelously titled *Murder, Chop Chop* (0-915230-16-X, $13.00) is a wonderful example of the eccentric detective novel. "The book has the butter-wouldn't-melt-in-his-mouth cool of Rick in *Casablanca*."—*The Rocky Mountain News*. "Amuses the reader no end."—*Mystery News*. "This long out-of-print masterpiece is intricately plotted, full of eccentric characters and very humorous indeed. Highly recommended."—*Mysteries by Mail*. Meet Gimiendo Hernandez Quinto, a gigantic Mexican who once rode with Pancho Villa and who now trains *guerrilleros* for the Nationalist Chinese government when he isn't solving murders. At his side is a beautiful Eurasian known as Mountain of Virtue, a woman as dangerous to men as she is irresistible. First published in 1942.

Sheila Pim. *Ellery Queen's Mystery Magazine* said of these wonderful Irish vil-lage mysteries that Pim "depicts with style and humor everyday life." *Booklist* said they were in "the best tradition of Agatha Christie." Beekeeper Edward Gildea uses his knowledge of bees and plants to good use in *A Hive of Suspects* (0-915230-38-0, $14.00). *Creeping Venom* (0-915230-42-9, $14.00) blends politics and religion into a deadly mixture. *A Brush with Death* (0-915230-49-6, $14.00) grafts a clever art scam onto the stem of a gardening mystery.

Craig Rice. *Home Sweet Homicide.* This marvelously funny and utterly charming tale (set in 1942 and first published in 1944) of three children who "help" their widowed mystery writer mother solve a real-life murder and nab a handsome cop boyfriend along the way made just about every list of the best mysteries for the first half of the 20th century, including the Haycraft-Queen Cornerstone list (probably the most prestigious honor roll in the history of crime fiction), James Sandoe's *Reader's Guide to Crime,* and Melvyn Barnes' *Murder in Print.* Rice was of course best known for her screwball mystery comedies featuring Chicago criminal attorney John J. Malone. *Home Sweet Homicide* is a delightful cozy mystery partially based on Rice's own home life. Rice, the first mystery writer to appear on the cover of *Time*, died in 1957 at the age of 49 (0-915230-53-4, $14.95).

Charlotte Murray Russell. Spinster sleuth Jane Amanda Edwards tangles with a murderer and Nazi spies in *The Message of the Mute Dog* (0-915230-43-7, $14.00), a culinary cozy set just before Pearl Harbor. "Perhaps the mother of today's cozy."—*The Mystery Reader*.

Sarsfield, Maureen. These two mysteries featuring Inspector Lane Parry of Scotland Yard are among our most popular books. Both are set in Sussex. *Murder at Shots Hall* (0-915230-55-8, $14.95) features Flikka Ashley, a thirtyish sculptor with a past she would prefer remain hidden. It was originally published as *Green December Fills the Graveyard* in 1945. Parry is back in Sussex, trapped by a blizzard at a country hotel where a war hero has been pushed out of a window to his death in *Murder at Beechlands* (0-915230-56-9, $14.95). First published in 1948 in England as *A Party for None* and in the U.S. as *A Party for Lawty.* The owner of Houston's Murder by the Book called these two books the best publications from The Rue Morgue Press.

Juanita Sheridan. Sheridan was one of the most colorful figures in the history of detective fiction, as you can see from the introduction to *The Chinese Chop* (0-915230-32-1, 155 pages, $14.00). Her books are equally colorful, as well as examples of how mysteries with female protagonists began changing after World War II. The postwar housing crunch finds Janice Cameron, newly arrived in New York City from Hawaii, without a place to live until she answers an ad for a roommate. It turns out the advertiser is an acquaintance from Hawaii, Lily Wu. First published in 1949, this ground-breaking book was the first of four to feature Lily and be told by her Watson, Janice, a first-time novelist. "Highly recommended."—*I Love a Mystery.* "Puts to lie the common misconception that strong, self-reliant, non-spinster-or-comic sleuths didn't appear on the scene until the 1970s."—*Ellery Queen's Mystery Magazine.* The first book in the series to be set in Hawaii is *The Kahuna Killer* (0-915230-47-X, $14.00). "Originally published five decades ago (though it doesn't feel like it), this detective story featuring charming Chinese sleuth Lily Wu has the friends and foster sisters investigating mysterious events—blood on an ancient altar, pagan rites, and the appearance of a kahuna (a witch doctor)—and the death of a sultry hula girl in 1950s Oahu."—*Publishers Weekly.* Third in the series is *The Mamo Murders* (0915230-51-8, $14.00), set on a Maui cattle ranch. The final book in the quartet, *The Waikiki Widow* (0-915230-59-3, $14.00) is set in Honolulu tea industry.